NBC Great
ESCAPES

THE
SECRETS
OF LAKE
SUCCESS

CREATED BY DAVID STENN
WRITTEN BY JANET QUIN-HARKIN

THE CRAMER COMPANY IN ASSOCIATION
WITH NBC PRODUCTIONS

Copyright © 1993 National Broadcasting Company, Inc.
The Secrets of Lake Success™ is a trademark of
National Broadcasting Company, Inc. Used under license.
NBC Great Escapes™ is a trademark of National
Broadcasting Company, Inc. Used under license.
All rights reserved.

ISBN 0-87086-014-3

A Tom Doherty Associates Book
in association with
A Creative Media Applications Book

10 9 8 7 6 5 4 3 2 1

Printed in U.S.A.
First printing, September 1993

NBC Great Escapes
Credits for "The Secrets of Lake Success" Mini-series

Created and written for television by:	David Stenn
Executive Producers:	Douglas S. Cramer
	& David Stenn
Director (Premiere):	Jonathan Sanger
Producers (Premiere):	Frank Fischer
	& Naomi Janzen
Unit Production Manager (Premiere):	Ron Grow
Casting:	Denise Chamian
Director of Photography:	Roy H. Wagner
Production Designer:	John T. Walker
Set Decorators:	Barbara Cassel
	& Brenda Meyers Ballard
Costume Designer (Premiere):	Jane Trapnell
Makeup (Premiere):	Charles Blackman
Produced by:	The Cramer Company
	in association with
	NBC Productions.

STARRING:
Samantha Eggar as Diana Westley
Valerie Perrine as Honey Potts Atkins
Brian Keith as P. Stuart Atkins
Liz Vassey as Suzy Atkins
Stan Ivar as Tucker Reed
Gregg Marx as Dr. Martin Goldman

ALSO STARRING:
John Bradley as Rowan Atkins
Colleen Morris as Judy Grayson
Rebeccah Bush as Decker Atkins
Shawn Huff as Corinne Atkins
Edward Kerr as Tony Parrish
Chandra West as Jenny Grayson
Ryan Phillippe as Stew Atkins
Bryan Travis Smith as Adam Atkins
Lanei Chapman as Melanie Jones

THE SECRETS OF LAKE SUCCESS

See the passion, deception and betrayal of this remarkable novel come to life in an NBC mini-series!

Don't miss other riveting dramas like "Sisters" and "Against the Grain" — and when you're ready for fun, there's just one place to find the season's funniest new comedies. For passion, suspense, love and laughs, the stars are back on NBC!

SISTERS

Returning for its 4th season, this is an acclaimed series about families as they really are—fighting, loving, caring, ready to do anything, go anywhere, for a sister.

AGAINST THE GRAIN NEW SHOW

A father follows his dream, and takes his family with him. This new series about life in a small all-American Texas town makes you feel good about who you are and what you're doing.

MAD ABOUT YOU NOW ON THURSDAYS!

Voted "Best New Comedy of the Season" by the Viewers for Quality Television, "Mad About You" now joins NBC's Thursday night lineup for the greatest night of TV on TV!

*T*HE MOMMIES `NEW SHOW`

They're neighbors who share the pains and the (sometimes) pleasures of motherhood—they're real moms, they're real funny! Starring one of the hottest new comedy duos in the business.

*C*AFÉ AMERICAIN `NEW SHOW`

Valerie Bertinelli returns in a sparkling new comedy! She's a young woman who chucks it all and runs away to Paris in search of romance and excitement . . . only to discover that there's a waiting list for romance and excitement.

*E*MPTY NEST

This "empty nest" just keeps getting more crowded, more crazy. There are two great new additions to the cast: Marsha Warfield, from "Night Court," and Sophia herself, "Golden Girl" Estelle Getty!

*N*URSES

Loni Anderson returns to series TV as a hospital administrator. She joins the group of hardworking nurses who are so good with their patients, and always good for a laugh.

THE
SECRETS
OF LAKE
SUCCESS

CHAPTER 1

Old Man Atkins sat in his study and stared at the sheet of paper in his hands. He already knew the wording by heart, but he continued to stare until the words merged into a dark blur in the center of a white page. Only the word "terminal" refused to blur with the rest. It flashed in front of his eyes until he closed them, then continued to flash red against the blackness.

"Balderdash," he said out loud. "The fools don't know what they're talking about." He crumpled the paper into a ball and tossed it in the corner, watching it bounce from the embossed leather wall covering to the Persian rug beneath. He got up and began pacing.

He should never have listened to Martin in the first place. What did Martin know? He was a researcher—never had dealt with a real patient in his life. But the specialist at the Mayo Clinic—who had written the report—was supposed to be the expert on kidney disease. If he couldn't do anything, then that was that.

"Poor Martin," he said out loud again. His son-in-law, Dr. Martin Goldman, had been stuck with the task of breaking the news. He was a sensitive man and, Old Man Atkins thought, genuinely fond of his father-in-law. Earlier that day, he had certainly tried to be gentler than those few words on the sheet of paper.

"Of course you must realize that new breakthroughs are being made every day," he said gently.

Old Man Atkins looked him straight in the eye. "But as of today, my chances for making it through the year aren't too good?"

Martin looked away, avoiding his father-in-law's direct stare. "Maybe it might be as well to make sure your affairs are in order, sir," he said. Old Man Atkins noted that Martin, after twelve years in the family, always avoided having to call him Pop or Dad, or even Father. Terms of intimacy had always been in short supply around the Atkins household.

"Affairs in order?"

"Someone's going to have to take over all this when you've gone," Martin said. "I should imagine it's important to you which of your children it is. They're not all equally suited to run a billion-dollar business."

"Your wife?" Atkins asked. Another direct stare.

"Of course Decker thinks she could run the country, if asked," he said with the barest hint of a smile. "But I make no claims for my wife. It's up to you to decide."

Suddenly Old Man Atkins gave a short, brittle laugh. "Ironic, isn't it?" he demanded. "I own the company that is supposed to be coming up with the formula for eternal life—"

"Not exactly eternal life," Dr. Goldman interjected hurriedly. "Decker-Atkins isn't God, yet."

"We'll come pretty damn close to it if Vital-A actually works—if it does keep on renewing cells the way it seems to do in mice. I understand they're almost ready to begin clinical trials?"

"Don't ask me," Dr. Goldman said dryly. "It's Decker's baby, as you know. I'm only the guy who came up with the original theory. Now she won't let me anywhere near it."

"But you must have heard the rumors. We're close to witnessing the first miracle. Only too late for me."

Martin Goldman spread his hand apologetically. "Even Vital-A won't be able to regenerate what is already destroyed," he said. "But I promise you I'll do everything in my power to keep you going as long as possible."

"Not if it means becoming a vegetable," Old Man Atkins said quickly. "If I can't have full use of my faculties, I'd rather not hang around."

"I understand," Martin Goldman assured him.

"Can I see the report that fool at the Mayo Clinic sent you?"

Martin handed it to him.

"He's not God either," Atkins snapped. "He might be wrong."

"He might be," Martin agreed.

"Then there's always hope."

"There's always hope."

Atkins sat down at his desk. "Thanks, Martin. Now leave me alone for a while, will you? And keep that wife of yours away. This will take some digesting."

"Very well, sir," Martin said. He went out, closing the door quietly behind him.

Old Man Atkins walked over to the window. Below him, sprinklers moistened manicured green lawns, rainbow arcs of spray intersecting each other where the sprinklers overlapped.

His eye moved from the parklike grounds of his mansion and out across the town. He could see the streamlined glass-and-concrete buildings of the clinic glinting in the sun, the roofs of lakeside homes, ranging in design from Tudor to Colonial, from quaint European cottage to red-tiled Spanish. It had always been his aim that this should be a community of individuals. None of those dreary, unimaginative suburbs with identical ranch-style homes for him! And beyond the roofs, the sparkling water of the lake, and the gentle curves of green hills rising line after line into the distance. All of this he had created out of nothing! When he had first seen this valley, it had been empty except for marsh and waving grass and the stream winding through it. It had been his vision, his driving force, that had created the lake and built a community around it.

Old Man Atkins thumped his fist against his palm. He still had so much that he wanted to do: his clinic was coming up with new ways to treat manic depression. It seemed now that the illness might be linked to a childhood virus, which gave hope for inoculation. His pharmaceutical company was working on a promising new AIDS drug. And then there was Vital-A. If the hormone treatments really worked, he'd go down in history. Of course Decker would want to take the credit, and it was Martin's original research that had started the project, but it had been Atkins' vision and *his* money that had made it possible. So much to give, and apparently no more time in which to give it.

Which brought his thoughts back to the question of his succession. Which of his children could be trusted to carry on with his work? He was still chauvinistic enough to want to hand over to a son, but certainly not his oldest son Rowan. Rowan would like the title of CEO and the publicity and the money, but Rowan had never had the sort of brain that could grasp what doctors like Martin Goldman were trying to achieve. Rowan wouldn't know a promising project from a bum one.

Old Man Atkins decided that his first assessment of his son had been the correct one. He had tried to show two-year-old Rowan how to assemble a tower of stacking rings. He had demonstrated twice, but Rowan had still put the smallest one on first.

"The red one first," Atkins had stormed. "Can't you see that?"

Rowan had looked up defiantly. "I like this one best," he said.

Atkins had shaken his head as he looked at his wife. "You've given birth to a pretty-faced idiot," he said and walked from the room.

Definitely not Rowan then, and certainly not his second son, Adam, who was currently a patient in the famed Decker-Atkins Rehabilitation Center for the third time. This time it was for Quaaludes. Adam had always been too sensitive, kept too close to a mother who was constantly popping pills herself. Adam couldn't even handle his own life and certainly not a multibillion-dollar empire.

Which brought him to his daughter, Decker. Of the three, she had the most going for her. She had inherited her father's drive, but her ruthlessness scared him.

He thought of himself as ruthless when necessary. All his life he had known what he wanted and had gone for it. Sometimes he hadn't been completely honest or ethical about getting it, either. But he had always sensed that deep down he still had a code of ethics, which had made him, for example, shy away from Thalidomide the first second the rumor of birth defects surfaced.

Decker was restrained by no such code. Whatever Decker wanted, Decker went after. She had proved that by snaring her husband before the poor fool knew what was happening to him. And Decker demonstrated a greed for power and material things that Atkins himself had never possessed.

He had never wanted to be rich for the sake of the money alone. He had always set out to prove a point, to do something that couldn't be done. The riches had been merely a by-product. Decker would market Agent Orange to get rid of dandelions if she thought it would make money for her.

Atkins sighed and turned away from the window. None of them then. No child a fitting heir to his empire. He shook his head and smiled as he realized he had almost overlooked his two youngest children. Excusable in the circumstances, since he hadn't seen them since they were tots. Of course they were both too young to take over his company, and probably not too hot in the brain department if they took after their mother.

He went over to his desk and opened the center drawer. Under some papers was a silver-framed photo. He took it out and studied the picture. It was of a rather silly face, like a young Marilyn Monroe, with a lot of blond curls, wide, baby-blue eyes, and very red lips mouthing a kiss to the camera. She looked what she was—a common, uneducated, small-town girl turned Las Vegas showgirl. And yet there had been something about her—something that had captured the heart of a middle-aged billionaire who could have had his pick of women. Even in the posed photograph, a kind of innocent, ethereal quality showed through. Here was someone who was constantly surprised and delighted with any little thing life chose to give her. He'd loved to give her presents, just to see those huge blue eyes open wide with surprise and to hear the little squeak of delight. So childlike in many ways, he thought, and yet everyone else seemed to think that her sweet, innocent exterior hid a sharp, cunning little mind, a mind that had plotted a very clever escape . . . He closed his eyes as a spasm of pain contorted his face. He stuffed the photo back into the drawer and slammed it shut.

He wouldn't think about her anymore. He didn't even know why he kept her picture, after all these years. It was just that he couldn't bring himself to throw it away.

It was time to get down to business. No more sentimentality. No more painful memories. He wasn't going to have them fighting over Decker-Atkins when he'd gone. He pulled up his chair and began to write.

"I, P. Stuart Atkins, III, being of sound mind . . ."

That made him pause and smile. He could just imagine how his children would react if they found they'd been deprived of their fair share of the estate. They'd each rush to a lawyer and try to have their father proved of unsound mind, even though they all knew that his mind was still as sharp as a young man's.

Sharper than most, he decided. He'd had one of the best brains at Yale, where good brains were two a penny. He'd definitely been the smartest boy in his school. He'd realized that at a very early age, the first time one of the other boys paid him to do his homework.

P. Stuart Atkins . . . He wrote the name again, doodling around it in bold black squiggles with his wide-nib black fountain pen. Funny that he should remember about the homework now, after all these years. He'd grown so used to thinking of himself as P. Stuart Atkins that he'd almost forgotten he'd once had another name and identity.

CHAPTER 2

PROVIDENCE, RHODE ISLAND, 1937

Woodrow Wilson Austen stood on his bicycle pedals to propel the heavy load up the hill. Rain blew in his face as he neared the crest, snatching his breath away. Leaves were piled in sodden drifts across the road, making the going treacherous. A car sped past, spattering him with mud, and he almost lost his balance as he swerved out of its path. He glared at it as it sped away, its occupants safe and dry inside. The suburban street was deserted, its maple trees standing bare-boned and dejected as water dripped from them. Only a fool would be out on an afternoon like this, Woody thought. Only a fool or someone who had no choice. He was the latter.

"Take this box of groceries over to Mrs. Atkins on Elm Street," old Mr. Gianni had said just as he was preparing to go home.

"Now?" Woody had thought he was done for the day.

Mr. Gianni frowned. "Late order. Just came in," he

said. "And Mrs. Atkins doesn't like to be kept waiting. She needs this stuff for a dinner party. You know the Atkins' house, don't you?"

Of course he knew the Atkins' house. He went by there often enough to drop off Ronald Atkins' homework. He always had to pretend that he was a friend, to keep Ronald's parents from suspecting that Ronald wasn't doing his own homework. But both boys knew that they were anything but friends. Ronald despised him yet would have been shocked to learn that the feeling was mutual.

Ronald Atkins was one of those parasites carried through life by rich parents. He and his friends did little work in school, were rude to teachers, and thought it was fun to deflate bike tires and throw smaller boys' caps into the river. They did all this secure in the knowledge that their parents would bail them out of any situation and that the principal of Benjamin Franklin High School would never upset the families who made such generous donations to the sports field fund.

They were the haves in this part of Providence, but Woody was a have-not. He had a father and mother and damp, dingy room in a tenement down by the river in the worst part of town, but that was all. His father hadn't managed to find a job since he was laid off back in 1933. However, he hadn't actually looked for work in several years and spent his time in the local taverns whenever he could find the money.

Woody had been the family's only breadwinner

since he was twelve. He delivered papers before school and worked in Gianni's Grocery after school every day. At first he felt proud when he handed over his paycheck, and knowing that he kept his family from starving. But as he grew older and realized what he was missing, anger seethed deep inside him.

Most of the other kids in high school took it for granted that life was a big lark. They played football and skated on the pond in winter, and went to parties and dances, but Woody never could. His athletic ability made him a natural for the football team, but he couldn't attend practices. His English teacher urged him to join the new debate squad, but his jobs wouldn't allow him to practice after school and compete in tournaments.

Woody also knew that he didn't have the right clothes to appear in debates. Most of his were so patched and worn that he was the subject of constant teasing at school.

"Hey, Austen, is that breeks you're wearing on your patches?"

"Hey, Austen, is that a quilt or a jacket? Is the rainbow look in fashion this year?"

He always pretended he hadn't heard. He had no influential father to stick up for him if he hit back. For the same reason he never went to dances. He didn't want to be humiliated when the girls in his class turned him down and laughed at him. This irked him, particularly because he knew he was more charming and handsome than the popular boys. He had inherited his father's rugged Irish features and bright blue eyes, strikingly framed by blond hair inherited from his Scandinavian mother. To comfort him, his mother told him that missing dances was no great loss. "A lot of cheap, common floozies go to those dances," she said. "No nice girl goes to a dance without a chaperon."

This was probably true in her youth. She had been forty-one when he was born, a plain, big-boned woman who looked as if she had a perpetual bad smell under her nose. Although she came from near poverty herself, she had big ideas. Why else would she have named her only child after the President of the United States? She would never have sunk to marrying a returned army private like Duncan Austen had she not been almost forty, with no other prospects. She found out immediately that she had made a big mistake. The only thing Duncan ever provided for her was this unexpected child.

Nothing Woody's father could do was ever good enough for her. Her constant tirades against her husband's failure just caused heavier drinking and louder abuse. Woody didn't remember a day in his childhood when his parents spoke pleasantly to each other. At least his jobs kept him out of the house. At other times he escaped to the public library and lost himself in adventure novels.

CHAPTER 3

Woody coasted down the other side of the hill, gently applying the brake. This was the area where the "best" families in town lived, in tall square houses set back from the street. He rode up the Atkins' driveway and around to the back of the house. Once he'd delivered groceries to the front door, and Mrs. Atkins, who was usually so friendly, had severely reprimanded him.

"Deliveries to the back door, Woodrow," she had said. "That is the tradesmen's entrance."

A maid took the box from him this time and shut the door in his face without giving him a tip. He was just leaving the driveway when he saw three figures walking up the street toward him; they were laughing and sharing a bag of candy as they walked, protected by a large black umbrella. Woody recognized Ronald Atkins, with his two best friends, Joshua Paul and Harry Stuart.

Woody considered riding away before they reached the gate, but they had already spotted him.

"Is that Woody Austen or a drowned rat, would you say?" Ronald drawled.

"Looks like a drowned rat."

"Smells like a drowned rat."

"Makes a change from his father, who's a pickled herring!"

"Watch it, Stuart," Woody said, swerving his bike up onto the sidewalk to confront them. He was in no mood for this.

"I hope you didn't get our groceries wet, Austen," Ronald said. "My mother will make a frightful fuss if she gets wet flour. You might find yourself out of a job."

Woody knew that a smart answer wouldn't pay. Because their brains didn't work as fast as his, they only got more spiteful. But he did manage one jab.

"By the way, Atkins, you still owe me for the physics homework I did for you last week," he said loudly.

Atkins looked around in alarm. "Are you crazy? Keep your voice down. If anyone were to hear . . ." He reached into his pocket and pulled out a coin. "Here," he said, "although I don't really think you deserve this. You only got me a B plus."

He flipped the coin in Woody's general direction. Woody grabbed at it, but it slipped from his wet hands, rolled along the wet sidewalk and disappeared into a drain. If he hadn't needed it so badly, he would have ridden away. But he did need it. He concealed his anger as he leaned his bike against the fence and got down on all fours to reach down into the drain. He could see the coin lying in the mud, just out of reach. Tears of frustration burned in his eyes. He could hear the laughter behind him, but it seemed to be coming from far, far away.

"Of course I couldn't get you an A, you stupid fool," he muttered to himself. "As if any teacher would believe you were capable of A work!"

Grudgingly, he got to his feet. He would not stoop to ask Ronald for another quarter. He grabbed his bike and began to pedal away, the rain in his face cooling his rage.

At that moment he made a vow. He'd rather starve than do their homework anymore. He was going to put all his energy into his own schoolwork and graduate with such distinction that they'd have to give him a place at college. No longer would Woody Austen be the poor boy who had to grabble in the mud for a quarter. He was going to make something of his life, not to please his mother, nor to make up for his father's failure, but to show Paul and Stuart and Atkins and all the asses like them that Woody Austen was a somebody!

CHAPTER 4

When he got home, his mother was waiting by the door, arms folded with displeasure. "And where have you been?" she demanded.

"Old man Gianni gave me a last-minute delivery. I had to ride all the way over to the Atkinses."

"I hope they gave you a good tip for riding over on a night like this."

"They didn't give me a tip."

"You should have asked for one. People like that don't deserve to be community leaders. In my day, the rich were brought up to be gracious."

As Woody closed the door behind him and began to take off his sodden jacket, she noticed his disheveled appearance. "Just look at you! You look like a street urchin! No wonder they didn't give you a tip. What have you been doing to yourself? You haven't been fighting again?"

"No, Mother," he said wearily. "It's raining out there, in case you hadn't noticed. I got spattered by a passing car."

Instantly her tone changed. "My poor boy." She helped him off with his jacket. "You're soaked to the skin. I hope you don't catch your death of cold. Quick, take off those wet things and I'll heat some water for you to take a bath." She began unbuttoning his shirt.

"Mother," he said, pulling her hand away. "I'm seventeen years old. I don't need you to undress me."

"You're my little boy, Woodrow. You're all I have."

"You have father too."

"Huh. A lot of use he is."

"Where is he, anyway?" The house was strangely quiet.

"He's been gone all day. Where he found the money to spend all that time in the tavern is beyond me."

"You've checked the cookie jar?" Woody ran over to the mantlepiece. That was where they kept the rent money, under the cookies.

"It's safe. I told you he'd never look there. Now get those wet clothes off. I'll put the water on to heat."

Inside his own tiny room, Woody had just stripped and was reaching for his robe when he turned to find his mother.

"Mother! I wish you'd knock!" he told her angrily, snatching up his robe and holding it to cover himself.

"I only came to tell you that the water is hot!" she exclaimed with dignity. "Since when can't a parent come into her child's room?"

"I'm almost a man, Mother. It's not right," he said, his face hot with embarrassment.

She moved away. "Did you hear any more about the speech contest yet?"

"Mother, I've told you, I haven't a chance," he protested.

"You're a good speaker."

"I'm not the sort of person they'd choose to represent the school."

"I don't see why not."

"For one thing, I'd look a fool standing up in front of everyone at City Hall in pants that come above my ankles and a jacket with patches on both elbows," he said. "You can't seem to get it into your head that we're poor, Mother. We're nobodies. We're trash."

She slapped him hard across the face, almost sending him sprawling on the bed. "Don't ever talk that way again, Woodrow Wilson Austen," she said. "Just because you've a father who is a nobody, who comes from a long line of Irish peasant nobodies, doesn't mean you have to follow in their footsteps. I'm counting on you, Woodrow. I've raised you to be somebody. You've got to think big and you've got to seize every opportunity that comes your way. You've got to make up for your father's hopeless failure."

"I hope he's all right," Woody said, peering out of the window. "He's usually home for dinner. Should I go look for him?"

"Good riddance. That's what I say," Mrs. Austen said bitterly. "We'd be better off without him."

Woody looked at the hatred on his mother's face. He wondered how it was possible to dislike a parent as much as he did. Not that he felt much for his father, but at least he pitied him. "I'll take my bath in here," he said, and went to drag the old zinc tub from the closet.

Duncan Austen didn't return home that night. Woody lay awake, listening to the shutters clattering in the wind and the rain spattering on the window. He kept telling himself that it was his duty to get up and go find his father, but he shuddered when he thought of encountering the man after so many hours of drinking. By this time, he'd either be fighting drunk or weepy. Either was embarrassing.

Woody had just drifted off to sleep when he was woken by the sound of hammering on the front door. A policeman stood there. "Mrs. Austen?" he asked. "I'm afraid I've some bad news for you. Your husband's just been found dead."

Woody had to admit that his mother put on a good display. She clutched her bosom. "Dead? Oh, no. What happened, Officer? How did he die?"

"Seems like he drowned, ma'am."

"Drowned?" Mrs. Austen couldn't conceal her surprise. "Finlay's Tavern is nowhere near the river—"

"He wasn't in the river, ma'am," the young policeman said with obvious embarrassment. "Looks like he passed out and fell into a puddle behind the tavern. Apparently he drowned in three inches of water."

Woody's mother actually laughed. "What a fitting

end to a completely useless life," she said. She slipped her arm through her son's. "Well, child, it's all up to you now. You are your mother's only hope. Promise me that you'll make me proud of you."

Woody was fighting with conflicting emotions: anger that his mother should be taking his father's death so lightly, relief that he wouldn't have to walk on egg shells when his old man came home drunk, and guilt that he felt no great loss at his parent's death.

"Don't worry, Mother," he said. "I fully intend to make something of my life."

After his father's death, life improved slightly for Woody. There were now only two mouths to feed, and no need to hide money away. The principal gave a speech at assembly and urged the students to show sympathy for Woody's tragic loss. Atkins and his cronies sniggered and made remarks under their breath at this, but when Woody glanced around he saw that Mary Pilcher had tears in her eyes. Mary was one of the smartest people in the class. He often saw her at the library and nodded a polite hello. After assembly she came up to him and rested her hand gently on his arm. "Woody, I'm so sorry," she said. "If there's anything I can do . . . maybe you'd like to work on homework together sometimes. I know you like to read—"

It was an obvious invitation, and he saw warmth in those gentle brown eyes. "I could meet you in the library after I get off work, if you like," he said.

"All right." She smiled at him, and Woody felt his heart melting.

That night they studied together in the library, he asked her to stop off for a soda at Greenberg's Drugstore. They sat until the store closed, discussing their favorite authors and books. Then Woody walked her home.

It was dark when he climbed the stairs to his apartment, very conscious of the smell of cat and old orange peel in the stairwell and the crying baby at number five. How could someone like him ever have the nerve to ask Mary Pilcher to be his girl?

As he stepped inside, his arm was grabbed in a viselike grip. "And where have you been?" his mother demanded. She was all ready for bed, in her nightgown.

"I was working at the library. I had some things I had to look up," he replied quickly.

"The library closed over an hour ago."

"I met a friend from school there. We talked for a while afterward."

"A friend? What friend?"

"Her name's Mary. She's in my English class."

"A girl? I won't have it. I won't have you wasting your time with girls. At this stage of your career, you'll study and not let any little tramp get in the way."

"She is not a tramp, Mother. Take that back!" Woody said angrily. "She's one of the smartest students in the school. We discuss literature together."

"Huh! Literature, eh? Mark my words, Woodrow. Friendship with women leads to no good. All men have lust in their hearts and fire in their loins. It only takes a little closeness with a woman to waken it."

"Mother. This relationship is quite innocent."

"They all start that way, but they all end up the same way too . . . in lust, Woodrow. I'll not have you wasting your time with lust. Your first duty is to your widowed mother, Woodrow. Please remember that. As it happens, I was praying for you to come home because I am in considerable pain."

"In pain? What is it, Mother? Should I call the doctor?"

"No, we can't afford doctors. It's just my rheumatism playing up in this damp weather. I can bear it if you'd only rub on a little liniment for me."

"Of course, Mother. I'll fetch it for you."

"Come in my bedroom." She led the way and handed him the tube. "It's my shoulder and back, Woodrow. Right here." She sat on the bed and pulled her gown down over her right shoulder. Woody squeezed some liniment onto his hand and began to rub.

"Does that feel better now?" he asked.

"Don't stop, Woody. Don't stop," she murmured. Her eyes were closed and she was moving back and forth on the bed.

Woody pulled his hand away. "I've already rubbed it in," he said. "Now I have homework to finish." He hurried to his own room and shut the door.

CHAPTER 5

He never again told his mother when he was seeing Mary. He had precious little free time, between working and studying for graduation, but they managed to take walks together along the riverbank and to see an occasional movie. As the school year drew to a close, he fantasized about taking her to the senior prom.

"George Wentworth has asked me to go with him, Woody," Mary said as they walked home one evening.

"What did you tell him?"

"That I wasn't sure yet."

Woody kicked savagely at a rock, sending it bouncing across the street. "You know I'd like to take you, Mary. It's just not possible. I wouldn't want to embarrass you with the way I was dressed."

She stopped and touched his hand lightly. "Woody, if you need the money to rent a tux—"

"I couldn't accept charity from anyone, Mary.

Least of all from you," he said. "I want you to go with George." He could hardly get the words out, they were so painful. "I want you to have an evening to remember."

Her hand squeezed his. "I'd rather remember it with you, Woody, but I do understand how you feel."

"It's not as if I have any claim on you, Mary," he told her hopelessly. "I mean, there's no possible future for us. You're headed for Vassar in the fall and I'm going to be working like a slave trying to save enough to go to some college, sometime in my life . . ."

Her eyes were soft and warm. "It will get better, Woody. I know it will. You're smart and you're handsome. All you need is one good break in life and I know you'll make it someday."

"Oh, I intend to make it someday," he said. "Only it'll be too late for us."

So he stayed home while Mary went to the prom with George. He was one of several students graduating with a perfect 4.0, but he was not asked to be valedictorian. He did go to Mary's graduation party though, where he had his first taste of champagne and kissed her on the back porch.

He was humming to himself as he came home in the early hours of the morning. No sound came from his mother's room as he let himself into the apartment. He felt pleasantly relaxed and hopeful as he undressed and slipped between the cool sheets. It took him a moment to realize that he wasn't alone in the bed, and for a second he had the fantastic thought that Mary had somehow managed to slip into the apartment to wait for him.

"Mary?" he whispered.

"You don't need Mary, Woody," his mother's voice murmured beside him.

"Stay away from me," he warned as he began dressing again hurriedly. "Stay away, you hear. Don't ever touch me again!"

"Woody," the voice pleaded, "I only wanted to help. I don't want anything to come between us. You're my boy, Woody. I don't want to share you . . . you're all I've got."

Woody had crammed his feet into his shoes. Without waiting to tie the laces, he ran out, down the stairs and into the night.

CHAPTER 6

Woody's first thought was only of flight. He couldn't wait to put distance between himself and his mother. He ran until it hurt him to breathe, then he slid down to the railroad tracks and hopped onto a slow-moving freight train. He didn't even know which direction it was going in. All he wanted to do was to get out of town fast. The boxcar he had climbed into was piled with logs and he perched uncomfortably on top of them while black smoke from the engine coated him with soot. Every time he thought back to the scene in his bedroom, he felt almost physically sick.

He realized he had known for a long time that his mother's obsession with him was unhealthy, and now that he had a man's body, she wanted to possess him. He shuddered and tried to put her from his mind. He would never go back there again, no matter what happened to him, or to her. She was an able-bodied woman. Now she'd have to get herself a job or starve. He didn't care what she did.

The train was slow-moving and halted several times in the blackness while an express screamed past. Now and then he smelled the tang of the ocean and once saw lights glittering across the water. They must be heading down the Coast. He thought of New York City. He had always dreamed of going there one day. Maybe a place as big as New York even had jobs. He propped himself uncomfortably between logs and, lulled by the rhythmic motion, drifted into uneasy sleep as the train lumbered on.

He woke with a start as the train jerked to a stop with a loud clang. His neck was so stiff he could hardly lift his head. He could hear far-off shouts and he looked up cautiously. It was improbable that anyone should be searching for him, but he felt like a criminal on the run. He saw that the sky was streaked with dawn and that the car was now in what seemed to be a freight yard. There was no longer an engine at the front of the train, and cars were being shunted farther down the track. He decided to make his escape before he was discovered so he climbed down from the car, dodged across the freight yard and up an embankment.

Woody had no idea of where he was, but he was clearly in a town of some size. He passed solid brick houses set amid green lawns. A newsboy rode past, skillfully hurling papers and whistling as he went.

This reminded Woody that Mr. Hutchinson would be waiting in vain for him to show up for his morning route. How would his mother explain his absence? he wondered. He didn't even care. His stomach growled in hunger, and he decided that he should first find a job before he went any farther. It looked like a prosperous town, and he wasn't afraid of hard work.

He saw large buildings ahead and thought he was approaching the center of town when he came out into a square and stood staring, his mouth open in wonder. His gaze took in the brick Colonial buildings with their white columns and cloaks of ivy, the immaculate green lawns with paths crisscrossing, and the discreet sign at the front: Yale University, Founded 1701. It was as if he were having a vision. He knew without reservation that he wanted to be a student here, not someday in the distant future, but now, this fall, with all his contemporaries. He knew his was a hopelessly impractical vision, but his jaw was set with determination.

His present appearance was hardly appropriate for his first visit to his future campus. His old clothes looked even worse after a night in a sooty boxcar. His hair was tousled and his face grimy. He hurried from the campus in the absurd fear that a future professor would see him and later remember him. He needed clothes, a new image . . . and money, he reminded himself. It cost a lot of money to go to Yale, more money than he'd ever be able to save. And yet he wasn't ready to give up. He believed that he had been sent here by divine providence, brought to this place for a purpose and that a way would be found.

His first task, obviously, was to find a job, but not in town, where he'd be mingling with students and professors. He hitchhiked back out to the countryside and was hired by a local farmer to help bring in the hay. The job lasted a week. He was well fed, slept in the barn, and was a few dollars richer by the end of it. From there he moved to strawberry picking and earned a few more dollars. He considered that he now had enough to get some presentable clothes and went back into town to find some gray-flannel pants and a white shirt at a used-clothing store. Since he didn't have enough for a blazer, he was glad that the weather was very hot. Then he went to a stationer's and bought a sheet of fine linen bond writing paper and an envelope.

While was working long hours in the fields he had an incredible idea. He remembered reading in the library of a famous novelist who had entered Harvard under an assumed identity. If Harvard could be easily fooled, why not Yale?

He went into the public library, settled himself at a table in the corner and began to write:

"This is to introduce my great-nephew . . ." He looked around for inspiration. The name must reek of respectability . . . a good old-family name, that's what he wanted. A picture of those three spoiled oafs floated into his head. Paul, Stuart and Atkins—supposedly all from good families. Woody grinned to himself and

continued writing: *"my great nephew, P. Stuart Atkins III.*

"This young man comes from a fine old family, wiped out like so many others by this terrible depression. I am his one surviving relative and have been told that I don't have long in this world. I am therefore very concerned that young Paul Stuart should be able to make something of his life. His formal schooling has been interrupted by lack of finances." This would explain the absence of a diploma. *"However, he is a very able boy, hampered by adverse circumstances. If you would just let him take your entrance exam, you would see that he has a fine, scientific brain and is the sort of student who belongs at your university."*

Woody signed it in a suitably shaky hand, *"Yours truly, H. C. Atkins."*

There was an incredulous smile across his face as he sat back to admire his work. It was the craziest, audacious thing, and probably had no chance of succeeding, but he was going to give it a try anyway.

CHAPTER 7

Head high, he strode across those green lawns to the front entrance of Yale University. Still he had to command his legs to obey him; he was sure he would be flung out in disgrace. But he managed enough composure to ask for the admissions office.

The director, a distinguished old gentleman with wispy white hair and steel-framed spectacles, peered first at the letter and then at young P. Stuart Atkins.

"We'll consider this and let you know," he said. "To what address should an answer be sent?"

"I've just arrived in town and don't have an address as yet," Woody replied.

"Your home address?"

"I'm afraid, sir, that I'm the last member of my immediate family. We lost the family home due to financial disaster. I've been—living off my wits, so to speak."

The old man nodded with understanding. Such stories were all too common during the past few years. "I see," he said. "Well, young Atkins. Come back this afternoon and I'll see what I can do."

During the next few days, Woody took a series of entrance exams and at the end of the week, he was invited to see the registrar.

"You certainly have an exceptional mathematical and scientific brain," the registrar said, "and it is the feeling here that such brains will be needed in the coming years if that madman in Germany is not stopped before he swallows Europe. I am pleased to inform you that we would be prepared to admit you for the fall semester with a partial waiving of fees."

A partial waiving of fees put Yale as far from Woody as the moon, but he smiled graciously, shook the man's hand and accepted the offer. He would attend in the fall if it meant working five jobs around his classes.

He went straight back out to the countryside and worked on a succession of farms, picking fruit and vegetables all summer. By September he was bronzed and muscled, had a reasonable amount of money saved, and several items of clothing, donated by sympathetic farmers' wives.

He entered Yale, full of hope, in the fall of 1937. It was quite a shock to see the name on his dorm-room door: P. Stuart Atkins, III. He almost walked past before he realized that this was his name from now on. He must be careful never to let this new identity slip.

He took a deep breath before he opened the door and went into the room. It was Spartan by most standards, but it looked old and distinguished, exactly as he had imagined a dorm room would look. He had just put his small bag down on one bed when the door burst open and another young man came in, tall with a mop of reddish curls, and gangly limbs.

"You beat me to it and chose the best bed, you blighter," he said. "The last thing they said to me when I left home was to never get the bed under the window. There's always a draft."

"I didn't think. I took the nearest one," Woody said. "I could trade if it's important to you. I don't mind drafts."

"I don't either," the other boy said. He held out his hand. "I'm Theo, and I see that you are P. Stuart Atkins the Third. What a mouthful. It's even worse than Theodore Edward Brinkmeyer. What is one supposed to call you?"

"I don't mind," Woody said.

"You must have a nickname."

"Afraid not. I never stayed in one place long enough to pick up a nickname."

"Then I'll just have to give you one," Theo said with a friendly grin. "I'll call you Trip, for the triple digits after your name."

"Okay," Trip agreed. He liked the sound of it already. He also liked Theo.

Theo looked at the bag on the bed. "I say, when's the rest of your stuff arriving?"

"It will catch up with me eventually, I guess," Trip replied.

"I took my trunks on the train with me," Theo said. "The porters will be bringing them up any minute. I hope it all fits in here. If not, you can always sleep in the hall."

He grinned again and Trip grinned back. It was the first time he had been treated as an equal and he liked it.

He was determined that nobody would ever find out the truth about Trip Atkins. But assuming a new identity was not easy. Trip quickly discovered that compared to him the best families spoke such a different language and led such different lives that they might have lived on another planet. He had to back out of many conversations because he hadn't seen plays on Broadway, he didn't know the names of operas, and he hadn't been to Europe.

He learned this quickly after a series of horrible blunders over coffee one night. Henry Harrison, one of the young men down the hall, had spent the summer touring Europe.

"Personally, I can't say that I go for Cannes in a big way," he said in his bored drawl. "What about you, Trip?"

"Cans? Oh, we never ate anything out of cans at home," Trip replied. "My mother thought it wasn't safe."

There was a roar of laughter around the room. Trip flushed scarlet.

"He's talking about Cannes the place, not the tin

receptacle," one of the other boys explained.

"I'm sorry, I wasn't listening properly," Trip answered hastily. "I was thinking about tomorrow's physics test."

"I hope you're not going to turn into a brain, Trip Atkins," Theo said. "I give fair warning right now that I intend to do only enough work to get out of here with a diploma in hand and to shut up all the nagging at home."

"What did they nag you about?" Trip was interested.

"Not going to West Point. We're a military family. I was not enticed by cold showers and someone blowing a bugle in my ear at five in the morning. They all think there's something wrong with me."

"I tell you what I miss after Europe," Henry said pensively. "I miss escargots."

"Escargots? Henry, how could you? Nobody actually likes escargots, do they? Do you like escargots, Trip?"

"I've never actually been there," Trip replied.

More laughter.

"Trip, you are such a wag," Henry said. "I don't know how you can say all this stuff with a straight face. You have to write for the Yale humor magazine."

At least they thought that his blunders were jokes, but he decided to keep quiet until he read up about Europe and food and opera and everything else these boys took for granted.

But it was hard keeping the truth from Theo. When

they were invited to their first party, Trip put on his one good suit, which he had bought at the used-clothing store. Theo took one look at it and laughed. "You're surely not intending to wear that?"

"What's wrong with it?"

"Lapels like that went out with the ark, old man. How on earth long have you had it?"

Trip was intending to say that this style was all the rage in Berlin or Paris this year, but he couldn't lie to Theo. "To be honest with you, it's all I've got," he said. "It hasn't been easy since my family lost everything. I haven't actually been to Europe, either. I've been working for my living."

Theo put a friendly hand on his shoulder. "Look here, old man, I'm terribly sorry," he said. "You should have said earlier. It's no disgrace to be poor, especially not in these times. If we were the same size, I'd say borrow mine, only . . ." He peered down at his long, lanky legs.

"Thanks anyway. What do you think I should wear?"

"Stick to the gray flannels. You can't go wrong with them. And I tell you what—I'll take the suit to my tailor next time I go. He can usually work miracles."

CHAPTER 8

So Theo became a best friend, amiable, easygoing, bounding through life like a friendly St. Bernard puppy. And Trip too began to flourish. Theo persuaded him to go out for the football team and coaches soon began grooming him to take over from the senior wide-receiver. He joined the debate squad, and best of all, he began meeting girls. Theo's family lived in Westchester County, close enough for weekend visits from girl cousins and family friends. After he got over his initial shyness, Trip was amazed to find that the girls clustered around him and that he could have his pick. Theo got used to girls arriving at their dorm room announcing, "We won't pretend we've come to see you, Theo dear. I promised Daisy that I'd introduce her to Trip Atkins."

Trip wished he had the time and money to take them out the way Theo and the other guys did, but he was working at a bookstore and had just started a job as a busboy at swank Antoine's Restaurant. He was hopeful about this job. If he worked well enough, he'd be promoted to waiter and then the tips would be enormous.

Unfortunately, the job lasted only a week. On Saturday night a party of young people came in. Trip was heading to clear dishes from a table when he heard a squeal of delight.

"Trip! It's Trip Atkins, everybody. Who are you dining with?" It was Peggy Hochstetter, a friend of Theo's family.

"I'm not dining with anybody," Trip began uncomfortably.

"Then you must join us, mustn't he, Peter?" Peggy clapped her hands. "Antoine, could you possibly squeeze in another chair beside me for Mr. Atkins? We can't let him dine alone, can we?"

Trip tried desperately to find a way to tell her that he was working there, but the words wouldn't come. He allowed himself to be squeezed in beside Peggy and tried not to notice the stares of the waiters and Monsieur Antoine as they brought him his food. At the end of the evening, Antoine was waiting for him as he emerged to apologize at the back door.

"I 'ave no place for a busboy who fraternizes with my clients," he said. "Such things I never 'eard of. Take your things and go."

The loss of money was a blow, but Trip knew that he could never endure another evening like that one. So he managed to find a job tutoring two very dull high school girls in math and he scraped through the school year.

That summer he turned down an invitation to Theo's summer home and worked in the fields again, building muscles and a bank account for the year ahead. In the fall, he learned that the football coach had requested that he be put on full scholarship, and his financial worries were at an end. He had also made the dean's list. The next summer he spent with Theo, and by the time he entered his senior year, he had acquired the easy grace and confidence of a Yale starting wide-receiver, a debate captain, and a social success.

In the middle of his senior year, he fell in love. Trip and Theo had just come off the field after a football game when Theo heard his name called and turned to see two young ladies hurrying after them. They were dressed alike in fashionable wide-shouldered suits with neat little pillbox hats perched on top of their heads, but other than that, they were a study in contrasts: one of them very fair, the other very dark. The dark-haired one was waving a tiny gloved hand. "Theo, it's me, Lizzy."

"Good God," Theo said. "Lizzy Decker? I thought you were still in kindergarten. Weren't you in pigtails last year? How did you manage to grow up so quickly?"

The girl turned her big dark eyes on him, in a crushing stare. "Theo Brinkmeyer—still as horrid as ever, I see. Is that any sort of greeting to an old friend of the family? I brought Alice to meet you because I thought you might have become civilized and amusing after four years at Yale, but I can see you haven't."

Theo grinned good-naturedly. "I apologize, Lizzy. You caught me off guard. Really I had no idea you were . . . a young lady now. What are you doing here?"

"Alice and I are fellow sufferers at Miss Porter's Academy. It's supposed to finish us."

"Finish what?" Theo asked in amusement.

Liz gave him her withering stare again. "Finish our education, silly. We're going to come out completely equipped to marry princes or a Rockefeller, whichever comes first."

"Speak for yourself, Lizzy." The other girl spoke for the first time. She had a deep, melodious voice. "I have no desire to end up with either a prince or a Rockefeller. In fact, I don't even know if I ever want to get married at all. I might want to be another Amelia Earhart."

"That doesn't promise a long and successful career," Trip said, also joining in the conversation for the first time.

The girl looked up at him and Trip found himself looking into the most perfect cool gray eyes, ringed with sweeping dark lashes. He thought she was the loveliest thing he had ever seen.

"At least one wouldn't need a retirement fund," she said, and smiled. She had one perfect dimple in each cheek. Trip wanted to come up with an equally witty answer, but he was tongue-tied.

Luckily, Lizzy interrupted. "Aren't you going to introduce us to your friend, Theo? We're not really supposed to chat to young men we haven't been introduced to. Miss Porter says it's not correct in the best circles, like the British court."

"I wouldn't start thinking in terms of the British court, Lizzy," Theo said with a wink to Trip. "After that embarrassing abdication last year they're not exactly going to welcome any more American girls with open arms. But I will introduce you to the next best thing to the Prince of Wales. Elizabeth Decker, may I present my good friend and roommate, P. Stuart Atkins the Third, usually known as Trip."

Liz held out her tiny gloved hand. "So you're Trip Atkins? We've been dying to meet you. We've just watched you being brilliant on the football field."

"And your defense was equally good, Mr. Brinkmeyer," Lizzy's friend said. "I'm Alice, by the way. Alice Woodbury. I know your cousin Mary Lou. We went to ballet classes together once. She was as bad at it as I was. We were both frogs when other girls got to be butterflies." She laughed as she held out her hand to Theo.

Trip couldn't take his eyes off her. Everything about her was perfect, he quickly decided; her complexion was like rose petals, her hair like spun gold. She was as delicate as a china doll. And she was shaking hands with Theo. Trip wanted to push Theo out of the way. He could hardly conceal his impatience until she turned to him and said, "And I haven't officially said hello to you yet, Mr. Atkins."

"Please call me Trip," he said. He could feel himself blushing.

"Trip? What does that stand for?"

"I named him," Theo said. "I mean, who was going to stumble over all that P. Stuart nonsense? So I called him for the three digits after his name. It turned out to be very apt, because trip is what he usually does when he's running with the ball."

"Huh!" Trip said. "Who scored three touchdowns last week?"

The gray eyes turned to him. "That was an awfully good catch you made this afternoon. Quite spectacular."

"Thanks," Trip mumbled. Her presence had quite unnerved him. He was no longer the confident football star used to adoring women fans. He felt like a little boy again, praying not to say the wrong thing in front of her.

"Well, I don't intend to stand here listening to you two girls praise Trip Atkins," Theo said. "How about dinner tonight? Does Miss Porter's Academy allow such sinful things?"

"If we're in by ten," Lizzy said.

"Dinner should be over in the college dining-commons long before ten, shouldn't it, Trip?" Theo asked with a wink.

"Theo Brinkmeyer, if you think that Alice and I would consider eating with a lot of loud men in a college dining hall—" Lizzy began.

"Oh, I don't know. It might be rather fun," Alice said.

"Don't worry, Lizzy. I was only teasing. I know you're used to caviar and smoked salmon. We're not going to subject you to the unidentifiable pudding they serve in commons. We'll come up with somewhere suitable to take young ladies from Miss Porter's."

Trip was glad that Theo was making plans, because his own head was spinning.

It turned out to be a good evening. They laughed a lot and danced. As they walked up the stairs to their dorm room later, Theo exclaimed, "What a stroke of luck, running into Liz Decker after all these years. And she used to be such a bratty kid too. She hasn't turned out badly at all. In fact, I feel quite fondly toward her now—"

"You do?" Trip was relieved. He hadn't been able to tell what Theo's feelings were.

"She was the messenger of fate, wasn't she? She brought Alice to the game. Wasn't she a little honey? An absolute doll."

"You like Alice?" Trip stammered.

"Who wouldn't?" Theo said. He turned to look at Trip. "Don't tell me you've fallen for her too?"

"Like a ton of bricks."

"But I thought you were flirting with Lizzy."

"Only because I was completely tongue-tied whenever I looked at Alice," Trip said. He shook his head.

"What are we going to do about it?"

"Prepared to fight a duel for her?"

"To the death," Trip answered firmly. The smile left Theo's face. "You're serious, aren't you?"

Trip nodded. "I've never met a girl before who makes me feel this way. I'm in love, Theo. Head over heels. I never believed it would happen to me, but it has."

"This can't be Trip, famed breaker of hearts, love 'em and leave 'em."

"Afraid so."

Theo looked at him for a long while in silence before he said slowly, "Then I suppose I have to bow to the power of love. Go ahead. She's yours. Only, if she turns you down, I get a crack."

Trip thumped him on the back. "Theo, you're a swell guy," he said. "I don't know how to thank you."

"You can write my paper for me," Theo said with a grin. "No, seriously, Trip, our friendship is too important to fall out over some girl, no matter how lovely and adorable and exquisite she is."

"She'll probably turn me down anyway," Trip said.

CHAPTER 9

But she didn't turn him down. Alice Woodbury
was delighted when Trip telephoned her the
next day. "To be honest with you, Trip," she
said, "I've had my eye on you all year. I've been to all
the football games. It was so lucky that Liz Decker
knew Theo, wasn't it?"

"Yes, wasn't it?" Trip couldn't believe his luck.
They dined and danced and went out for drives in her
little red sports car. Trip took up tutoring again, so that
he would have money to entertain her with and to buy
her flowers, which she loved. When Trip showed up
with a posy of fresias or jasmine, she would plunge
her face into it, breathing in the scent and looking up
to exclaim, "Heavenly!"

Trip wished that he had enough money to send her
orchids or roses every day. Luckily, she loved doing
things that were not beyond his reach. She loved
walking in the countryside. She loved curling up by a

fire and reading poetry out loud to him. She loved sentimental movies. She sobbed all the way through "How Green Was My Valley." Trip also adored movies with her, but for a different reason. In the darkness he could put his arm around her and sit content with her head on his shoulder, until she turned her face up expectantly for him to kiss. Her kisses were warm and generous, and when he grew bolder, she never pushed him away.

By his fourth year at Yale, Trip wasn't exactly a novice when it came to sex. Theo had told him that virginity was okay in a freshman but no longer, and had taken him to the place where he had taken his own first lessons in the art. Since then, there were always girls who were anxious to entertain a football player. Not nice girls, of course. Nice girls went home to Miss Porter's or to their parents' house.

"It's really not fair that the only car we have use of is so cramped and open for the world to see," Trip complained when he tried to kiss her goodnight, down the street from Miss Porter's.

"Trip Atkins, I suspect you have evil designs on me," Alice said, laughing.

"If I do, they'll never come true," Trip said. "There's nowhere we can go to be alone. If we're out in the country, then some damn woman comes by walking her dog. If we're at Yale, someone always interrupts, and in this car we're visible to the whole world. I wish we could just drive up to the wilds of Vermont and be truly alone together."

"Wouldn't that be wonderful," Alice sighed. "Just think of it, Trip. Big fire, pine trees, heavenly smell, and just you and me—"

"Then let's do it!"

Alice laughed. "There are small matters that get in the way, unfortunately," she said. "For one thing, Miss Porter wouldn't give me permission to spend a weekend in Vermont with you, and for another, my parents rather expect me to stay a virgin until I marry."

"Then we'll get married and go to Vermont!" Trip yelled excitedly.

Alice put her hand on his cheek and drew his face toward her to kiss him. "My dear sweet darling, I don't want to think of marriage for ages yet," she said. "There's so much I want to do. I want to see the world, and I want to work for my living as a real person, not as somebody's wife. And then there's this terrible war in Europe. Maybe we should be doing something about that."

"Like what?"

"Train as a nurse, maybe?"

"You'd like to be a nurse?"

"Maybe."

"That's incredible," Trip said. "Because I'm going to be a doctor. We could work together. I can say 'Scalpel, Nurse,' and you can pass it to me."

Alice laughed. "I might say 'Get it yourself.' I'm not very good at taking orders, Trip. I see myself as an independent woman. I don't want to be bossed around by any man." Then she slipped her arms around his neck. "Although in your case, I might make an exception—if you asked me nicely."

"I'd ask you very nicely," Trip whispered. He brought his lips to meet hers, kissing her gently at first, then more demandingly. His hand undid the button on her blouse and slipped inside to touch the silk of her slip, the soft warmth of her breast. "Oh, Alice," he breathed.

Alice shot apart from him and sat upright. "Someone's coming," she murmured as footsteps came tapping down the street.

"Damn," Trip muttered under his breath.

CHAPTER 10

Trip's last year at Yale drew to a close. Theo had been accepted at med school. Trip had gone through preliminary interviews at the same med school, but couldn't take up his place there until he could afford to finance himself, which meant at least a year of hard work in the real world. But he was learning that a Yale graduate was a valuable commodity, even if he lacked most of his peers' connections. He had several job offers by the time graduation came around and had planned to take up a sales position with a pharmaceutical company, because the pay was good and because he'd be working in the medical sphere.

The week before graduation he invited Alice to a frat-house ball. It was a balmy night and the air was heavy with the scent of blossoms. As he put on his tux, he thought back to the senior prom at high school and how he'd had to let Mary go with another boy because he couldn't afford the tux rental.

"Never again," he decided, looking at himself in the mirror. He was never going to be poor again. He was never going to miss an opportunity. And he wasn't going to let Alice slip away from him!

After they had danced for a while, Trip took Alice out into the gardens and they kissed on a bench under a tree.

"I can't believe I'll be out of here soon," he said. "It's become my life."

"Will you go home for the summer?"

"I've no home to go to," he said. "There's just me left now. No relatives. No home."

"Poor Trip," Alice said. "If only you were a puppy, I could adopt you."

"Oh, don't worry about me," Trip said. "I'm planning a great future. I'm going to graduate top of my class from med school and become a brilliant surgeon and save lives and live in one of those big brick houses with a beautiful wife and lots of adorable children around me."

"Sounds like a nice dream," Alice remarked.

"Not a dream, Alice. A plan. It's my plan," Trip said.

"And does the beautiful wife look at all like me?"

"Very like you."

"That's good," she said, "because by the time you're a brilliant surgeon, I'll probably have tired of being an independent woman and traveling the world."

Trip's heart beat faster. "Then I have a chance, Alice? Just tell me that I have a chance someday."

"Of course you have a chance, silly," she said, fondly stroking his cheek. "You know how I feel about you, Trip."

He took her hands in his. "Look, Alice. I know I have nothing now, but I promise that I'll make you proud of me someday."

"I'm sure you will, Trip," she told him. "You're so determined. I'm sure you'll make all your dreams come true."

"So I may continue to call on you when you leave Miss Porter's?" he asked as she stood up and started to walk through the darkened gardens.

"Of course. I want you to meet my parents."

"I hope you've told them that I'm poor but very respectable."

"Of course I have. They agreed that lots of good families were wiped out in the Depression and that being poor isn't a sin. Anyway," she said, laughing, "my father is a football fan. Anyone who can score all those touchdowns has to be okay."

They walked hand in hand through the gardens while the moonlight made shadows dance on the gravel paths. Trip felt that he wanted to yell with happiness. His whole future was stretching ahead of him, anything was within his grasp. He felt that he could leap up and grab the moon.

It was almost two in the morning when Alice waltzed into her room at Miss Porter's. She flung herself down on her bed with a sigh of ecstasy.

"You're back really late," Elizabeth Decker said, peeking around her door. "Did you get in trouble?"

"No, they understood. College balls are okay," Alice said. "It was wonderful, Lizzy. The most romantic evening of my life . . . he sort of asked me to marry him and I sort of said yes."

"Trip Atkins?" Liz demanded sharply. "You're going to marry Trip Atkins?"

"Not for ages yet. He has to become a famous doctor and I have to do something special with my life too."

Liz came in and sat down on her bed. "When do you meet his family?"

"He doesn't have one. He's a poor orphan. His father shot himself because he lost everything in the Depression, and he was brought up by his ancient grandfather, Colonel P. Stuart Atkins the First, until he died and left Trip all alone. Isn't that the most tragic, romantic story?"

"So he doesn't actually have any money? Your parents won't approve of that."

"They won't mind," Alice said. "As I told you, Lizzy, we're not going to marry until he becomes a doctor. By then they'll be so relieved to get me off their hands that they won't care who I marry."

"My parents would certainly mind who I marry," Liz said.

Alice laughed. "Your parents would let you marry King Kong if you begged them to," she told her friend. "You know very well you've got them eating out of the palm of your hand."

Liz smiled sweetly. "I suppose that's true," she said. "One of the benefits of being an only child."

Alice glanced at her watch. "Two o'clock. I can't believe it's so late and I'm not tired. Oh, Lizzy, the way he kissed me! I feel like I'm floating and on fire. If only we really had gone away for a weekend, like he suggested, I know I would have given myself willingly to him."

"Alice!" Liz said in a shocked voice. "You're not supposed to think about things like that until you're married."

"I can't help thinking about them," Alice said. "If you'd ever been in love, Lizzy, you'd know how I feel. I want him so badly it hurts." She sat up and beckoned Liz close to her. "I have to tell you—if we have the opportunity out at the Cape this summer, I have the feeling I'm not going to push him away, Lizzy."

"He's going out to the Cape this summer with you?" Liz asked.

"I'm going to ask Father if he can come and stay."

"What fun," Liz said in a tight little voice.

Alice looked up. "It was so sweet of you to wait up for me, Lizzy," she said, "but now you really must get some sleep. And so must I."

"You're right," Lizzy said. "I have lots of things to do in the morning."

CHAPTER 11

Liz went back to her room and flung herself back onto her bed. "Damn her," she said out loud. So her worst fears had come true. Alice really was going to marry Trip Atkins. Everything had gone wrong since Lizzy had met Trip and Theo at the football game. Alice was supposed to fall for Theo and she was supposed to get Trip. She had fallen in love with him the first time she saw him on the football field, his fair hair flopping boyishly across his forehead as he ran. He had scored a touchdown and then looked up with the most wonderful smile, waving the ball above his head. Liz thought he looked like a young Greek god.

But he had noticed Alice instead. In spite of everything she had done, he had still chosen Alice. And Liz had had to suffer all year through Alice's accounts of her wonderful evenings with Trip. She knew that listening to all the details would only make her feel worse, but she had to do it anyway. It was like wiggling a loose tooth when she was a child. She knew it would hurt, but the compulsion was so strong that she couldn't stop herself. And all year she had waited for Alice to tire of him, or for Trip to tire of Alice.

But it hadn't happened and now they were actually talking of marriage. Liz sat up in bed and clenched her fists. There was no way that she was going to let Trip Atkins marry Alice Woodbury. She'd stop it if it was the last thing she did!

Next morning she phoned her father's young secretary, Sheldon, and asked him to meet her on urgent business. Sheldon was rather stupidly in love with her and would do anything she asked.

"Sheldon, I've a small favor," she said when they sat at the small table. "I want to find out everything there is to know about a Yale man called Trip Atkins. If you have to hire a detective, I'll pay for it. Only, find out every detail, please."

Sheldon looked amused and interested. "May one ask what this is for?"

"My friend is thinking of marrying him and I'm sure she's making a big mistake," Liz said sweetly. "I'd like her to know the truth about him before she commits herself."

"I see," Sheldon said. "Very well, Miss Lizzy. I'll see what I can do."

"Here," she said. "This is what he looks like." She handed across a snapshot of the four of them, Theo,

Trip, Liz and Alice, sitting on a country wall, laughing. Trip's arm was around both girls and he was grinning with pure happiness. Liz's heart lurched as she handed it over. "It's a good likeness," she told Sheldon.

Liz waited impatiently for news while she packed up her things and prepared to move back home from Miss Porter's. After a few days, Sheldon called her. "It's rather like looking for a needle in a haystack," he reported. "Atkins isn't an uncommon name. They've no next of kin in his records at Yale. Any idea what part of the country he comes from?"

"I think he once mentioned Rhode Island," Liz recalled.

"Ah," Sheldon said. "There is a prominent family called Atkins living in Providence. Do you want me to go visit them?"

"That would be very sweet of you, Sheldon," Liz answered.

The next evening he called excitedly. "You were right to be suspicious," he said. "There seems to be some funny business going on."

"They recognized the photo, then?"

"Yes, they did, but his name's not Atkins. The photo's of a young man called Woody Austen. His widowed mother still lives in a run-down tenement. I have the address. Do you want me to visit her and confirm this?"

"No," Liz said. "Let me visit her myself."

CHAPTER 12

In the train on the way to Providence, Liz thought about turning back a hundred times. Deep down inside she knew she shouldn't go through with this. Trip had always been nice to her. Could she really go on, calmly knowing that she would wreck his life? I'm not really going to wreck his life, she decided. Whatever she found out today she'd keep to herself, unless she could use it to make sure that Alice and Trip never married.

The tenement was worse than she expected. It had been raining and foul-smelling puddles lay across the crumbling street. Mosquitoes whined and flies buzzed around garbage. She pushed open the door and went up the staircase, hearing babies crying and a radio blaring. Nobody came to the Austen door for a long while. Then Liz heard the sound of a lock being pulled back and the door opened an inch or so.

"Yes? Who is it? What do you want?" a slurred voice demanded.

"I'm a friend of your son's, Mrs. Austen," Liz said.

"Son? What son? I haven't got a son," the voice said belligerently.

Liz was half glad, half sorry that she was wrong. "I'm sorry," she said. "They told me that someone called Woody Austen used to live here."

The door opened slowly to reveal an old woman, the skin shrunken around her face like a skull. Her eyes were sunken and blinked in the daylight. Her hair was wild and unkempt, and her clothing looked like a collection of rags. "You know my Woody?" she asked in a cracked voice. "He's not dead? They said he was dead."

"He's very much alive and doing well, Mrs. Austen," Liz said.

The tired face lit up. "Well, come in then. Come in," she invited Liz, brushing off a chair. "Some tea? Can I make you some tea? I'd offer iced tea but there's no refrigerator, I'm afraid."

"Thank you, I'm not thirsty," Liz said, looking at the dirt and clutter. She took out the photo. "I've brought this with me."

The old woman took it with trembling hands. "Yes," she said after a while. "That's my Woody, all right. Where is he? What's he doing?"

"He's a Yale man, Mrs. Austen. A football star."

"He is? I always knew he'd make something of

himself," Mrs. Austen said proudly. "I always told him, you have to work hard so you don't end up like your father."

"What happened to his father?"

"He was a lazy, no-good, drunken Irish bum, Miss. He fell down dead drunk and drowned himself. Never was good for anything. That's why I made Woody work so hard. And it's paid off. I'm so proud." She grabbed Lizzy's arm, making the girl pull back. Her breath stank of alcohol and decay. "So tell me. Where can I find him now? When can I see him again?"

"I . . . can't tell you that, Mrs. Austen," she said. "But I'll mention to him that I've seen you and that you'd like him to visit."

The old woman wiped her eyes. "You're too kind, bothering to visit his mother."

"Not at all, Mrs. Austen. You've been a big help," Liz said. She opened her purse. "I hope you won't be too proud to take a little money—to help with expenses?" The hundred dollars seemed to hover in mid-air before the old hand shot out and took it.

The next day Liz visited Mrs. Woodbury.

"I just hate to tell you this, but I wanted to save poor Alice from making a big mistake," she said.

Mrs. Woodbury's face was white. "But he sounded like such a nice boy," she said. "Alice was very smitten with him. This is going to break her heart." She leaned over and patted Liz's hand. "We're very grateful to you, my dear."

"I thought it was my duty," Liz said. "Only please don't tell Alice how you found out. I wouldn't want her to think that I let her down."

"Of course not. Her father will be relieved, I fear. He had his sights set on someone quite different for her. Someone with money." She got up and went over to the window, pulling back the lace drapes to peer out. "Ah well, she's only eighteen. At that age one doesn't yet know what one really wants from life."

How wrong she is, Liz thought. I know exactly what I want. She got up and went over to Mrs. Woodbury. "I must be going now. Please give Alice my love when you see her. Tell her I'm sorry I missed her today."

Trip was whistling as he walked up the front path to the Woodbury's elegant home in Scarsdale. In his hand he held a big bouquet of roses. A maid came to the front door. Before he could say anything, she said, "I'm afraid that Miss Woodbury cannot see you."

The smile faded from Trip's face. "Is something the matter? Is she sick?"

The face remained expressionless. "My orders from Mr. Woodbury were to tell you that you are not welcome here and must leave immediately. Miss Woodbury doesn't wish to see you ever again."

"But why? What have I done? Let me see her for just a moment," Trip begged. "I'm sure this is all a misunderstanding. Let her tell me herself if she doesn't want to see me. If she tells me herself, then I'll go."

"I'm afraid that Miss Woodbury cannot see you, sir," the maid told him firmly. "Please go. Mr. Woodbury instructed me that I was to call the police if there was any unpleasantness."

"The police? What am I supposed to have done? I'm not a damned criminal!"

"Miss Alice doesn't want to see you, sir. Just go."

"But can't I at least know why? Won't somebody tell me what I've done?" Trip was yelling now.

"I really don't want to call the police, sir," the maid said shakily. He could see that her composure was beginning to crack. "Please go." She shut the door firmly, leaving Trip standing on the front steps.

He waited there forever, his head reeling, trying to decide what to do. He wasn't prepared to go away and leave Alice. He couldn't believe that she didn't want to see him again. Obviously, something must have happened to change her parents' or Alice's mind about him. He had to set them straight, but it was quite possible that only servants were home and they really would call the police.

Reluctantly, he went down the steps. He was halfway down the path when he heard Alice call his name. He looked up and there she was at an upstairs window.

"Alice!" he yelled. "Alice, what's wrong? Tell me what I've done."

Tears were streaming down her cheeks. "I can't, Trip. I'm not allowed to talk to you. They won't let me see you ever again. They're taking me out to

California . . . I'm so sorry, Trip."

"But why, Alice?"

"I can't tell you. Good-bye, Trip. I really loved
you."

"I love you, Alice. I won't give up. I'll be here,
waiting for you to find me again."

"It's no good, Trip. Please go away and get on with
your life," she begged him. She was crying so hard
now that he could hardly understand the words. "I
want you to be happy."

Before she could say any more, she was jerked
away and the window was slammed shut. Trip stood
alone in the empty street, staring up at the window for
a long time before he finally walked away.

CHAPTER 13

On December 7, 1941, the Japanese air force bombed Pearl Harbor.

Trip Atkins was walking through New York City at the time. A salesman for a drug company, he had just made a successful sale of the new sulfa drugs to a large pharmacy. It was late afternoon and a watery sun hung like a red ball low in the smoky sky. Fifth Avenue was festive when Trip entered the building an hour earlier. Pre-holiday shoppers streamed out of Bloomingdale's and Gimbels, their arms piled high with bags and boxes. There was definitely more money to spend than last Christmas, now that the war in Europe was fueling the economy. Street corner Santas were doing better too as they stamped their feet to keep warm, chanting "God bless you, sir, Merry Christmas, lady" as coins clanged into kettles. Carols were blaring from open storefronts, "God Rest Ye,

Merry Gentlemen" fighting against "Angels We Have Heard On High" from across the street. The air was crisp and cold, with the promise of Christmas snow.

Trip was exhilarated. He had received a holiday invitation from Theo's family, and he'd finally see what a real Christmas was all about.

He was humming to himself as he came out of the medical building but he noticed instantly that something had changed. There was a conspicuous quiet, almost as if snow had fallen and muffled all sound. The carols weren't playing anymore and the shoppers were standing around in nervous little groups, talking and glancing up at the sky. Trip glanced up, too, but the sky was clear and glowed red on the horizon between the buildings on Forty-second Street. As he came around the corner into Times Square, he saw that a crowd had gathered. He looked up at the billboard and read the words: "Japs bomb Hawaii. We're at war."

Like most of the crowd, he was stunned as he made his way down the subway and home. That a year that had started off with so much promise should end like this!

Trip was only now beginning to get over the shock of Alice's rejection, though he still didn't understand it. She hadn't attempted to contact him again; he feared that being a penniless nobody had mattered to her and her family after all.

Although the ache in his heart hadn't completely subsided, his life wasn't unpleasant. He was making good money and gaining experience which would be useful at medical school. If all went well, he planned to join Theo at Johns Hopkins next fall. He was even studying in the evenings, in anticipation.

Every time Theo wrote or telephoned, it was to complain about how hard he had to work. He wasn't even sure that he wanted to be a doctor if it meant actually having to learn so much unnecessary stuff, he said half-jokingly. He was sure he was never going to join a leper colony, so why did he have to know the history of leprosy? And did all the bones of the foot really have to have Latin names? Trip wasn't sure of how serious Theo's complaints were. He knew that Theo had breezed through Yale without any serious attempt at studying. Maybe med school was a horrible shock to him.

"You darned well better not give up before I get there," Trip said. "I'm counting on you to introduce me to girls."

"Girls? Who has time to meet girls?" Theo responded.

Trip didn't have much time to meet girls, either. He worked long hours for the drug company and often tutored in the evenings. When he wasn't working, he was studying. He rationalized that he had to save every penny to put himself through med school, but in reality he didn't want to get involved with a woman again. Women were naturally drawn to Trip—he was tall, broad shouldered, and handsome, with striking blond hair and bright blue eyes. He was content to pick up a girl in a bar occasionally and take her somewhere for the night, but that was all. From now on, women were to be for physical enjoyment, nothing more.

On the train home, Trip realized the Japanese bombing of Pearl Harbor shouldn't have taken him by surprise. He was all too aware that war was raging in most other parts of the world. As a drug salesman, he knew that his company was making tremendous profits from sales to both the German and the British governments. In his visits to hospitals, he often met refugee doctors from Europe with horrifying tales. He dismissed most of these as exaggerations. After all, would even a madman like Hitler deliberately set out to destroy the best and brightest brains in his own country just because they belonged to people of a different religion?

At Yale, he had joined in a number of heated discussions over American's isolationist policies. Some of his fellow students were anxious to join in Europe's fight against Hitler, while others saw no moral obligation to do so. Trip found that he could look at the matter objectively. He had no family ties to the military or to armaments sales. He felt sorry for those people being bombed in Europe, but no great affinity with them. In fact, privately he thought that war was a complete waste of time and money. Who had ever gained anything from a war, apart from profiteers? Every single country in history was worse off in victory than it had been before the war started. He had no desire to fight and hoped President Roosevelt managed to stay out of the conflict.

That night he listened to Roosevelt's speech on the radio, prepared to go on with his life as before and leave the vengeance on the Japanese to those who wanted to fight. He just hoped that his connection with the pharmaceutical industry was enough to keep him out of war. If not, then surely his future admission to medical school would get him a deferment?

A few days later Theo burst into his room.

"What are you doing here?" Trip exclaimed, jumping up with delight. "I thought you had another week before vacation. Don't tell me they kicked you out already?"

"I've taken leave-of-absence," Theo said, grinning excitedly at Trip. "I'm off to do my bit for my country."

"You're what?"

"Going to heed the call and join up and fight for Uncle Sam, apple pie and the American Way, and I've come to drag you with me."

"Are you crazy?"

"No, deadly serious," Theo replied.

"But we don't have to join up," Trip protested. "Medical students are a protected occupation. We'll get a deferment until we graduate and we're of some use to them."

"The war might be over by then," Theo said. "I can't wait that long, Trip. I've got to do something now. I'm going to join the Marines, and I want you to come with me."

"The Marines? Why the Marines?"

"Because they're the roughest, toughest bunch in uniform," Theo said with a laugh. "When I appear in my Marine uniform, even my grandfather can't go on calling me a pansy."

"You're joining the Marines just to prove something to your grandfather?" Trip demanded.

Theo flushed. "I want to join up anyway," he said. "I can't sit home and let other people fight a war for me. It was just the choice of services. If I joined the Army, my family could always compare me to all those generals and colonels who went before. But a Marine, Trip. Nobody says anything bad about a Marine."

"There's the Navy or the Air Force," Trip suggested. "Doesn't it sound like a better idea to drop bombs on the enemy from the safety of twenty thousand feet?"

Theo grabbed Trip's shoulders. "You don't understand, Trip. This is my chance. They've been disappointed in everything I've done so far. Now I can prove that I can take anything they could take."

"I still say it's the wrong reason to risk your life," Trip said.

Theo's face clouded. "So you're saying you're not coming with me?"

"You were the one who said you couldn't put up with cold showers and a bugle in your ear every morning."

"It will be different in wartime. They'll train us in things that really matter, real survival training, hand-to-hand combat. They won't care about polished buttons and all that other peace-time crap. And then, off to action and pretty girls throwing themselves at us. And we return home heroes."

"If we return home."

"We will. We're Yale men. We'll be officers and we'll be able to stand back and yell, 'Get in there and give them hell, men.'"

Trip had to laugh. "Theo, you're something else," he said. "You're serious about this, aren't you?"

"Absolutely, Trip. And I really want you to come with me. Remember how I backed off from Alice because our friendship meant more to me? Now I'm asking you to return the favor. Come with me, Trip. Let's go fight the enemy together."

He looked at Trip, his clear blue eyes pleading.

At last Trip laughed. "I must be mad," he said, "but you've talked me into it. Okay, when do we start and where do we go to sign up?"

Theo threw his arms around him and thumped him on the back.

"I should never have gotten into this friendship in the first place," Trip said. "I knew it could lead nowhere but to trouble."

CHAPTER 14

They spent Christmas at Camp Pendleton in southern California. It wasn't the Christmas that Trip had been expecting. Contrary to what Theo had predicted, there was a bugler at five every morning and there were cold showers, and kit inspection, and polished buttons. They tramped for miles with packs on their backs and new boots pinching. They clambered through obstacle courses. Theo never had been good at following orders and got on the wrong side of the sergeant major right away.

"I'm sorry, Sergeant," he'd say in his bored, patrician way, "but I didn't think that order could possibly be meant for me. No, I didn't hear the bugle, was there one?"

Trip, amused by the sergeant's reaction, swiftly developed his own methods of getting around blind authority and boring assignments. His quick mind was constantly thinking of ways to get them out of obstacle courses without doing the obstacles. But when he doubled back through a wood and cut three miles off a hike, he was caught by the same sergeant major and made to repeat the hike with double kit.

After three months, they were summoned to the commanding officer. "I understand that you two have applied for Officer Training School," he said. He looked down at their records. "I see you're both Yale men."

Theo looked at Trip and gave him the thumbs-up sign.

"But my sergeant major tells me that you've never yet managed to get your blankets folded correctly, Private Brinkmeyer," he said.

Trip grinned.

"And that you question every order you're given, Private Atkins. I think you still have to learn what the Marines are about. I want officers who will obey any order immediately without thinking and pass that order on to their men, however stupid it sounds. Marines who think are dead Marines, privates. I'll review your request in three months. Let's see if you've learned anything by then."

"We're staying here another three months?" Theo asked in horror.

"Oh, no. Your unit is being shipped to Hawaii tomorrow. Dismissed."

Outside, Theo slapped Trip on the back. "Shipped to Hawaii, eh? What did I tell you? We've certainly fallen on our feet this time. Beaches, tropical moon, willing girls . . ."

* * *

"We've certainly fallen on our feet this time? Is that what you said?" Trip asked bitterly. They were crammed with a hundred other Marines into a landing craft, riding a heavy swell as it headed for a craggy green island. They had spent just over a month on Hawaii, most of it up in the mountains, learning the rudiments of jungle warfare, before they loaded onto a ship and sailed east.

On their last night in Hawaii, a strange thing happened. They had been given a twelve hour pass before shipping out and had spent an improbable day on the beach. A few miles away from the base, the world was still going on as before. Children were digging sand castles and splashing in the shallows. Boys were surfing, girls were tanning. And in the evening, before reporting for embarkation, they had gone to the Moana Hotel for a drink in the Banyan Lounge. An orchestra was playing with soft Hawaiian sounds. Couples were dancing. The tropical breeze was wafting in through open archways, and the giant banyan tree was floodlit. It was dark and romantic, and Trip felt a surge of restless longing.

Then, across the room, he heard a laugh. He searched for her and found her. She was dancing with a naval officer, his crisp white uniform a contrast to the tanned arm which rested against him. Bronzed and healthy in a turquoise-blue strapless dress, she looked lovelier than ever. He opened his mouth to call her name, then saw her wrap her arms around the officer's neck and gaze up at him with an adoring smile. Trip started to back away. He only wanted to get out of there fast.

"Hey, Trip, old buddy. Where are you going?" Theo called. Alice looked up at the sound of his name and saw him. Instant recognition flashed in her eyes.

"Why, Trip! What a lovely surprise. What are you doing here?"

"Leaving in a couple of hours to go fight the Japanese," he replied stiffly. "Good to see you again, Alice. You're looking well. Now, if you'll excuse us, we have to get back to base."

He took Theo's arm and firmly escorted him out.

Alice stared after them, not conscious of her dancing partner.

"Someone you know?" he asked.

"An old boyfriend," she said.

"And shipping out tonight, poor bastards," the officer said. "I wouldn't want to be a Marine with the kind of fighting they're called on to do right now. Those Japs are devils when it comes to close combat."

Alice shuddered. "I never saw Trip as a Marine," she said. "Nor Theo, either."

She tried to go back to her dancing, but it was no good. She had no idea of what her partner was saying. Impulsively, she grabbed his arm. "Do you have your jeep here? I'd like to go down to the docks and say good-bye."

"I don't have a jeep, but I could get one," he said.

"I'd appreciate it," she said.

"But I don't know how close to the docks they allow civilians."

She looked at him appealingly. "You're an officer. Couldn't you wangle something? Couldn't you say that I was your driver or a nurse or something?"

He smiled. "I could try, if it means that much to you."

"It does."

They took a taxi back to base and waited for him to sign out a jeep. Then they rattled past deserted warehouses and around areas still blackened and twisted by the Pearl Harbor bombing.

"I'm afraid we can't get any closer than this," he said. A dark channel lay between them and the lighted wharf, the focus of activity.

Alice got out of the jeep and began to walk along the edge of the channel as a line of Marines, kit bags over their shoulders, was marching along the dock and up a gangplank. Vehicles were being winched aboard. She thought she saw him and yelled his name. She even thought he looked up and waved. But she couldn't be sure.

"Can we go now?" her escort asked. The last of the vehicles had gone aboard. The gangplanks were being raised.

"Not yet," she said.

Slowly the ship began to move away from the dock and started to steam down the channel toward open water. Alice began to run, trying to keep up with it. "No, Trip, don't go!" she screamed. "Come back. I love you! You hear me? I love you!"

But the boat steamed away, leaving a silver trail on the dark water.

Trip thought of her again as he stood packed in the landing craft, waiting to go ashore. He remembered every detail of how she had looked, how she had smiled. He had half-convinced himself that he saw her, waving on the dockside, but he told himself it was just his overactive imagination and wishful thinking on his part. Already the vision of her seemed unreal, like a dream.

CHAPTER 15

As they steamed out of Honolulu, none of the Marines could guess where they were going. Japan now occupied all the island chains east of Hawaii, so it was probable that their captain didn't know their final destination either. A couple of weeks later they heard that U.S. troops had recaptured Midway. That first victory against Japan had boosted morale below-decks.

Morale certainly needed boosting. Their journey had been long, monotonous and uncomfortable, crammed below-decks as they zigzagged to outwit enemy submarines and avoid enemy bombing. Another ship in their convoy had been hit by a torpedo and it sank before many of its men could be rescued. Those pulled aboard had severe burns or missing limbs. It was Trip's first taste of the reality of war and he knew that his instinct had been right. War was a ridiculous waste.

They came at last, after a long cat-and-mouse game, to the southern Pacific at the end of July. No one had ever heard of the island. It was in a group called the Solomons, and its name was Guadalcanal.

"I thought that was in Central America somewhere!" Private Dinkins, in the next bunk, exclaimed.

"That's the Panama Canal, you moron," Theo said, winking at Trip.

"I don't care where it is, I just want to get at 'em," Private Winetsky said. "This bayonet is itchin' to stick in some fat Jap gut."

Trip said nothing. From his first day in the Marines he had felt that he had made a horrible mistake. He had no wish to kill or be killed. In fact, he often wondered whether he'd be able to kill a man, even one designated The Enemy. Most of the other Marines around him had no such reservations. They were spoiling for a good fight. Trip thought that probably Theo was too.

On August second, they finally came within sight of land and got their orders to prepare to go ashore. They came up on deck, blinking in the bright sunlight. A shaggy green island lay low on the horizon. The ocean was a deep, clear blue, changing to purest turquoise as it neared the coral reef. But the deep rumble of guns from the island peaks and the bright line of tracers made Trip realize he wasn't in a South Sea idyll.

The Marines were herded like cattle into shallow landing craft, which headed immediately for the beaches. Their orders: to secure the beaches and then move inland. Shells whined over their heads and exploded in the water around them. One man was praying a rosary, his mouth moving silently as his hands slid over the beads. Trip wished he had some form of religion. At Yale it had been fashionable to mock such things; now Trip wanted it, as a straw to grasp.

"You were right," Theo muttered into his ear.

"About what?"

"Joining the Air Force. It would have been more sensible to drop bombs from twenty thousand feet."

"Now he tells me!" Trip hissed.

The two friends exchanged a grin.

"I hope I can do this," Theo said. "I hope I don't let them all down at the last moment."

"Listen," Trip said under his breath, "we don't need any heroics, understand? These guys can't wait to run people through with bayonets. Let them go first. As I see it, we dig ourselves a sensible hole on the beach and take our time."

Theo was staring out at the line of breaking surf ahead. "I had such a nice spade once," he said. "When we used to go to Cape Cod for the summer. It was red, I remember. A good solid spade that you could build great castles with. And a matching bucket with a picture of a duck on it. I wonder what happened to that spade?"

Trip looked at him fondly. There was something about Theo that brought out good thoughts in people.

It was impossible not to like him. Who else would remember a childhood spade right before entering hell?

"I don't think the Japs would give you time to build a sand castle with it right now anyway," Trip said.

"It could dig a good hole," Theo replied.

"Okay, men, this is it!" the officer yelled. "Keep your heads down, move up steadily. If I give the signal to retreat, then get the hell out of there."

"You bet we will," Trip muttered to Theo.

The gate clanged open into shallow water. The first men poured out, rifles ready, bayonets aimed, yelling as they charged. They didn't even make the beach. They were mown down in the shallows, where they splashed face-forward. But more followed them. The second and third and fourth rows didn't hesitate. Like waves coming in with the tide, each man got a little farther. Trip was already scouting out the beach, noting coconut trees that would offer protection. Beside them, the water was full of similar landing craft and men were pouring ashore like ants. None of them had yet made it to the coconut trees.

Trip grabbed Theo's arm. "This is madness," he said. "Suicide. The only way to survive is to play dead as soon as we step ashore. Find a pile of bodies and fling yourself down behind it."

"We can't do that!"

"We have to, Theo. This isn't warfare, it's mass suicide—it's lemmings going over a cliff. We're not lemmings, Theo."

They reached the front of the boat. "Go! Go!" the officer was yelling. "Come on, move it, move it."

Cold water clung to their legs, seeped into their boots and squelched as they moved. Waves rushed past, almost tripping them. Bodies floated, bullets whined. A man beside Trip fell without a sound. One second he was running forward, the next lying in the water.

Trip had already located the pile of bodies where he intended to fall. A bullet grazed his shoulder. He hardly felt it, but he cried out and dove for the soft sand. As he fell, he looked for Theo, to pull him down beside him, but Theo was charging at full speed up the beach and a primal yell was coming from deep within him. Firing as he went, he was farther up the beach than any of the other Marines.

"Get back, you fool!" Trip shouted, but his voice was drowned in the boom and crackle of guns. Theo had almost reached the palm trees when he was hit. Trip watched as his body seemed to leap in the air, flip and land in a heap on the sand.

"Damn him, damn him," Trip heard himself saying. Theo would be blasted to pieces if he lay there, so close to the enemy in the trees. He had to get him out of there fast. He put his head down and ran, stumbling over bodies, feeling the passage of bullets close by, but he reached Theo's crumpled form and threw himself down beside him.

"Come on, old buddy. We've got to get out of here," he murmured. "Can you walk?"

Theo's clear eyes opened. "Oh, hi, Trip," he said. "I did pretty well, didn't I? I almost made it to the trees. You'll tell them that when you get home, won't you?"

"You're coming back with me, you idiot," Trip told him. "I'm going to get you back to the boat if I have to drag you all the way."

"Not much point really," Theo said. "Get back yourself while you can."

"I'm not leaving you here. You're going to be okay."

"I wish I were," Theo said. "There was so much I wanted to do, Trip. We were going to have . . . such a great life . . ." He paused, fighting for breath. ". . . So stupid, really."

A shell whined close to them. Tears were running down Trip's cheeks, blinding him. He covered Theo's body with his own as the world exploded with orange fire. He could feel his leg and shoulder burning.

"Stupid," he agreed, as the world faded to black.

CHAPTER 16

It was February, 1943, before Trip finally found himself in a taxi, riding through the snow-covered landscape of Westchester County to visit Theo's parents. He had spent several months recuperating, first in a hospital in Hawaii, then in California, where he had undergone reconstructive surgery on his leg. He now had two metal plates holding his bones together and he walked with a stick. He had been invalided out of the Marines with the Purple Heart.

After the sticky heat and brilliant colors of the tropics, New York looked like a Christmas-card scene. Snow lay on rooftops and glittered like icing on tree branches. Icicles hung from eaves. Little children had made a slide on the sidewalk and were yelling encouragement to each other as they slid down it, their snowsuits making bright blurs of color against the whiteness. There were snowmen in front yards.

Everything was so peaceful and ordinary that it was

hard to believe that the war was still raging on in the rest of the world.

Trip knew that he was one of the lucky ones. More than half his platoon had not returned. Now he had to face Theo's family, and he was dreading it. But he had promised Theo, and it seemed the least he could do. After all these months, he still found it hard to believe that Theo was dead. Theo had been his one close friend, the brother he never had, and he felt a great, gnawing hole inside him in the place that Theo had occupied in his heart.

The taxi drew up outside the Brinkmeyers' mansion. He was glad he had written to say he would be in the neighborhood and would like to pay them a visit. At least they would be somewhat prepared.

Mrs. Brinkmeyer came to the door herself. He noticed that she looked older and thinner than he remembered. Her hair now had gray streaks in it and she was wearing a severe black dress. She took a moment to recognize him, but then she opened her arms and wrapped him in an embrace. "Trip," she said, "welcome home."

She led him through into a living room where a big fire was burning. "You must excuse the austerity. We're trying to do our part for the war effort," she said.

Trip couldn't see any austerity. It looked like paradise to him. "We had to let almost all the servants go, of course," she went on, talking brightly. "They all wanted to do their part. Of course we don't mind the inconvenience, but Henry's arthritis makes things . . . a little difficult . . ." She forced a cheerful smile. "We've put you in your old room. You can make the stairs, can't you? I didn't think to ask."

"Oh yes, I'm fine, thank you," Trip said. "Almost as good as new."

He winced at his own words. What a trite thing to say.

"We're all very proud of you," Mrs. Brinkmeyer went on, "and what you did for Theo."

"Theo's the one you should be proud of," Trip said. "You should have seen what he did. He—"

She held up a hand. "Let's not talk about him now. I know my husband and father-in-law are looking forward to hearing all the details, but I'd rather not hear them twice." She moved closer to him. "Between ourselves, I'd like to know just one thing. He didn't suffer long, did he?"

Trip shook his head. "He wasn't in any pain," he lied. "He talked and joked with me until that last shell."

Relief flooded her face. "That's good then. A mother always worries about that sort of thing. It makes it easier to accept, knowing that he had a peaceful end and that . . . you were there with him." She collected herself and flashed him another bright smile. "Well, I mustn't stand here talking. I should be seeing about lunch and I expect you'd like to freshen up." Trip took the hint and escaped upstairs.

That night at dinner he gave the full account of

Theo's heroism on the beach. "Men were falling all around us," he said, "but Theo didn't hesitate for a second. I think he would have been the first one to reach the enemy lines if he hadn't taken that one bullet."

"I always knew he'd prove himself in the end," old Colonel Brinkmeyer said gruffly. He swallowed hard. "A Marine, too. The finest fighting men. *Semper fi*, right, Atkins?"

"Right, sir."

"What about you, Trip?" Mr. Brinkmeyer asked. "Are they going to let you back into action?"

"Heavens, Henry, the boy's been given the Purple Heart. He's done more than his share."

"I'd like to go, sir," Trip lied, "but unfortunately I've been invalided out. I'm not much use to them with this leg."

"So what are your plans, Trip?" Mrs. Brinkmeyer asked.

"I'm not sure yet. I don't think I could get my old job back. I can't do the walking, but I expect I'll find something in an office."

"You must consider this your home now," Mrs. Brinkmeyer said, reaching over to pat his hand. "Mustn't he, Henry? Stay as long as you want. Take your time to recover." She smiled at him warmly. He returned the smile but felt like a fraud. He was welcomed, treated like a hero, when he'd only wanted to stay out of the fighting and save his own skin. But he also sensed that Theo's parents wanted him here, as a final link to their son.

* * *

And so he remained. It was the first time in his life—aside from his hospital stay—that he hadn't been fully occupied. It was pleasant to learn to play bridge and billiards and to walk through the gardens with Mrs. Brinkmeyer. As the weather warmed, a succession of visitors came to the house, many of them the young female cousins he had met at Yale. They looked at him adoringly and told him how brave he was. Trip felt uncomfortable at their praise but nonetheless continued to use his stick, even though his leg was now strong enough to support him.

One thing he came to realize was that the war had eliminated much of his competition. These young girls, who would have turned him down as penniless before, were now interested because so many of his contemporaries had been killed. Mrs. Brinkmeyer was always reporting on someone like "poor Jack Haversham, you remember him, don't you? His parents just got the telegram yesterday." It seemed that the Class of '41 was thinning by the minute, and it made Trip realize that he should plan his future while he could still capitalize on his war-hero status.

One day he was reading in the front garden when he heard the neat tap of heels passing outside. He looked up and his heart lurched. A young lady was going by, elegantly dressed, delicate, graceful. Her wide-brimmed hat half-covered her face so that he couldn't be sure, but he could almost swear that it was

Alice. He got out of his chair to call to her, but to his amazement, she already had her hand on the gate. As she turned to face him, he saw that it wasn't Alice. The build and the rosebud mouth were similar, but the hat hid sleek, dark hair and shadowed big, dark eyes. What's more, those eyes lit up with recognition.

"Good heavens, it's Trip Atkins. What in the world are you doing here?" she asked.

"Lizzy Decker. What a surprise," he greeted her. He had overcome his initial shock and was as pleased to see a familiar face as she was. "Are you coming to visit?"

"Yes. I'm staying with my godmother just around the corner and I always come to visit the Brinkmeyers when I'm here. I came to say how sorry I was about poor Theo. I heard the news only recently. What a shock. He was the sweetest boy in the world. Do you have any idea of where he was killed?"

"Yes. Guadalcanal. I was with him," Trip said.

"You were?" Her large eyes widened, then she noticed the stick beside him. "And you were wounded too. My poor Trip. Are you going to be okay?"

Trip smiled. "Let's say that I'll never win the hundred-yard dash again," he said, "but they tell me my leg should heal completely. I still get headaches from the head injury, but I know how lucky I am. Most of the men with me didn't make it."

"How terrible," she said. "But I'm so glad to find you here. Are you staying long?"

"I've been here several months already," he

explained. "I don't know how long I can go imposing on the Brinkmeyers' hospitality."

They started to walk together toward the house.

"How is Theo's mother taking it?" she asked. "Pretty hard, I should imagine."

"She's being very brave," Trip said, "and she tries to keep busy. That's why I haven't tried to leave yet. Having me here gives her something to do, and someone to talk to."

Liz laid her white-gloved hand on his arm. "Dear Trip, you always were so thoughtful."

"How long are you here for, Lizzy?"

"Only a few days. It's too hot for me in Westchester in summer. Our place is on the water. You must come out and visit sometime."

"I'd like that," he said. "You know, you gave me quite a shock. I thought for a moment that you were Alice."

"Alice?"

"Yes, Alice Woodbury."

"Alice Kaiser, you mean?"

"Kaiser?"

"Yes, you know. Kaiser steel. Kaiser aluminum. I heard that she's planning to marry this spring. Out in California, I gather."

"Oh, I see," he said. "Well, good for her. I hope she's happy."

Liz gave him a little smile. "That sounds like sour grapes to me. She turned you down, did she?"

"You could say that."

"You and half of Westchester County. She's broken hundreds of hearts."

Trip said nothing. It had never occurred to him before that Alice was a flirt or that any other men had been in the picture. How could he have been so hopelessly naive? He remembered how she had smiled up at the naval lieutenant. Well, he'd never make that mistake again. Never again would he let his heart rule his head.

Mrs. Brinkmeyer invited Liz to stay to lunch and Trip really enjoyed her company. After she had gone, he realized that he didn't know much about her. He knew she was at Miss Porter's and that she was rich, but that was about it. When they'd been together, he'd only been interested in Alice. He'd hardly noticed what Lizzy was saying.

From Mrs. Brinkmeyer he discovered that she was the only child of retired banker Conrad Decker, owner of one of the largest estates on Long Island and worth millions. Trip admitted to himself that he felt none of the overpowering sexual attraction he had felt for Alice Woodbury, but he was determined not to let his feelings get in the way again. Lizzy Decker was pretty and witty and very well bred. She would be an ideal choice for a wife. He decided to plan his courtship with the same determination with which he had secured a place at Yale.

The next time Theo's young cousin Mary Lou came to visit her relatives, Trip cornered her after lunch.

"Look, Mary Lou, I need a big favor," he said.

"Anything for you, Trip," she said, smiling up at him adoringly.

"I want you to arrange to have me invited to any gathering that's likely to include Elizabeth Decker."

Mary Lou's eyes opened wide. "Liz Decker? My, we are setting our sights high, aren't we?" She patted his arm. "Be warned. She's an only child and her parents think the sun shines out of her head," she said. "I think they're planning on a Rockefeller or a Kennedy, or at least a European prince, for her. I hardly think a Trip Atkins has a hope in you-know-what."

"I'm willing to take my chances," he said, "if you can just arrange to get me alone with her."

"I don't see why I should put myself out to set up dates with other women for you," she told him, pouting. "Frankly, that's asking rather a lot, Trip Atkins."

"But you'll do it anyway, because you adore me?" He put his fingers under her chin and drew her face toward his.

"You have too much charm for your own damned good," Mary Lou muttered. "Of course I'll do it."

Two weeks later Trip found himself at a boating party on Long Island Sound and acted completely surprised when he came upon Liz Decker, dangling her feet over the side of the dock. She was wearing a blue and white nautical outfit, her dark curls were blowing across her face, and he thought she looked like a charming child.

"We meet again, Lizzy. What a coincidence," he said. "Almost as if we were fated to know each other better."

"It does seem to be that way, doesn't it?" Liz said. "I'm a great believer in fate. How about you?"

"Absolutely," he agreed as he sat down on the dock beside her. They went out sailing together and he made her laugh. He saw right away that she was a very different type of girl from Alice. She told him she'd been to a convent school before Miss Porter's. To Trip, that convent upbringing definitely showed. She blushed when one of the young men uttered a profanity and when another told a mildly risqué joke. Trip took note of both incidents.

Liz Decker was like a hothouse plant, he told himself. Coddled by her parents, protected by the nuns. He would have to proceed very carefully.

The next day he sent her flowers and spent a morning at the library copying suitable love poems. He met her again at a party the next weekend and she nestled her head on his shoulder when they danced. They met regularly after that and on the third occasion, he kissed her. She turned her little face up expectantly and shut her lips as well as her eyes.

It was clear that she was not going to be another Alice. And now Trip had been through a war. He was used to girls who couldn't wait to unzip his pants while he unbuttoned their blouses. But when his hand slid inside the low neckline of Liz's dress, she pulled away and slapped it.

"Don't do that. It's not nice," she said.

Trip wanted to say he suspected that her round, firm breasts would be very nice, but he apologized and muttered that any man would get carried away when he was with someone as lovely as she.

"The nuns said we should wait to give our bodies until we were married," Liz said primly.

"Then I'll elope with you tonight," he said jokingly. "Would that do?"

"Oh, no." She looked at him seriously. "I couldn't elope with anyone. My mother's looking forward to planning the wedding of the century. I couldn't cheat her out of that."

Trip went home content. The subject of marriage had been mentioned and not completely rejected.

Back at the estate on Long Island, Elizabeth rushed into her parents' room. "I've met the most dreamy man," she said. "I want you to ask him for the weekend to see if you approve." She couldn't believe how easy it had been to arrange everything and how smoothly it was going. After almost two years of waiting, it finally seemed that Lizzy's dream was coming true. Now all she had to do was to make sure that her parents didn't find out too much about Trip and that they could visualize him as a future son-in-law. The secret was to present him as a war hero, she decided.

Long before the weekend, Conrad Decker had made his own inquiries. "He seems like a nice guy, decorated veteran, Yale man and all that," he confided to his wife, "but he hasn't a bean."

"Lizzy certainly seems to be smitten with him," Jeanie Decker said. "He writes her love poems every day."

"Love poems," Conrad snorted. "Love poems won't pay the rent. We'll soon see if the guy's a gold digger."

Trip was on his best behavior all weekend and on Sunday afternoon Conrad took him aside. "So what career plans do you have, young man?" he asked.

"I was planning to go into medicine," Trip said, "but the war sort of put a stop to that. Now I'm a little old to begin years of med school, so I'm thinking more in terms of my own business. I've been recuperating all year, and I have to say that I wasn't born to be idle. I'm like a horse chafing at the bit right now, ready to get going again. I figure there will be an explosion in all the technical fields the moment this war is over and people have money to spend again. Labor-saving devices, television, it's all going to boom."

"And what's going to finance this . . . business?" Conrad asked, giving Trip a direct stare.

Trip's gaze didn't waver. "I put myself through Yale with no money, sir," he said. "I figure I can build a business from scratch if I need to. You should know about that. I understand you are a self-made man who started with nothing, and look at what you've accomplished."

Conrad nodded.

After Trip had gone, he confided to his wife, "Either he's a good liar or he's not content to live on Lizzy's money. He's got a good head on his shoulders too. All the same, I'd rather she hitched up with someone we know a little more about. None of my men can tell me a thing about these supposed Atkinses. We'll bide our time and make them take it slow. She's only twenty after all. Maybe she'll change her mind."

At that moment Liz burst into the room. "I've just finished saying good-bye, Daddy," she said, "so tell me, what do you think?"

"He seems nice enough," her mother said cautiously.

"Nice enough? Mommy, he's perfect!" Liz said. "He's the most wonderful man I've ever met. I've got to have him. If I can't marry him, I'll just die."

CHAPTER 17

Trip and Elizabeth's wedding wasn't exactly the wedding of the century, as her mother had hoped, but it came pretty close to it. Maybe if young Joe Kennedy hadn't been killed, or if the king of England had had a son instead of Princess Elizabeth, something more spectacular would have been arranged. But marriage to a P. Stuart Atkins, who had no family and few friends, seemed hardly worth a truly spectacular ceremony. The Deckers decided to have a simple home ceremony and to limit the guest list to five hundred. Elizabeth's parents made it clear that they were not overjoyed about her marrying a penniless nobody, even if he was Yale-educated and good-looking. But they were used to granting their daughter her every wish. She had only to shut herself in her room and sob that she couldn't live without Trip and they reluctantly gave in.

"You'll receive a considerable income on your

twenty-first birthday," Conrad Decker had said to his daughter. "Let's just hope that your young man hasn't gone through it by your twenty-second."

"Not Trip," Liz exclaimed in horror. "He's clever, Daddy. He really wants to make something of his life. You'll see. He'll end up even richer than you." She went up to him and wrapped her arms around his neck. "I'm so happy, Daddy. I want you to be happy for me."

Conrad looked down at her fondly. "All we want is your happiness, darling child," he said. "If this marriage is what you really want—"

"I do, Daddy. So does Trip. He can't wait."

"So I imagine," Conrad said dryly.

But he had insisted on their waiting until the war was over. At the back of his mind was the worry about what would happen to him and his fortune if Germany and Japan should pull off a surprise victory. Also, what might happen to him when it was found that he had made pre-war loans to the Krupps that were undoubtedly used for the production of armaments.

In reality, Trip wasn't finding it very hard to be chaste around Elizabeth. Her behavior didn't exactly arouse desire in him. They had known each other for almost a year before she allowed him to put his hand on her breast, and then she clearly thought she was being very daring. She also made it clear that she was granting him a favor and that the presence of his hand there didn't excite her. Trip found himself wondering whether her appetite would be aroused after they were married. He blamed those nuns for instilling such strong morality in her that almost any physical contact was a sin. But maybe she was really a little volcano, just waiting to erupt with the right conditions. He fantasized about it sometimes, and he was certainly looking forward to teaching her. He'd never been with a virgin before.

The wedding took place in her parents' home on Long Island. The main staircase was decorated with gardenias, and an arbor of gardenias and camellias had been created in the palatial living room. Lizzy's dress alone cost ten thousand dollars. It was made of heavy white silk and embroidered with thousands of tiny pearls. It took eight bridesmaids to carry her train. As she came down the curved staircase on her father's arm, her delicate face hidden under yards of frothing veil, Trip thought she was the most exquisite creature he had ever seen. She was like a princess from a fairy tale, as fragile as porcelain, sweet and gentle. And as he raised the veil at the end of the ceremony and she turned her sweet red lips up for him to kiss, he told himself he was the luckiest man alive and that he was marrying the only woman he wanted.

They set sail for a honeymoon cruise to Europe. Liz had been insistent about seeing Europe, although neither Trip nor her parents were sure this was a good idea. Europe, still recovering from the effects of a terrible war, had severe shortages and refugees and lots of devastation.

"It might be upsetting for you," Trip warned.

"Then we'll just go to the nice parts where there weren't any bombs," Liz said sweetly. "I'm sure nobody bombed the Riviera."

And so they embarked on the Queen Mary. It was her maiden voyage since she had been converted back from a troopship, and every cabin was filled. Since the rich and famous were traveling back to Europe for the first time since the war, Liz had to content herself with an ordinary cabin.

"I don't mind. We'll want to be together every second anyway," she said when her father had exhausted every means to get a Saudi prince turned out of the royal suite.

As soon as the ship steamed out of New York Harbor, they went down to dinner. Trip noted the looks of admiration and the whispers as they came into the dining room. His bride was certainly the best-dressed woman among all those celebrities, and he beamed with pride as he pulled back her chair for her. After dinner they danced until Trip suggested they go back to their cabin.

"I'll undress in the bathroom, so that you have some privacy," he whispered.

Liz blushed. "All right," she said.

"Don't take too long," he murmured, nuzzling at her ear. She giggled and pushed him away.

After what he considered a suitable length of time, he opened the bathroom door. Liz was already in bed and the light was out. He slipped into bed beside her.

She was wearing a flimsy silk nightgown and he could feel her warm, young body through it. He was aroused. It was a long time since he'd been in bed with a woman. He must remember to go slow with Liz.

He leaned over her and kissed her gently on the mouth. He could feel her heart hammering through the thin silk as his chest brushed against her breasts. "Don't worry, I'll be very gentle," he whispered. "You don't have to be scared. I know this is all new to you."

He had meant to take it very slowly, to start with kisses and then to explore her body with his hands until he had her excited and ready, but he found his own desire and impatience growing. He lifted the skirt of her nightgown and lowered himself onto her.

"Don't! That's not nice."

"We're married, Lizzy," he said, getting exasperated by now. "Whatever the nuns told you doesn't apply any longer. Married people do these things. It might hurt a little the first time, but I'm going to try to be gentle. Just relax."

He nudged her back down on the bed and kissed her again, forcing his tongue into her mouth. Surely she must be warming up by now. He couldn't wait much longer. He tried to enter her and met resistance. Just one good thrust, that was all it needed. He was breathing heavily now, desire humming red in his brain. As he thrust into her, she screamed, so loudly that he pulled back in alarm. He started to say something soothing, but she leaped out of bed and ran to the far corner of the room.

"You hurt me," she said accusingly. "You were hurting me. I didn't like it."

Trip felt like a brute. He tried to tell himself that he was her husband and he was only taking what was his by right, but he felt like a brute all the same. He got out of bed and went over to her.

"Lizzy, darling, it's okay," he whispered.

"No, it's not okay," she said through clenched teeth. "You hurt me."

"I'm sorry."

"You were trying to do horrible things to me."

"I was doing what men and women do all over the world."

"I didn't like it."

"Sweetheart, it's very natural."

"No, it's not." She shook her head violently. "It's dirty. It's disgusting. Just go away from me. Leave me alone."

"Come back to bed, it's all right." He tried to touch her, but she shook him away.

"No. I won't!" she yelled. "I'm not going to let you hurt me again. I hate you. Go away. Just go away."

Her voice was rising to a hysterical level.

"All right," he said. Hastily, he pulled on some clothes. "I'm going out of the cabin. You can sleep here alone tonight if you want to."

He went out and walked up and down the deck. He was angry that she had made him feel like a heel when he was only doing what every other husband did on his wedding night. He had tried to be gentle and considerate about it. He imagined that many men would have just gone ahead and not cared if they hurt her or not. He had cared. He had known that she was an innocent child, but not that innocent. He slammed his hand down onto the railing. Christ, how could any American girl in the 1940s not know even the basics about sex? Had she been living in a bubble all these years? Had she been the one woman whose mother never had a little talk with her?

A figure passed him, then paused at the railing beside him. He looked up expectantly, hoping that it was Liz coming to apologize and invite him back inside. But instead, it was a ravishing, black-haired beauty whom he had noticed at the captain's table at dinner—elegant, sophisticated, dressed in a backless red evening gown and seated beside an Arab.

"Got a light?" she asked, handing him an open cigarette case. He took a cigarette and lit hers. She took a puff, then gave him a quizzical smile. "Not the place I would have expected to find a newlywed husband on his wedding night."

Trip returned the smile. "My wife was tired and overwrought. It was a big day for her, a lot of pressure."

"I know how I'd find a way to relax after a big day," she said. Her voice was low and seductive. "You're Trip Atkins. I read about your wedding in the papers. I'm Lita Wentworth."

"I thought I recognized you," he said. "I've seen your movies. You were very good in 'Dawn Chorus'."

"Flatterer," she said.

"No, I mean it. I rarely enjoy that sort of movie, but Lizzy wanted to go and I thought you were fabulous. Are you going to make a movie in Europe?"

"No, sweetie. I'm on a little R and R," she said. "I've spent the war entertaining the troops. Now it's Lita's turn. I have an invitation from a certain Egyptian king who is very infatuated with me at the moment to join him in Monte Carlo."

"You go for . . . Egyptians, do you?"

"Darling, I go for anybody with that kind of money," she said, laughing. "I bet you've never been weighed in rubies."

"You might wind up in a harem."

"There could be worse fates," she said, smiling. "Three meals a day and night duty only once every three months. As long as he let me have a lover on the side, I wouldn't mind at all."

She extended her hand and rested it lightly on his sleeve. "That little china doll in the cabin doesn't know what she's missing. If I were you, I'd go establish right away who's boss, or she'll have you dancing on a string for the rest of her life."

She began to move away down the deck. Trip watched her go, noting how her hips swung beneath the clinging red sheath. There was definitely a grain of truth in what she said too, but when he went back to the cabin, the door was locked.

Trip spent an uncomfortable night on a sofa in the lounge. Next morning Liz let him in but told him that she wasn't feeling well and that she had told the steward to have all her meals delivered to her cabin. He tried sitting with her, bought her flowers, candies and magazines from the shops on board, but she flinched when he came near her and looked at him coldly. That night she sent him for cigarettes and when he got back, she had locked him out of the cabin again.

He stood in the empty hallway feeling his anger rising. This had now gone too far. "Lizzy," he said, trying to keep his voice calm, "open the door, please. Don't be silly. You have no reason to be afraid of me."

He waited. There was no response from inside.

He rattled the doorknob. "I'm your husband, Lizzy. This is my cabin too," he told her. "Open the door this instant or I'll go get the steward with a passkey."

"Go away," came the muffled voice through the door. "I don't want you in my room. My daddy paid for it and I can shut you out if I like."

He stood there in the hall, his hand on the doorknob. A couple passed him and made him feel like a fool. He was torn between getting the steward and risking a possible scene, or leaving her alone for another night. In the end, he gave in. Would it be any better to sleep on the floor of his cabin than on a sofa in the lounge?

"Very well, if that's how you want it," he said.

As he made his way back along the corridor, a door opened.

"Not having too much luck, are you?" a husky voice demanded. Lita Wentworth was draped against the doorway, wearing a black negligee that left little to the imagination.

"I can't force my way in there," Trip said hopelessly.

"Maybe she's not worth bothering with," Lita said. "I have a very comfortable cabin, if you're interested. A big, beautiful bed—"

"And you're all alone?"

"Until you came along."

Trip looked back down the hall. Lita read his thoughts. "It's not your fault that you're a normal, red-blooded American male with a healthy appetite and she's on a diet. Why should you starve?" She ran her hand down her thigh. "Besides, you'd be doing me a favor. I hate sleeping alone."

Trip glanced back quickly once more before stepping inside and firmly closing the door behind him. Lita took his hand and led him across to the bed. With one fluid movement, she slipped the negligee off her shoulders and stood naked before him. Her body had acquired the voluptuous curves of maturity and Trip feasted his eyes as she began to unbutton his shirt. "I hope it hasn't been so long that you've forgotten how," she murmured. As Trip was fumbling with his belt buckle, Lita laughed and took over, undressing him skillfully and quickly.

"Do you want me to turn the light off?" he asked as she lay back on the bed.

"Do you want to?"

"I think I'd rather watch."

"Naughty boy," she said. She opened her arms to him and he sank onto her voluptuous body. He heard her laugh again, deep in her throat, as his passion exploded.

* * *

He woke next morning to an empty cabin and saw that it was past nine o'clock. Hastily he dressed and made his way back to his own cabin, feeling somewhat guilty. Liz had probably been searching all over the ship for him and was worried sick. He found the cabin unlocked and entered to see her sitting at the writing table, fully dressed. An untouched breakfast tray was beside her.

"I've just finished cabling my father," she said, eyeing him coldly. "I've told him to get the marriage annulled."

In a flash Trip saw how close he was to losing everything he had worked for. "But Lizzy, sweetheart, you haven't even given it a try yet," he said. "You can't judge a marriage by a first night disaster. We have to give it time."

Her eyes were like dark, icy pools as she gazed at him steadily. "I can judge an unfaithful husband by one night's adultery," she said. "I'm not staying married to a man who can't keep his hands off other women. Who even has the nerve to desert me during my honeymoon and slink to some tart . . ."

"Why should you care?" he demanded. "You made it very clear that you didn't want me anywhere near you. I didn't want to sleep a second night on a sofa in the lounge where all the world could see me."

"I know. I realized that," she said abruptly. "I changed my mind and I went to find you. I heard your voice in that woman's room. You really blew it, didn't you, Trip Atkins? You could have been one of the richest men in the United States. Daddy's cable should be coming back any second now. I bet he's already contacted the lawyer. You'll probably have to spend the rest of the journey on that sofa, unless your lady friend wants you back."

As if on cue, there was a discreet knock at the door. A steward came in with a sealed envelope on a silver tray. He bowed and presented it to Liz. She ripped it open, read it and flung it down with a cry of anger. Trip tipped the steward, then picked up the paper. The message was brief and to the point: YOU MADE YOUR BED NOW YOU MUST LIE IN IT. STOP. DADDY. Trip started to laugh.

"I'd say you were the one who's blown it, sweetheart," he said. "It looks like you have to stay married to me after all."

Liz gave a howl of rage and flung herself across the bed. "I won't!" she screamed. "Get out of here. I hate you. I never want to see you again!"

Trip thought it might be discreet to leave her alone for a while.

CHAPTER 18

All that day Liz lay sobbing in the cabin. She refused to eat. She refused to speak to anyone. Trip was alarmed at this other side of her that was surfacing. She was no longer the sweet, delicate child, but the spoiled brat, used to getting her own way. But knowing that his father-in-law was on his side gave Trip the confidence he needed. He went to meals in the dining room, dressed for dinner, and completely ignored his wife's temper tantrum. It wasn't until they were finally heading into Southampton that he sat on her bed and spoke to her. She turned away instantly.

"Lizzy?" he said calmly.

"Go away. I hate you," came the muffled response.

"May I ask what you plan to do as soon as we go on shore?"

"Get the next boat back to New York, go straight to a judge and file for divorce."

"On what grounds?"

"That you're a brute and an unfaithful rat and I hate you."

He laughed, which infuriated her. "I don't think any judge is going to be on your side," he said. "I think you'd find you were the one to blame, for denying me my conjugal rights."

"Your what?"

"I'm your husband. I'm supposed to be able to have sex with you if I want to."

"Who says so?"

"It's the law."

"A stupid law, obviously invented by men," she growled. "As soon as I get home, I'm going to get the women of the world to unite against stupid laws and stupid men."

He laughed again. "Strangely enough, most of the women in the world seem to enjoy it."

"They can't. It's brutish and disgusting."

"Most women don't think so. I think you'll find that you're the odd one out, my dear."

She turned toward him. Her face was blotched and tear-stained, her eyes puffy, her hair uncombed. "That woman," she said hesitantly. "The one down the hallway. Does she enjoy it?"

"She can't get enough of it."

"But it hurts."

"Only the first couple of times maybe. After that, you'd like it. It's a wonderful tingling sensation all over your body, and afterward you're so relaxed you just fall asleep in each other's arms."

"Did you fall asleep in her arms?" she asked softly.

"Let's not talk about it anymore," he said. "I would have preferred to fall asleep in your arms, but you locked me out."

She lay there silently. Trip put his hand on hers, and she didn't shake him off this time, which he took to be a good sign. "Lizzy," he said, "let me ask you something. What exactly did you expect from marriage?"

"My own home," she said quietly, "and my husband to look after me and make me happy, and adorable little babies someday."

"Ah, that presents a problem," Trip said, smiling triumphantly at her.

"What do you mean?"

"I mean, my sweet Lizzy, that you can't have any babies if you kick your husband out of bed."

"Oh," she said. "So if I don't let you . . . we won't ever have any babies?"

"You got it."

He stood up and began taking suits from the wardrobe, calmly packing his suitcase.

"Trip?" she asked in a small voice.

"Yes?" He didn't turn around.

"Is it really going to get better and not hurt anymore?"

"Yes, it is."

"Then could we try it again?"

"Now?"

"Yes, now."

"But we dock in Southampton in an hour or so."

"I know. But I have to know what it's like right now."

"Okay." He closed the drapes and locked the door. He just hoped that the porters wouldn't arrive and that he'd be able to perform. Liz lay back and closed her eyes tightly. He undressed and eased himself onto her as gently as he could. He could tell he was hurting her by the way she screwed up her face and bit her lip, but she didn't cry out. He tried to be as gentlemanly as possible, but he found her virginity strangely exciting.

"There," he gasped as he collapsed onto her. "That wasn't so bad, was it? And now you're not a virgin anymore." As he said it, he realized that he was safe for the time being. Now she couldn't make her father change his mind and help her get the marriage annulled.

CHAPTER 19

London was dreary and gray. Even the Dorchester Hotel smacked of postwar austerity. There were piles of rubble on almost every street where buildings had once stood. The people looked tired and dispirited, as if they were the losers of a great war, not the victors. All the headlines on the newsboards talked of strikes and power cuts. They stayed only two days, then went on to Paris. Paris was equally depressing, in spite of the food at Maxim's, which was still at its prewar excellence. They stayed long enough to visit the Louvre and the Eiffel Tower and for Liz to be measured for dresses at Dior. Then they caught a night train to Monte Carlo.

There they finally found a place untouched by war. Beautiful people were driving convertible cars, sunning on the beaches and filling the casino at night. Liz was delighted with everything. She loved playing roulette and was quite excited about losing a thousand dollars in an evening. She loved showing off her clothes and being admired and having her hand kissed by distinguished foreigners.

Trip hoped that this atmosphere would finally get her to relax enough to enjoy sex with him. He had tried twice more with her since leaving the boat, and both times she had lain there, not complaining, her face the picture of martyrdom. In fact, she reminded Trip of the pictures he had just seen in the Louvre of saints suffering incredible tortures. It was not conducive to passion, and he found himself dreading returning to their room at night.

After a couple of evenings of losing heavily at roulette, Liz complained that she was tired and went to bed at nine. Trip lingered alone in the casino and found no shortage of interesting women who were only too anxious to slip him the key to their rooms. He knew he shouldn't. He told himself that it was his duty to hurry back to Liz, but he couldn't help himself. He needed to prove to himself that it wasn't his fault that his wife didn't enjoy being with him. And he was very discreet. Lizzy was sound asleep and she'd never know.

Elizabeth Decker Atkins sat alone in her bedroom in the Hotel Majestique and brushed her hair. A gentle Mediterranean breeze wafted the scent of jasmine through her open window. Looking out, she could see the yachts bobbing in the harbor, their strings of lights dancing in the black water. There were lights on the promenade too, and the sound of laughter and singing floated up to her. It was as if the rest of the world was involved in a festival and only she was excluded. She knew that it was her fault she wasn't having a good time, that she could be down in the casino with Trip right now, but she didn't want to be there.

The last few days had confirmed her worst fears from the voyage on the Queen Mary. She might be naive, she decided; she might not know much about men or life, but she wasn't completely blind. She hadn't been mistaken, on a hot night when she couldn't sleep, when she had looked out of her window and seen a beautiful woman hurrying across the garden, followed a few minutes later by Trip. It was dark in the garden, but she was sure it was Trip. He still walked with a slight limp, for one thing, and he had stopped to light a cigarette, illuminating his features for a brief second. And Liz had instinctively known that he was following the woman up to her room.

"What a fool I have been," she exclaimed to her image in the mirror. "So stupidly naive. I didn't realize!" She had been so head over heels in love with him, it had never crossed her mind that he wasn't in love with her. Now she saw that he had never loved her. He had played his part well, but not well enough.

The question was, what to do next? She could do what she had threatened and file for divorce as soon as they returned to the States, but that would mean going back home to her parents in disgrace and failure. Her mother would be angry about the expense of the wed-

ding for nothing, and she'd be a little girl again, coddled and overprotected, until she found the next can-
didate for husband. And even then, she'd never be
completely sure that it wasn't her money that attracted
him.

"Damn," she said, throwing down the silver-backed
hairbrush so that it slid along the polished surface and
onto the floor. The trouble was that she still wanted
Trip. She still loved him, in spite of everything. And
at the back of her mind was the nagging thought that
he turned to other women only because she was somehow failing him. She knew he got little satisfaction
out of sex with her. She still hated it, and it must be
obvious to him. "But that's his bad luck," she said to
herself. "He married me and now he's stuck with me,
just like I'm stuck with him."

When Trip let himself quietly into the room around
one in the morning, he found Liz sitting up in bed,
waiting for him.

"Lizzy, you're awake. Is something wrong? Are
you not feeling well?" he asked.

She turned cool eyes on him. "You and I have to
talk, Mr. Atkins."

"Okay. Talk away." He sat easily on the end of the
bed.

"You must think I'm very stupid," Lizzy said. "But
I've been watching you. I know you go to other wom-
en's rooms after I've gone to bed."

"Liz, it's not like you think," he began, but she held
up her hand. "I'm going to tell you right now, Trip

Atkins," she said. "I'm an only child. I wasn't brought up to share. I realize now that it was my money that attracted you to me in the first place. Very well. I accept that. But I'm not going to share you, Trip. You and I have to make a little bargain: if you want to stay married to me, and you want to get your hands on one penny of my money, then you agree to stay faithful to me. And I don't mean appear to stay faithful, or only meet women you think I can't find out about. I'm hiring a detective to follow you day and night, Trip. You make one slip and I'll have you in the divorce courts so fast you won't know what happened to you. And I'll drag in every single woman you've been with. My detective will supply me with names." She paused and looked at him defiantly. "So what's it going to be, Trip? All or nothing?"

He nodded. "You're growing up fast, Lizzy," he said. "And you know I'm not a fool. I have no choice but to agree to your conditions."

"Good," she said. "And to keep you out of temptation for a little while, I'm going to charter a yacht tomorrow. We'll sail down the Mediterranean together—just us and a male crew."

Trip spread open his hands. "Your wish is my command, apparently," he said.

The next morning they set off on a sleek, white yacht, bound for Nice. During long days basking in the sun, swimming or going ashore to shop, they achieved a certain degree of happiness and contentment. Liz was adoring and attentive, happy in the knowledge that she had won and she wouldn't ever have to worry about her husband again. Trip decided there could be worse fates than being held captive by a millionaire wife who was prepared to grant his almost every wish.

A month later, as they sailed back to Monte Carlo to take the train to Paris and then to sail back home out of Le Havre, they were holding hands and pausing to kiss like any other newlywed couple.

In Monte Carlo Liz stopped off to consult a doctor. She had been plagued by seasickness on the last mornings of the trip, even though the sea was as calm as a pond. She worried that she might have picked up a bug from swimming in polluted water.

But she came out of the doctor's office, her face radiant.

"Good news, darling," she yelled clear across the courtyard. "We're going to have a baby!"

CHAPTER 20

Back in the States the couple moved into their own mansion in Oyster Bay. The house had been a wedding gift from Liz's father, not too far from her parents' estate and furnished to their taste. Liz, plagued with morning sickness and dizziness, was advised by her doctor to rest. This was a good excuse for Mrs. Decker to come over every day, even though there were servants enough to look after Liz and Conrad Decker had hired a nurse.

Trip wandered from room to room, feeling strangely detached and like an outsider in his own house. The Deckers had even unpacked all the wedding gifts and displayed them where they saw fit. Trip winced as he passed a huge Della Robbia vase in the entry hall and the stags' heads in the library. It was as if he, Trip, had no existence and no personality outside of his wife. Her trust fund gave her complete control over her money and she gave him a generous allowance. Trip hated it. He felt like a kept lapdog.

"Is this what you wanted?" he asked himself often. "Is this what life is going to be about?"

He would have willingly gone out and gotten a job, any job, even as clerk at one of Decker's banks, but Liz made it clear that she wanted him with her. She worried when he was away from the house, and the doctor had told her that worry wasn't good for the baby. So Trip stayed, trying to make *The New York Times* last the whole morning and praying that when the baby finally came, Liz's attention would be diverted sufficiently to allow him some freedom. After October, he told himself, he could start living again. Liz would have the baby to fuss over. By then he should have some idea about the sort of business he wanted to start. So he brought home technical books and financial reports and spent hours in his study, doodling over designs for vacuum cleaners and television sets and rocking baby cradles.

As the period of morning sickness passed, Liz began to devote every minute to preparation for the coming baby. She consulted with decorators and child pschologists about the design of the nursery. She spent hours pouring over wallpapers with chicks or puppies on them. "It's important he gets the correct amount of stimulation at an early age, Trip," she said. "He's got to grow up to be President someday."

"I wouldn't wish that fate on the kid," Trip said, laughing.

Liz frowned at him. "I don't think you're taking

this at all seriously," she said. "It's a big responsibility, raising a child. We have to give him the very best from the first day. He has to be raised to know he is someone special."

"And if he's a she?"

"Don't be silly," she said. "One has to have the boy first. I've already told him that. I talk to him, you know. Dr. Hauser says that babies can detect their mother's voices from the womb."

She turned to him, her eyes glowing. "I still can't believe it, Trip. My own little baby. Soon I'll be holding him in my arms and I'll be able to play with him and sing to him and he'll love me and call me Mommy."

He bent to kiss her forehead. "I'm glad you're happy, sweetheart," he said.

"Meaning you're not happy? You don't want a baby? You're not looking forward to it?"

He put his arms around her. "Of course I am, you silly thing. It's just that men are different. We don't go into raptures over babies and chicks on the wallpaper. And I have to think about getting my own career started. He needs to look up to his dad, you know, and he won't look up to me if I'm loafing around the house, doing nothing."

"But I need you right now, Trip," Liz said, pouting. "You're such a comfort when I don't feel well."

"Your mother comes over," he pointed out, "and the nurse is paid to comfort you too."

"But they're not the same as you," she protested.

"All the same, Lizzy, I don't want you to count on my being around forever," he said. "A man needs a career. He needs to make something of his life. Your parents wouldn't think very highly of me if I spent the rest of my life sponging off your money, would they?"

"I suppose not," she said, "and I know I'm being selfish. It's just that I'm scared something will happen if you're not around."

"What could happen, you silly child? There are servants galore to take care of you. The only thing I'd worry about is tripping over a servant!" And he laughed and kissed her.

The next day Trip went for a brief trip into New York City. He wanted to check out a company that was importing European wines. Having developed a taste for French wines, it occurred to him that the standard of New York wines could definitely be improved. Maybe he should look into a winery and bring over a French wine master. While he was walking down Wall Street, he ran into Tony Hall, one of his classmates from Yale, who was now a successful stockbroker. The two men went to have a drink together.

"I hear you've got it made, you lucky dog," Tony said. "I saw the wedding in the newsreels. I said to myself, Trip Atkins, of all people. He started with nothing and now look—he's dining on caviar while the rest of us have our noses to the grindstone."

"Frankly, I'd rather have my nose to the grindstone," Trip said. "There is such a thing as too much leisure. That's why I'm in town today. I'm looking into the possibility of growing French grapes in New York." He looked up from his glass. "I have to do something, Tony. I have a good brain. I can't spend my life watching the flowers grow and the artwork appreciate as it hangs on the walls."

Tony laughed. "You have to be born to it, old man," he said. "My family has lived off private money for generations and I'd willingly trade places with you tomorrow. But let me give you one little hint. Don't bother trying to grow good grapes in New York. Too much humidity in the summers. You're always going to get a wine that's too sweet. If you want something resembling a European wine, then you'd better look at California."

Trip didn't want to say that he was sure his wife wouldn't let him go to California. "California's too far away," he said. "I might start looking into an import business then. I've got to do something," he repeated, putting his empty glass back on the table.

Back at the Oyster Bay mansion, Liz had been keeping a careful eye on the workmen painting the nursery. She had decided that light yellow would be the right color for the woodwork and would go well with the chick-and-duck wallpaper she had selected. It wasn't until the workmen packed up for the night that she realized she hadn't seen Trip all afternoon.

"Trip?" she called.

A maid appeared at the foot of the stairs.

"Maria, where is Mr. Atkins?" Liz asked.

"Not back from the city yet, Mrs. Atkins," the maid replied.

"But he went hours ago. He said he only had an appointment with a man at an import company. It couldn't have taken that long."

"I expect he was held up in traffic," Maria said comfortingly. "Don't worry, Mrs. Atkins. I'll have some tea sent up to you."

Liz's mind was racing. This import idea had been one she hadn't heard him talk of before. Was it a cover for a woman he had met? Was he cheating on her in spite of his promise? Why else should a simple meeting keep him away so long?

She went down the stairs, conscious that it was growing dark. She had reached the bottom step when the maid looked up at her and smiled. "There's a car in the driveway now, Mrs. Atkins. That will be him coming home. You see, you had nothing to worry about."

Outside, a car door slammed. There was the sound of footsteps on gravel. "Trip!" Liz called and ran across the marble foyer strewn with Persian rugs. As she put her foot on one, it began to slide. She screamed and fought to regain her balance, but her feet shot from under her and she went crashing onto the hard, white marble as Trip opened the front door.

She was rushed to hospital, bleeding, and around midnight the doctor came out to Trip to tell him that she had lost the baby. "I'm very sorry, Mr. Atkins," he said quietly. "We did everything we could, but the blow separated the placenta from the wall of the uterus. She would have bled to death if we hadn't intervened."

Trip found himself blinking back tears. "Thank you," he mumbled gruffly. "I'm sure you did everything possible."

"Don't take it too hard," the doctor said. "You're both young. There's no reason why you shouldn't have many more children."

"My wife . . . is she going to be okay?" Trip asked.

"She's lost a lot of blood. We had to give her a transfusion. But she should make a complete recovery."

"When can I see her?"

"She's still sleeping. The anesthetic should wear off in an hour or so," the doctor said. "She doesn't yet know about the baby. I thought perhaps you should be the one to break it to her."

Trip's heart lurched as he thought of approaching the task. Liz had lived for that baby. It had become the center of her universe. What could he say that would ease her pain? He followed the nurse through to Liz's private room. Liz looked so small and frail, lying between the crisp white sheets like a sleeping child. He felt a surge of protectiveness and at the same time, a stab of guilt. Maybe if he hadn't gone into the city. . . . But he couldn't be a lapdog for the rest of his life. She had to realize that. It wasn't as if he'd done anything in the city that normal men didn't do every day of their business lives. He'd been home in good time for dinner. What more did she want, for Christ's sake?

It was an accident, he told himself. Accidents happen. Tragedies happen. They were part of the fabric of life. Liz was going to be fine. They would have other children.

It was close to dawn when she opened her eyes.

"Trip?" She looked around, bewildered. "Where am I?"

"In the hospital, darling. You had a bad fall. You slipped on the rug."

"I heard the car," she said. "I was running to you . . . "

He winced. "You shouldn't have run. You know how slippery that floor is, with all those damned rugs. I'm getting rid of them all."

"Is the baby going to be okay?" she asked in a small voice.

He took her hand and told her gently what the doctor had said. Then he kissed her forehead and told her that there was nothing to stop them from having another child as soon as her strength returned. He thought she took it remarkably well. There was no tantrum, no screaming. She didn't even cry, except for one teardrop that trickled down her cheek. He left her alone to sleep then and went back to Oyster Bay for the rest of the night.

He had scarcely gotten in the front door when he received a call from the hospital. His wife had sneaked out of her room, found a surgical instrument and tried to kill herself by slashing her wrists.

CHAPTER 21

After that, a nurse was with Liz day and night. She was heavily sedated, even after she was brought home from the hospital. Again, doctors were encouraging. They told Trip that postpartum depression was common and that the childbearing process often produced irrational behavior and psychosis, even without the shock she had been through. She'd snap out of it after a while, they said, but they suggested that he lock up the razors and sharp knives and take away the sleeping pills, just in case.

Trip was deeply shocked by this second tragedy. From his own experience he knew that life was full of misfortune and violence, but he had never come across suicide before, especially in one as young and hopeful as Lizzy.

He stayed close to her side, waiting to see her come out of the depression that engulfed her. But the months went by and still she showed little interest in life. If the nurse didn't wash and dress her, she wouldn't get up. She would speak only if spoken to, and then answer in monosyllables. She would walk only if Trip walked with her, holding her arm. She showed no interest in anything she had enjoyed before, not music or sewing or drawing. Trip bought her an adorable Pekinese puppy, and this did evoke a response. She sat for hours hugging the sleeping puppy and became quite upset when the little creature wanted to run or play and left her side for a moment.

Trip felt as if he was caught in a pit with no escape. Lizzy had turned into a stranger who didn't even want to talk to him, and yet she became upset when he left the room. He sent for the best nerve specialists and tried to pump them for answers to Liz's condition and when it might show improvement. They didn't seem to know any more than he did, and kept reassuring him that she could come out of her depression at any moment.

Strangely enough, he found unexpected allies in Liz's parents. They were shocked and bewildered by their daughter's behavior. There were days when she wouldn't even talk to them.

"How long do those damn doctors think this can go on?" Conrad muttered to Trip. Liz had been particularly unresponsive, hugging the Pekinese to her and not even appearing to notice that they were in the room.

"They keep telling me that she can snap out of it at any moment," Trip said hopelessly, "but to be frank with you, I think they're talking through their hats. They admit that they don't even know what's wrong with her. It's either simple depression, or manic-depression, or maybe a hormonal imbalance . . ."

"Damned fools," Conrad muttered. "It was the shock. Shock can do that sort of thing to the best people. I saw it in World War One. Even with tough soldiers. It doesn't mean she's crazy . . ."

Trip could read what his father-in-law was trying to say. There was no insanity in their family. A logical explanation for Lizzy's behavior had to be found.

"Of course she's not crazy," Trip said.

"Maybe if she could just have another baby . . ." Conrad said hopefully.

"Not in the foreseeable future," Trip said. "She won't let me anywhere near her."

"Maybe a cruise to get her mind off things?"

"Not yet, I'm afraid," Trip said. "It's all I can do to get her to leave her room on fine days for a walk in the garden. And then she gets hysterical if that stupid dog disappears behind a bush."

Conrad put a big hand on Trip's shoulder. "I'm deeply sorry for you, my boy," he said. "I know what this must be like for you. No chance to get on with your own life. If you feel you have to get away for a day or so, you know my wife and I will be happy to take over for you."

Trip's face brightened. "If you really would, sir," he said. "I've just received an invitation to join the Brinkmeyers at Newport for the regatta. That's not too far away and I'd dearly love to go. I haven't seen them in months."

"Of course, my boy. Explain to Lizzy that we'll be there to take care of her."

Trip went up to Lizzy's room that night. She smiled at him, which was a good sign. "Look what I've taught Yin-Yin to do," she said. "Okay, Yin-Yin, shake hands."

The dog lifted a paw. Trip clapped. "Very good, Yin-Yin," he said. "You must show your folks when they come to visit tomorrow."

"Tomorrow? Are they coming tomorrow?"

"Yes. They're coming to keep you company while I go visit the Brinkmeyers. They're going to Newport for the regatta and they've asked me to go along with them. Your father thinks I need a dose of fresh air."

Her face had lost all color again. "You're going to a regatta?"

"Only because I want to see Theo's parents. I haven't seen them in a while, and they were so good to me."

"I don't want you to go," she said, pouting.

"I'll be away for only one day, and I promise you I won't talk to any female sailors." He said it jokingly, but he saw her face. "I've never broken my promise to you, Lizzy," he said. "You can trust me completely. I just need to get away once in a while."

"Why?"

"Because . . . because it's hard staying here all the time."

"You don't like being with me!"

"I don't mind being with you, sweetest," he said soothingly, "but you must admit it's not natural to stay in one room all one's life. I'm getting cabin fever. Like your father says, I need fresh air. And your parents will be with you every moment while I'm gone."

"I still don't want you to go," she said.

"I'll be back before you notice it," he said, kissing her on the cheek.

CHAPTER 22

He set out early the next morning and met the Brinkmeyers in Newport. It was a beautiful day, clear, bright, and not at all humid. The ocean was blue and a good, stiff breeze was blowing.

They sailed out of the harbor on a friend's yacht, calling out to fellow yachtsmen and encouraging competitors as they passed. Most of the boats were decorated with flags and the atmosphere was very festive. Champagne was poured and canapes were passed around. Mary Lou Brinkmeyer and her latest boyfriend were there and she made them all laugh with her stories of her new job in Manhattan. Trip realized that laughing was a new sensation for him. His face muscles felt as if they hadn't been stretched into a smile in ages. Mrs. Brinkmeyer was laughing too. It was good to see the frown lines melt from between her eyes.

"We've been so worried about you, Trip," she said.

"I do hope the worst is over now for Lizzy."

"She seems to be recovering slowly," he said, hoping this was true. When would she be well enough to come with him to take part in social events like this again, he wondered. He couldn't picture her here now. As the day progressed, he realized with a sinking heart that he would soon have to go back. It was like a day's furlough from prison. Other boats were heading back into port, and good-natured banter passed between the crews. As they came close to another yacht, Mr. Brinkmeyer shouted something to the helmsman and received a rude reply that made them all laugh. Trip was laughing too as he looked across, straight into Alice's smiling face.

The boats parted then and he had to sit there, watching the other yacht sail ahead of them into port. As soon as they docked, he excused himself and ran to find her. She was just being helped ashore, her cheeks glowing from a day in the wind and her hair windswept. She looked glorious.

"Hello, Trip," she said. "What are you doing here?"

"I'm here with the Brinkmeyers," he said. "How are you, Alice?"

"Oh, just fine, thank you. And you?"

"Fine." Now that she was beside him, he was lost for words again.

"I read about your wedding last year. Not quite up to Westminster Abbey, but almost."

She smiled at him and he felt himself melting. Dammit, why did she still have this effect on him?

"You're looking wonderful," he said. "Married life obviously agrees with you."

"Married life? Who told you I was married?" she asked.

"I heard you'd married a Mr. Kaiser."

"Jack Kaiser? Oh please!" She made a face. "That was my father's choice, not mine. He stuttered and slurped his coffee. I turned him down. No, I'm still free and easy, enjoying my independence until the right man comes along." She said it brightly, but he read the longing in her eyes.

"I hope he does, one day, Alice," he said.

"So you recommend married life, then? Lizzy spoils you shamelessly and waits on you hand and foot?"

He looked away. "Lizzy's not been too well lately."

"I'm sorry to hear that, Trip. She's on the mend, I hope?"

"I hope too," he said.

"Nothing too serious?"

He cleared his throat. "She lost a baby last year. She hasn't quite gotten over it yet."

She touched his hand. "I'm so sorry, Trip. It must have been very upsetting for you."

He realized with a jolt that nobody had expressed sympathy for him until now. Everyone had told Lizzy how sorry they were about the baby, but they had assumed that as a man Trip could handle it.

"Thank you, Alice," he said.

"You should have brought Lizzy with you. Fresh

air and fun are probably what she needs."

"I'm afraid she hasn't come that far yet," he said. "She . . . she tried to kill herself after the baby. We have to have a nurse with her day and night."

Alice's clear, gray eyes held his. "Oh, Trip. I'm so sorry. It must be beastly for you. Come and have dinner with us tonight. We're going to be a very lively party, and we're going to be silly and laugh a lot."

"I really should get back."

"You say she has a nurse with her. She'll understand. You can drive back after dinner. A few hours won't make much difference."

Now that she was with him, he couldn't bear to be parted from her. "All right, you've talked me into it," he said. He went to the phone and told his mother-in-law that the Brinkmeyers wouldn't be returning from the regatta until later than planned. She seemed to think that it was fine.

The dinner was fun, as Alice had promised. He laughed and drank and feasted his eyes on Alice across the table.

He arrived home in the early hours of the morning to find that Liz had been rushed to the local hospital. She had been found slumped over a toilet seat. Acute food poisoning had been diagnosed as the cause. It was only when Trip was alone with Dr. Martin, the family physician, that he found out the truth. She had been rushed to the hospital and her stomach had been pumped out just in time. It appeared that she had taken rat poison.

CHAPTER 23

"I t's hopeless," Trip said to himself. He sat in a lawn chair on the terrace of his home, looking out across Long Island Sound. A brisk breeze was blowing and sailboats were out in force, their bright sails dotting the blue water with color. To Trip they represented a freedom he had almost forgotten. It seemed like an eternity since he was free to move around as he pleased. Months had gone by and he couldn't really say that Liz had turned the corner back to normal life. Just when she seemed to be more stable, she would do something to show that she was far from her old self. There had been a couple of weeks of hope. She had even gone out shopping with her mother and bought new clothes—and now this.

Trip shuddered as he thought of her latest behavior. It was too bizarre to think about, making him realize that the suicide attempts and the depression might not just reflect one shock, but might indicate that Liz would always be unstable and need treatment.

Trip felt as if there was a great weight around his neck. He had tried his hardest to do something for her, and now he didn't know what else to do. Even the so-called experts seemed to be divided. Some doctors told him that Liz's mental illness was the result of a chemical imbalance and should be treated with drugs; others recommended electric-shock therapy, and still others hinted that it was an inherited weakness and all he could do was to make sure she was always watched.

"Ah, there you are, my boy," Conrad's voice boomed across the terrace.

Trip got to his feet. "Hi, Conrad," he said.

"Beautiful day, isn't it?"

"I suppose so."

"Cheer up, Trip," Conrad said. "She's on the mend, isn't she? My wife said she was quite chirpy when they went shopping last week."

Trip looked at him quizzically. "You haven't seen her today then?"

"Not yet."

"Ah."

"Meaning what?"

"Just that there's a new complication." He sighed and turned to stare out across the Sound. "It's never-ending, Conrad. She needs treatment, not just a nursemaid to watch over her. There must be somewhere, some sort of treatment center, that actually tries to return people like her to normal."

"And there isn't?"

"Normal private hospitals don't like to handle psychiatric cases. They're scared of being sued if the patient escapes, I suppose. There are the mental hospitals, of course," Trip said, "but I wouldn't wish those on a dog, let alone on my wife. I went to visit one, Conrad. The patients were lying in their own excrement. There was the unearthly sound of wailing and screaming all the time, and a woman came up to me and told me that she was Joan of Arc."

"A mental hospital would be quite wrong for Lizzy anyway," Conrad said brusquely. "She's not crazy. There's nothing wrong with our family, you know. It's the same as shell shock in the war."

"I understand that, sir," Trip said, "but I think you also have to understand that Lizzy may be mentally ill without being what you'd call crazy."

"She's getting better, I tell you. This stupid phase is wearing off. She went shopping with her mother last week, dammit."

They broke off talking as Liz appeared on the terrace. She was dressed in a flowing caftan and her dark hair was up in a ponytail, making her look about sixteen again. "Hi, Daddy," she called, and hurried over to him.

"There you are," Conrad muttered, grinning at Trip. "She looks in the very bloom of health. Back to normal, like I've said. You've nothing to worry about, my boy."

Liz reached her father and stood on tiptoe to kiss him. "So good of you to come, Daddy," she said. "I wanted to ask your advice about where I should hang a musical mobile in the nursery. Trip's no use at all. He's not interested in nurseries. It's important where I hang the mobile, you see. I want him to be able to see it, but I don't want him to grow up squint-eyed because it's too close."

Conrad's eyes widened. "My dear girl, are you trying to tell me . . . that there's another baby on the way?"

She looked surprised and laughed. "Of course. Didn't Trip tell you the good news?"

"When's it due?"

"Oh, any moment now," she said. She smiled at him happily. "It's going to be a boy this time. Maybe we'll call him Conrad. I have to go. The nursery needs to be finished and the doctor says I shouldn't do too much in my condition."

"I'm delighted for you, my darling," Conrad said, "and I'm thrilled to see you so happy again."

"Oh, yes," she said. "Very happy. See you at dinner, Daddy."

They watched her walk back up the terrace.

"You didn't tell me," Conrad said. "Congratulations to the pair of you." He thumped Trip on the back, not noticing that Trip shuddered. "Maybe this will make everything right again for her. As soon as she's got her baby to take care of, there will be no more thought of this ridiculous depression or these suicide attempts."

"There's only one thing, Conrad," Trip said in a tired voice. "She's not pregnant."

Conrad looked up. "What do you mean?" he asked sharply.

"She hasn't let me touch her since she lost the baby," Trip said, "and the doctors have examined her more than once. They've told her there's no evidence of a baby, but she won't believe them. She's showing all the symptoms. She's had morning sickness, and now she's even starting to put on weight."

Conrad stared out past his son-in-law and sighed. "Then she really is . . . crazy?" he asked.

"Doctors tell me these so-called hysterical pregnancies are not uncommon in a woman who has recently lost a child. But I also think it's possible that she's manic-depressive, I'm afraid."

Conrad covered his face with his hands. "My little Lizzy, crazy? How could it have happened? We gave her such a happy childhood. I can't believe—"

"Look, Conrad," Trip said gently. "If you found out she had diabetes, you wouldn't feel angry and repulsed by it, would you? You wouldn't try to blame yourself or your family. You'd want to help her."

"Yes, but this—" Conrad began.

"Mental illness is an illness too. It's one of those things that just happens and we don't yet know why. But it's not because of anything you or your family did. Some part of the delicate mechanism of her brain got cross-circuited, or failed."

"I created the Decker Bank with my brainpower, Trip," Conrad said in a choked voice. "I was always known for my level-headed thinking and my logic.

They always said, 'Ask Conrad Decker, he's got a good head on his shoulders.' It hurts me to know that my daughter is somehow imperfect in that department."

"She needs help, Conrad," Trip said. "She needs to be treated, not watched. There must be someplace where there are doctors who can combine psychotherapy with the latest drug treatments and bring her back to her old self. Why don't they have such places in this country? I hear there are good clinics in Switzerland, but I'm scared that another country and another language might push her even farther over the edge right now."

Trip started pacing up and down the terrace. "It's not as if we don't have the doctors here now. Before the war I met German refugee doctors who were top experts in their fields. How many more have been freed from those terrible slave camps and come here, with all their knowledge? They're way ahead of us in Europe in the treatment of mental illness. All it needs is—"

He broke off and stared at Conrad excitedly. "You once asked me what I wanted to do with my life. I told you that I wanted to work on something new, something that didn't exist. I don't have the medical training, Conrad, but I do have a good scientific brain."

"What are you trying to say, Trip?"

"That I'm going to build a clinic." Trip's face was animated as it hadn't been in years. "A clinic specifically for people like Lizzy. It will shatter the stereotyped image of mental institutions and the treatment of mental illness. No barred windows and padded cells and padded cells and sadistic nurses . . . It will be like a luxury hotel, peaceful, elegant, out in the country, and I'm going to staff it with the best doctors money can buy—doctors who are experimenting with the latest treatments and drugs. And I'll give them a place to do their research, too."

Conrad's face was animated now. "You really think a place like that could help Lizzy?"

"I think it's her only chance," Trip said, "and I don't like to bring it up at a time like this, but I think it could be very profitable too. I bet there are families all over the country who would pay anything to have their mentally ill loved ones treated humanely, with dignity . . . and maybe even cured."

"I think you might be on to something, Trip," Conrad said. "A venture like this wouldn't come cheap, but I'd be prepared to make an investment if Lizzy's money doesn't cover it."

"We'll call it the Atkins-Decker Clinic," Trip said, grinning like a schoolboy.

"Decker-Atkins," Conrad said shrewdly.

After that, Trip wasted no time. He found what he was looking for in Woonsocket, Rhode Island. It had been built as an oil magnate's mansion and lately used as a country club. Surrounded by acres of lush grounds and with a view out across sparkling water, it conveyed a feeling of peace and isolation while being close to urban areas and transportation. It was also close to Trip's birthplace, but that thought didn't even enter his mind. He had so completely become P. Stuart Atkins, III, that he had erased any memory of Woody Austen from his consciousness.

In a tenement in Providence, however, a severe-faced, elderly woman cut another picture from the local paper. The headline read, "Millionaire Atkins To Found Revolutionary Clinic." The woman stuck the picture into a scrapbook that already included wedding pictures and other tidbits about the boyishly handsome millionaire. She wasn't deceived at all. She knew her own son when she saw him, and she showed the pictures to neighbors in her tenement, who privately joked behind her back that she belonged in the new loony clinic as a patient!

On the advice of architects, Trip had the entire interior of the mansion gutted and a succession of pleasant, spacious rooms created, wallpapered in soft pastels, furnished with elegance, all with specially designed, accident-proof bathrooms and easy access to central nurses' stations. There would be a monitoring system, but otherwise the ambience would reflect that of a luxury hotel or country-club environment. Patients would be encouraged to choose their meals from an extensive menu prepared by a chef from an exclusive hotel in Bermuda. There would be tennis courts and a croquet lawn, a bright studio for painting or sculpture, music rooms, gardens and a small farm of young animals to pet.

Trip was in on every stage of the planning and design, and was solely responsible for hiring his team of doctors. He wanted men with brilliant brains and inquiring minds, but also with gentle compassion for the patients. He turned down several bright young doctors who were using new drug combinations, because they envisioned the clinic as a wonderful source of human guinea-pigs. Trip did manage to learn, however, the combinations of drugs they were trying, and noted them for further experimentation.

He felt reborn, recharged with energy and ready to tackle anything. Those who came up against him were impressed by his vitality and his determination to learn all he could about every specialty. Any doctor who spouted a pet theory to him in airy-fairy terms was likely to find Trip quoting a 1946 study from Guys Hospital in London, which had contraindicated that particular method. Trip felt like a sponge, ready to soak up all the knowledge in the world and manipulate it to his bidding. He felt truly alive again for the first time since his marriage.

The clinic was ready for its grand opening in the spring of 1948. Ironically, the founder's wife, Elizabeth Decker Atkins, became its first patient. On the day that she realized her pregnancy had gone on for ten months and that no baby would arrive, she was caught by her nurse trying to fling herself from the second floor window.

CHAPTER 24

Within five years, the clinic had acquired an international reputation. Eminent doctors from all over the world were offering their services, and Trip had a conference center built so that worldwide knowledge could be pooled on a regular basis. There was a waiting list, pages long, of prospective patients, and every day the receptionists had to politely turn down the most incredibly blatant bribes to have loved ones' names moved to the top of the list.

"You don't know how lucky you are to have such an honest staff, Mr. Atkins," one of the girls told Trip. "An Arab sheik just offered me my weight in diamonds if I'd erase a name on the front page and substitute his wife's instead."

"That's why I pay you so well, Angela," Trip said, smiling. "So you're not tempted by your weight in diamonds."

But as he left the room, he was reminded of the last

time he had had such a conversation. He thought back to Lita Wentworth, on board the Queen Mary, who had boasted that a Middle Eastern potentate had offered her her weight in rubies. Did she ever find happiness with her Middle Eastern king? he wondered.

Trip remembered the fabulous night he had spent in her cabin. It seemed like a dim memory, another lifetime, another world away. Had sex really been that good?

He had kept his promise to Liz, even though she was rarely able to accept him in her bed. It was years since he had been with a real woman, he thought wistfully. But he was all too aware that Lizzy's money had built the Decker-Atkins Clinic and that he had a moral obligation to uphold his part of the bargain, especially with a wife whose mental health was so fragile.

"It's lucky that I'm working so hard—I don't have any energy left at the end of the day, or time to meet women who aren't nurses," he decided with a wry smile. All the same, he was approaching thirty, conscious that he was now at the peak of his manhood and that life was slipping by him. Maybe when the clinic had made enough money so that he was wealthier than Liz, he'd no longer feel bound by his obligation. But by that time, a lot would depend on her mental state.

It was a source of annoyance to him that the clinic, for all its fame and its eminent doctors, had not been able to work a miracle cure on Liz. She went home cured and was bright and happy for a few months, only to declare herself pregnant again or to fall into depression. Trip had to face the reality that she would never be the friend and companion he wanted, and he threw himself with renewed effort into future plans for the clinic.

One of his frustrations in those early years was that the drug industry was in its infancy. There was aspirin, penicillin had been invented, sulfa drugs worked, but new drugs were notoriously slow to appear on the market. Too often he heard one of his doctors say, "If only there was a drug to treat schizophrenia, or there was a really effective antidepressant without all the side effects," and Trip's immediate reflex was to rush out and invent one. He realized that if he was to keep pace with the research being done at his clinic, he'd have to open his own pharmaceutical company. But he was running out of space at the site in Woonsocket, with no room for expansion. And land in the area was now at a premium, being sold for ridiculous amounts.

Trip put his ideas for expansion on hold, until one day in 1953, when he was trapped in San Francisco by one of that city's famous fogs. He had gone there to try and woo a professor of neurology away from the University of California Medical Center and to his clinic. The trip hadn't been successful from that standpoint. The professor liked the West Coast and had no desire to relocate to the crowded East, no matter what salary Trip waved under his nose. Trip, unaccustomed to being turned down, stalked back into the Mark Hopkins Hotel in a foul temper, ready to check out and catch the evening flight home. As he pushed through the doorway of the Mark, he almost collided with a woman who was leaving.

"Excuse me," he muttered without really looking at her, then heard her gasp.

"Well, that's a fine way to greet an old friend—almost mow me down!" she said.

"Alice!" he exclaimed, the scowl leaving his face. "What on earth are you doing here?"

"I live here," she explained. "I came into town to meet a friend and go to a show. What about you?"

"Whirlwind business trip. I'm just about to check out and catch a flight home."

"It's hello and good-bye then," she said, laughing uneasily.

He glanced at his watch. "I suppose I don't have to leave right this minute. Would you have time to join me for a drink before your show?"

"A quick drink, maybe."

"Terrific. Let's go up to the Top of the Mark."

They rode the elevator up to the top-floor bar and sat watching the lights come on all over the city and sparkle in the dark waters of the bay, while the twilight faded behind the western hills. "It's very beautiful here," Trip said. "You sure picked the prettiest spot to live in. What made you choose San Francisco?"

"My husband works here," she said.

"Oh, I see." The news that she was married threw him completely off balance. "You found the right man, then?"

"Pretty much," she said. "At least as close to the

right man as I was going to get. In the end, I got fed up with my parents constantly finding men for me and decided to keep them quiet by finding my own."

"Is he rich? I'm sorry, that's a crass question."

"Not at all. Yes, he's very rich. He owns factories and vineyards and we live in a mansion in Hillsborough. He travels a lot on business."

"And takes you with him?"

"No. Hardly ever. But I'm fine. I've a lot of friends. The social life is good."

"Any children?"

"Not yet. We're trying. What about you?"

"Not yet."

"You're still married to Lizzy, though?"

"Oh, yes. I'm still married to her."

She sensed what he was feeling. "Are things any better than they were?"

"Not much. I built a clinic."

"I've read all about it in *Time*. You're world famous."

"But it hasn't really helped Lizzy. I still never know…from one day to the next…" He paused and sighed. "It's like living on a roller coaster, Alice."

"I'm sorry, Trip. Who ever would have thought it? Liz Decker? She had the most energy of any of us at Miss Porter's. She was the one who always got us to do things—always laughing, always flirting."

"That's funny, she always said you were the biggest flirt."

"Me?" She looked amazed. "I don't know where

she got that idea. I met you close to the beginning of the year she knew me. I was with you all my free time."

He was staring at her hungrily. Her little-girl features had matured into elegant full bloom. She had superb bone structure, and her golden hair was styled in a sleek cap of waves. Her dress was simple gray cashmere, with a string of pearls at her throat, and there was a large, square-cut emerald on her finger.

"Don't go to your show," he said suddenly. "Stay and have dinner with me."

"I thought you had to catch a flight."

"Damn the flight."

"I have a friend meeting me at the theater."

"Call her and tell her that you have developed a terrible migraine in the last five minutes and can't come."

"I can't do that."

"Of course you can, if you want to."

She looked at him steadily. "All right," she said.

She went to the phone. When she came back, he had ordered a bottle of champagne.

"I hope you're not attempting to get me drunk, Trip Atkins," she said, laughing.

"This is to celebrate the renewal of our friendship," he said.

"I'll drink to that." She held out her glass for him to pour.

They dined in the restaurant, but Trip was not conscious of what he was eating. Course after course came, was eaten and cleared away. He was only conscious that Alice was sitting across the table from him. He didn't want the meal to come to an end. When the coffee was served, he had to ask the question that had been on his mind since the summer of 1941.

"I have to know," he said.

She looked up, curious.

"Why did your parents suddenly not want you to see me anymore? I never did find out what I was supposed to have done."

Her gaze was steady and unnerving. "You lied," she said.

"About what?"

"You pretended to be somebody you weren't. My parents found out that Trip Atkins was all a sham. They also found out who you really were."

"And that made you reject me?" He was outraged. "Alice, I wouldn't have wished my upbringing on a dog. I was the poorest boy in the school. They made fun of my patched clothes and my drunken father. Every day was a living hell, and you can't understand why I wanted to forget that boy ever existed? You condemn me for trying to make a real life for myself?"

Her gaze was still steady. "No," she said, "I don't condemn you for any of that. But I couldn't forgive you for lying to me. It hurt terribly that you couldn't tell me about yourself. To find out things like that from my parents, Trip! I felt like a fool—a betrayed fool. I began to wonder what else you hadn't told me."

"I would have told you," Trip said, "before I asked you to marry me. It's just that I'd tried to shut out all memories of my old life. I'd really convinced myself that I was born Trip Atkins. I had no secrets I was ashamed of."

They sat looking at each other in silence.

"I ran after your ship in Honolulu," Alice said at last. "I don't know what I expected to do if I caught up with it." She was laughing, but she put up her hand to brush away a tear.

"I thought you were happily in the arms of a sailor."

"I'd met him only that afternoon."

She reached out her hand across the table and held his. "Oh, Trip, what a comedy of errors," she said.

"Except that it's a tragedy."

"Is it really? You're unhappy with Liz?"

"Would you be happy with someone who spends half her time in a mental clinic and the other half on tranquilizers?"

"I suppose not."

"And you? Are you happy?"

"Not unhappy. Content, I suppose is the word. Just not over the moon."

"Not like we were."

"No, not like we were."

He squeezed her hand. "I don't want to leave you, Alice. What time is your husband expecting you home?"

"My husband is in Tokyo," she said evenly.

"And you're all alone in that big mansion?"

"Except for the servants."

"Who would understand if you called to say you were spending the night in the city?"

"It doesn't matter if they understand or not."

"Then don't go home tonight."

"I thought you had a plane to catch," she said shakily.

"To hell with the plane. To hell with the clinic and to hell with everyone else. This is our one chance for happiness, Alice. I can't let you go."

They rose from the table without saying a word and rode the elevator together down to his suite.

"It's very nice," she said, walking across to the window and looking out. "You have a lovely view."

He came up behind her and slipped his arms around her waist. "Not nearly as lovely as the view I have now. You are the most beautiful woman in the whole world, Alice. I've never stopped loving you for one minute."

She turned to him, wrapping her arms around his neck. "Nor I you, Trip Atkins," she whispered.

Their lips came together in a desperate kiss. He was fumbling with the buttons on the back of her dress while she loosened his tie.

"We should close the drapes," she said as he eased the dress over her head.

"We're on the twentieth floor, who can see us?" he said, laughing.

"Low-flying aircraft?" She was laughing too. "No, you're right. Let's admire the view, but turn the light out." Trip reached for the light switch and all they could see were the twinkling lights across the bay.

"It's like being among the stars," Alice said. She let fall the last of her undergarments and stood naked in front of him. There was still enough light in the room for him to feast his eyes on the curves of her body— the body he had fantasized about so often and knew only through touch. "Oh, Alice, you're so lovely," he said.

With a sigh they sank into each other's arms. Afterwards he didn't move away from her, but lay motionless, conscious of her body against his, the feel of her cheek, the arch of her neck, the smell of her perfume. It reminded him of the fresias he used to bring her and of how she always thrust her face into the posy.

"I don't want to leave you, Alice," he said simply.

"I know. I don't want to leave you either, but we mustn't do this again," she said. "It's wrong, Trip. I have a husband, and you have a wife who needs you."

"I know," he said. "If she were whole and healthy, I'd let her divorce me in a minute and I'd snatch you away from your husband and run off with you to Australia or Katmandu."

"But she's not healthy and you can't leave her."

"No," he said simply. "I can't leave her the way she is. It wouldn't be fair."

"We mustn't do this again."

"No," he said. "We mustn't do this again."

"But we still have the rest of tonight," she whispered. She lay with her head on his shoulder and fell asleep with his arms around her. When he woke in the morning, she was gone.

CHAPTER 25

Outside, the room was a sea of white. Fog had come in overnight and even the closest buildings were now invisible. He showered and dressed and took a taxi to San Francisco International, only to find that the fog had socked in the entire Bay Area. "We've had to cancel our nine-o'clock flight to New York," the girl at the airline counter said. "We'll try to find you space on the six-o'clock tonight, although it doesn't look good right now."

Trip wasn't prepared to hang around an airport all day. He took a taxi back to the city and was just in time to hop on the California Zephyr as it pulled out of the station bound for Chicago and all points east.

Riding the train was a novelty for him. Always hurried, he was used to flying everywhere. Now the forced idleness intrigued him. He gazed out of the window like a tourist as the track rose into the Sierras, crossing impressive chasms and thundering streams. There was still snow on the highest peaks. Soon after the crest, they stopped in Reno. From the train, it appeared a dreary, one-horse town, with none of the glamorous image associated with the divorce capital of the West. The stop was long, and Trip dozed in the heat. He didn't feel the train pulling out of the station again.

When he woke, they were crossing a desert landscape. Scrub and rocks stretched out in every direction toward craggy brown mountains. There was no sign of man as far as the eye could see. A bird of prey wheeled in a clear blue sky, but otherwise nothing moved.

I bet you could get land cheaply here, Trip thought with a laugh. Then the smile faded from his lips. He sat upright, staring out of the window, his mind racing. It was almost as if he were having a vision: a whole community, miles from anywhere, centered around the Decker-Atkins clinic. Peace and tranquillity, ideal climate, all the room in the world for expansion, research facilities, his own drug company. Trip's heart began to race. Land dirt cheap, as much as he wanted. A chance to create his own dream. How many people were given that opportunity? He took out a notebook and began jotting down figures. It was crazy, it was impractical, and he knew he had to try it.

When the train stopped in Denver, he got out and put through a call to his financial analyst, Bill Leviton, in New York, telling him to hop on the next flight west and meet him. Bill arrived the next morning to find that Trip had already lined up real estate people and geologists, and had chartered a private plane.

"Would you mind telling me what this is about?" Bill Leviton asked as he and Trip shook hands at the airport.

"We're going land-hunting, Bill."

"For what?"

"Enough land to build a town on." He laughed at Bill's astonished face. "Yeah, that's right. Enough land to build a whole town. I had this vision, Bill. A whole town centered around Decker-Atkins."

"Are you out of your mind, Trip?" Bill stammered. "You want to move the clinic out here?"

"And start my own drug-production facility. Room to expand. Room to grow, Bill. That's what I need."

"Nobody will come, Trip. And where are you going to find suitable land? Water's a big problem. And what about Indian rights? And transportation? How's anyone going to get here? I see a host of problems, Trip."

Trip laughed. "I don't care, Bill," he said. "I've got to do this." He put his hands on his friend's shoulders. "Do you believe in fate? I do. I have to. This is the second time in my life that fate has shown me what can be mine if I take it. Both times were unexpected train trips. I hopped a train once and landed outside Yale University. I took that as an omen, and I take this as an omen too."

Bill laughed. "You don't seem like the superstitious type to me, Trip."

"Just call it hunches, Bill. I have hunches and my hunches are always right. Could the clinic in Woonsocket have been any more successful?"

Bill shook his head. "No, you definitely found a need and filled it there."

"Then trust me with this."

Bill shrugged. "You're the boss. You want land, let's go find it."

"I was hoping you'd say that," Trip said.

"I just hope that you can persuade your clients to come to some godforsaken desert hellhole."

"It isn't going to be a hellhole, Bill. It's going to be paradise," Trip said.

They flew out on the Piper Cherokee and looked at several sites. Most of them suffered from the same problem: lack of available water. The geologist thought that they could drill artesian wells, but it would be costly and the water probably would be contaminated with salts. Bill looked at the dusty desert valleys and shuddered.

"If we find nothing better that this, can we go home and forget the whole thing?" he asked hopefully.

"We'll find it," Trip said. "I know we will."

On the way back to Denver, they were flying over a landscape where the Rockies dropped to meet the Great Plains. As they passed over a round valley basin, surrounded by gentle hills and with a marshy stream running through it, suddenly Trip yelled, "This is it! Fly down and see if you can land."

"There's no landing strip," the pilot said.

"I don't care a damn. See if you can touch down over on the other side of the river."

The plane banked sharply, came in between the hills and bounced to a bumpy landing. There was sweat on the realtor's forehead. Trip opened the door and jumped down. The air smelled fresh and was scented with herbs. A gentle breeze ran through the long grasses.

"This is it," Trip said with satisfaction.

"You want to relocate here?" Bill asked.

"Sure, why not? It's got everything I want. Not too far from a major highway. Gap in the hills over there where we can put in an airstrip, and we'll build the houses around a lake—"

"What lake? It's a marsh."

"Now it is," Trip said. "But when I've dammed the stream, it's going to be a lake, right in the middle of the valley. This place will be paradise, you'll see."

"We don't even know if this land is available," the real estate broker said nervously. "It's not on my books."

"Then find out who owns it and make them an offer they can't refuse," Trip said impatiently.

"I'm really not sure—" the man began, but Trip cut in. "Go with him, Bill, and make an offer that only an idiot would turn down. I want this place and I'm going to get it."

"I'm sure there are other sites, closer to major population areas," Bill said cautiously. Trip was pacing, which was a bad sign.

"I don't want another site. I'm going to build my town here," he said. "I can see it already. I can see the lake and the green lawns and the clinic buildings and the pharmaceutical factory and parks where kids can play and a downtown with a real old-fashioned Main Street feeling. People will want to live here, Bill. It will be the ideal small town. They'll want to raise their kids here. I'll call it Lake Success."

"Lake Success," Bill Leviton said with a laugh. "I'll believe it when I see it."

CHAPTER 26

Bill Leviton wasn't the only skeptic among Trip's friends and advisers. In fact, almost every one of them, firmly rooted to East Coast civilization, gaped in horror at the thought of anyone wanting to go live in the Western desert. "You can build all you like, but no one will come," was the general consensus of opinion. Even his father-in-law, who had been his ally and admirer during the past few years, couldn't go along with this new venture.

"It will ruin you, Trip," he said. "It will eat up all your profits from the clinic here . . ."

"But I don't intend to keep the clinic here once Lake Success gets going," Trip said.

Conrad's jaw dropped. "You're planning to close Woonsocket altogether?" he asked. "Not even have one sensible investment to fall back on?"

"It wouldn't make sense to keep it open," Trip said. "I want the best staff with me out at Lake Success.

That would mean I'd have to hire second-rate people to keep Woonsocket running and I'm not prepared to do that. If patients want to come to my clinic for treatment in the future, they'll have to come out west to find me."

"Do you realize what a risk you're taking?" Conrad demanded. "Gambling away your whole future?"

"Don't worry," Trip said calmly. "There's not one penny of your daughter's money involved in this. It's all mine to gamble with. And you should know that I thrive on risk, Conrad. I've precious little else to make my life exciting."

Conrad nodded with understanding. "But how do you think that Lizzy will adapt to the change? You know how easily she's upset—"

"That's one of the miracles I'm hoping for," Trip said. "I'll build her a beautiful, tranquil house, away from all the pressures of the East Coast. Maybe when she's in the middle of a new town, surrounded by contented young families, we might even be able to have the child of our own she longs for."

"Do you think that would be wise, considering?" Conrad asked.

"I'd like to make her well and I'd like to make her happy," Trip said simply. "You have to admit, Conrad, that she's not doing much right now. In and out of the clinic every few months, scared to travel, scared to go to the city: what sort of life is that anyway?"

Conrad nodded. "Maybe you're right. Maybe the change might work miracles. We can only hope."

Trip touched his arm. "I wouldn't mention it to her until it's finished," he said. "I don't want any unnecessary worry."

Privately he believed that an improvement in his relationship with Liz would be too much to hope for. Since her bouts of mental illness, he found he watched her like a hawk for signs of instability. He couldn't relax around her, and behavior that would have been normal in anyone else made him jumpy. If she forgot someone's name or jumped at the slamming of a door, he would ask when she'd last seen Dr. Gibson, which would make her nervous and defensive. The consequence was that they skirted around each other like two boxers stepping into the ring.

At night he rarely went to her bedroom and she rarely invited him. When he did go, it was obvious that she was merely doing her duty and took no pleasure from it. The way she'd lie there unmoving, often with her eyes open and staring at the ceiling, was enough to turn off the most ardent man, and Trip had never been ardent toward her.

But his home life didn't matter so much anymore. He knew that Lake Success was being built with his own money. Whatever promise he had made to her was no longer relevent. He had been faithful longer than most men would have been. The only time he had yielded to temptation had been with Alice, and Trip knew he would have risked immediate execution or life in prison to have been with her. But he accepted, as calmly as he could, the fact that they would now never be together. They had shared one blissful night and that would be all. From now on, he would find other sex partners, but never another woman to love.

Finding other partners was as easy as blinking. Approaching forty, Trip's rugged good looks had been enhanced by age. He sported a healthy tan and was muscled from tennis and swimming. His former blond hair was gradually showing streaks of attractive gray and his aura of power was magnetic. When he went away to lecture or consult, he usually found a willing partner, so the conferences became more frequent.

At first Liz didn't suspect anything. He had been faithful to her for so long, she even ignored the first rumors. But then she saw a newsreel of the World Health Conference in Geneva. There was Trip in the background, behind the presidents and United Nations officials, and as Liz watched, she saw a woman slip her arm through his. There was a possessiveness about that gesture, the sort of liberty people take only when they have just made love.

After that, Liz watched more closely. She called his room at odd hours and once a woman answered. Liz put the phone down, trembling. She wanted to confront Trip about it, but she couldn't. She was scared that if she pushed him too far, he'd leave and she'd be all alone. Instead she called Dr. Gibson over at the clinic. "I'm all out of sleeping pills," she said. "Do you think you could have some sent over?"

* * *

As Lake Success was being built, Trip had little time for women or anything else. He threw himself into the new venture with wholehearted enthusiasm. It was he who designed the layout for the new town, who suggested designs for the clinic buildings and was actually present when the first drops of water gushed up from the drilling pipes. Progress was much slower than Trip would have liked. He chafed impatiently while the lake filled, while streets were poured, sewers were dug and electricity brought in. Gradually the skeletons of new buildings went up. Lawns were laid and sprinklers went day and night. Main Street was built and the first permanent residents began to move in. Trip had given all his staff a generous relocation allowance and encouraged them with low interest loans to buy their own plots and build their own houses. An interesting medley of houses began to go up in the best section of town with lake views: in the middle of large lots Spanish and Tudor, Colonial and Ultra-modern houses sprang up. Further away from the lake Trip had the builder put in more modest suburbs of simple ranch style homes. But even these had large back yards with room for pools and garages big enough for two cars. At last construction began on Ridgehaven, the mansion he had selected for himself on a knoll overlooking the lake and the township. He wanted a place where Liz would feel at home, so he had created the best features of her parents' home and their own. He brought Liz out for the first time to show her when the house and lawn were almost finished and encouraged her to choose the interior decoration and furnishing.

Surprisingly, she didn't object to the move and threw herself with enthusiasm into her task. With her mother's help, a tasteful English castle rose by the lake, furnished and decorated with the finest antiques, wallpapered in silk and leather.

"What do you think of it, darling?" Liz asked, leading Trip inside on the day that the last of the furniture was installed.

Trip looked up the carved wood staircase, taking in the artworks and tapestries on the wall, the suit of armor in the corner, the chandelier that had come from a convent in Spain. The place reeked of good taste. He found his thoughts going back to his first semester at Yale and of how impressed he had been by everything, or how he had looked around with wonder and longing at the interior of Theo's house. And yet this was grander than anything he had ever dreamed of. If there was one moment in his life when Trip Atkins knew he had arrived, this was it. Suddenly the world was full of hope. Liz stood there, looking pleased and excited, just like the young girl who he had met on the football field all those years ago. Her eyes were clear and bright as they once had been and it struck him that maybe the move was the miracle he had been hoping for.

"It's beautiful, Lizzy, and so are you," he whispered, kissing her gently. "Let's make this a new beginning for both of us. This is the sort of house that should have a family in it."

She looked up at him, eyes shining. "Oh, yes, Trip. Let's hope it works this time. If only we could have children of our own."

"I'm working on a new drug, Liz," he said. "The researchers at Decker-Atkins are coming up with a new fertility agent. Would you like to be our first human trial?"

She looked up at him with scared eyes. "It would be safe, wouldn't it? I mean, you wouldn't try out something on me that could be dangerous?"

"I wouldn't try it on anyone until I was confident it worked," Trip said. "And the FDA has to approve it too. But I've read the reports, Liz. There is no reason why it shouldn't do what the scientists claim it can. As soon as we've settled in here and I've got the clinic going, we'll get down to the business of having our family."

She nodded excitedly. "I can't wait, Trip," she said. "I know everything will be better now. I'm so happy that you decided to bring me here."

CHAPTER 27

Contrary to all the pessimistic views, the new Decker-Atkins Clinic was an immediate success. It was still such a pioneer in the field of mental illness and substance abuse that the rich and famous were prepared to come halfway across the world to find it. Private jets landing at the airport became a common sight.

Trip had also built a less fancy wing to accomodate interesting or deserving cases who couldn't afford treatment at Decker-Atkins. A regular hospital wing provided free health care for all employees and the maternity unit was in immediate demand.

The mid-fifties was a time of hope and optimism, when many young families were moving out to the suburbs hoping to build better lives. This was the spirit at Lake Success during the early years. The parks and the shopping center were full of strollers, and the elementary school soon had to add an extra kindergarten.

Liz seemed really excited about the prospect of finally having a child. Trip was encouraged by the way she waited patiently for the FDA to approve human testing on his new fertility drug, and then submitted herself to a whole barrage of testing at the clinic. It didn't happen immediately, but, by late 1960, she was able to announce to a delighted Trip that her pregnancy had been confirmed by her doctor. Extra care was taken over her, nurses were hired to be with her day and night, and it was suggested that a trained nanny be brought over from England to take charge of the baby and Liz.

Liz was apprehensive about this. "I don't want a bossy woman telling me what to do and scaring me away from my own child," she said.

"Don't worry, darling. I'll stipulate that she should be another Mary Poppins," Trip said, giving her a gentle kiss on the cheek. It was surprising how tender he felt toward her, knowing that she would soon be bringing his child into the world. He was filled with hope for the future. A child to carry on his business—a son to carry on his name. He phoned his contacts in London and requested that they send a suitable nanny immediately.

A few weeks before the baby's birth there was a knock at the front door. Trip, who was passing through the hallway, went to open it. Outside stood a young girl. Her copper-colored hair was back in a ponytail, she had wide eyes, a freckled, fresh-scrubbed face, and she looked about fourteen. Even stranger, she had a large suitcase and several boxes and bags beside her.

"Yes?" Trip asked.

The girl's eyes were wide with alarm. "You're not the butler, are you? I don't think I could live in a house with a butler. I've always been scared of butlers." She had a clipped English accent.

Trip was still mystified. "I'm Mr. Atkins," he said. He was about to suggest that she'd come to the wrong house when he saw recognition dawn in her eyes.

"Are you the Mister?" she asked incredulously. "I'm Diana Westley. The nanny."

"The nanny?" Trip couldn't have been more surprised.

"Yes. Weren't you expecting me? They sent a cable to say I was coming."

"Yes, we got the cable, but, my dear girl, we were expecting . . . I mean, I know my wife would want . . . a mature woman, not a young babysitter. I thought the agency knew that."

Her face lit up then. "I'm trained," she said. "And I was the only one on their books who wanted to leave for America at a moment's notice." Then she added, "I'm older than I look. I always have trouble on the buses. They think that I'm half fare."

"Well," he said, holding out his hand to her. "I suppose you'd better come in, Diana Westley."

"Would you give me a hand with this?" she said, indicating the mound of luggage. "I can't manage it all by myself. Only, be careful with that one. It's my Elvis collection. I've got all his records. I'm his biggest fan."

Trip was amused. "I'll get one of the servants to bring it all up to your room," he said.

Her face turned bright red. "Oh, dear," she said. "Please excuse me. I shouldn't have suggested that you bring my stuff in for me. That was very rude. It's just that . . ."

"That what?" Trip prompted.

"That we were told in England that Americans don't stand on ceremony and don't really like being waited on."

"Well, I'm afraid you've come to one of the few exceptions, Diana," Trip said. "I'm too busy to help around the house, and my wife actually likes being treated like a princess. Just imagine you're in Buckingham Palace and you'll be okay."

"Very good, sir," Diana said with respect in her voice.

Trip hailed a passing servant. "Martha, get William to help this young lady with her things, and be extra careful of her Elvis records!"

He winked at Diana as he spoke and he saw her relax as she returned his smile.

Diana was taken up to her room and then met Liz. Liz was frostily polite to her. As soon as Trip had left Diana's room with Liz, he grabbed her arm. "Look, I can tell you're worried that she's not old enough and she doesn't have enough experience," he said, "but let's give her a try."

Liz looked at him coldly. "It's not her lack of experience that worries me, although it might concern you, I suppose."

"Excuse me?"

She gave him a withering smile. "Come on, Trip. I wasn't born yesterday," she said. "It's quite obvious to me why you brought her here. You picked up a young chick in London and you've smuggled her into the house, disguised as a nanny."

"What?" Trip was incredulous. "Do you believe I'd want an innocent eighteen-year-old in the first place, and do you think so little of me that you'd believe I'd bring her here? Think what you're saying, Liz."

"I am thinking," she said. "Don't think you can fool me, Trip Atkins. I know all about you and your women. Everywhere you go, you find yourself a cheap tart. You're completely sick. You just can't keep your hands off women."

Trip shrugged. "I admit that there have been a few meaningless affairs, Liz," he said, "but you also must admit that you've never exactly welcomed me to your bed. The only times you've shown any interest were when you wanted a baby. Surely even you can't expect me to remain celibate for the rest of my life."

Liz had turned away, her lips pressed together in anger. He touched her shoulder. "Liz, you have nothing to worry about. I have no interest in this Diana. I never saw her before in my life, and to me she will always be just another employee. Does that satisfy you?"

Liz still wouldn't speak, but shrugged him off.

"If I were you, I'd be more worried that she was old enough to manage our child," he said before he walked away.

* * *

Liz's labor and delivery, a couple of weeks later, were surprisingly normal, but the baby was a little girl, not a boy as Trip had dreamed. Liz had secretly been hoping for a girl all along. She had lain in bed during the last, languid weeks of pregnancy, fantasizing about the baby. Her little girl was going to grow up especialy close to her, just the way she and her mother had always been close. She would call her Decker, to keep her own family name alive. She pictured Decker as a small carbon copy of herself: long curls, white party dress, surrounded by dolls and tea parties and stuffed animals. Everybody would look at Decker and say "how adorable" the way they had always said it about her. The child would be passed from person to person as they hugged and adored her. And at night she would climb on her mommy's knee and snuggle up while Liz read her a story.

Liz had it all planned out—until the moment that Decker came into the world, squawling, tiny fists flailing, little red face screwed up in anger. No one could have described Decker as a pretty baby. Trip said she looked like a boiled lobster. Liz had planned to breast-feed Decker, but this proved impossible. Decker was not prepared to wait one second for the milk to appear. If she took one suck and there was no milk, she jerked her mouth away and screamed. For Liz, insecure enough about her ability to breast-feed, it meant disaster. After a week of fighting and weeping, Trip suggested gently that she give up and shove

a bottle in the kid's mouth. Though the bottle produced instant gratification, Liz saw it as another failure. She went back to the antidepressant pills she had-
n't used since before the child was conceived and
handed the care and feeding of Decker completely
over to Diana.

CHAPTER 28

As soon as Diana took over in the nursery, even Liz had to admit that she was good at her work and knew what she was doing. But she remained suspicious of her, and watched Diana like a hawk whenever Trip was in the house.

Trip had to admit that he was intrigued with Diana. He had always found Ridgehaven a somber place, like a museum. Trip never heard laughter or fun or even noise. Diana changed that. She was noisy by nature. She ran down the halls and took the last three stairs at a jump. She was always singing, too, as she went about her chores—usually her Elvis songs. Trip would look up and smile as he crossed the entrance hall to hear a high, clear voice belting out, "You ain't nothing but a hound dog," while Diana folded laundry. And when he looked out to see Diana frolicking in the pool with baby Decker, dressed in a red-and-white gingham bikini that was only three tiny triangles, Trip had to admit that his interest was aroused. She was so unlike anyone he'd met before—so completely innocent and honest and unassuming.

The fact that she seemed to be completely unaware of her lovely young body and sexuality made her all the more exciting, and Trip found that he was thinking distinctly unfatherly thoughts about her.

It was unfortunate that Liz was up and walking one day when she caught him staring out an upstairs window.

"You can't keep your eyes off her, can you?" she said. "I warn you. You make any move toward her and I'll send her home tomorrow."

Trip eyed Liz coldly. He was thinking of how this spoiled, willful side of Liz had surfaced on their honeymoon and now taken over completely. "I hired her, Elizabeth," he said quietly, "and I'll fire her."

"I'm in charge of the household and I decide what is to be done with my child."

"You wouldn't even have a child if it hadn't been for my new drug, and you wouldn't be living here if I hadn't built you this house in this town."

"Who'd want to live here?" she stormed. "Miles away from civilization. You dragged me away from my family and my friends."

"You saw little of your family and friends from a mental hospital."

"That's a horrible thing to say. It was your thoughtless, selfish treatment of me that drove me there in the first place."

Trip actually smiled. "No, I think it was the shock of finding that you wouldn't get your own way all your life. You're still a spoiled child, Liz, but your temper tantrums won't work on me anymore. It must be rather annoying to know that *my* money built Lake Success and this house, and that you can't make me dance on a string anymore." He gestured toward the door. "Very well, if you want to leave and go home to your mother, you're free to do so." Then, as she didn't answer, he went on, smiling broadly now, "That doesn't appeal to you as much as being First Lady of Lake Success? Then it looks like you're stuck with the nanny I chose," he answered, walking away triumphantly, pleased that he'd said what had been bottled up inside him for years.

Diana continued to be very much in awe of Trip. She only referred to him as "the Mister" and answered his questions in a tiny voice with eyes lowered. Trip was amused. She was refreshingly un-American to her boss as a superior being. The rest of the servants obeyed orders and opened doors for him, but only because he was paying them good wages, not because he was some sort of god. He realized he had made a big mistake in telling Diana to think of Ridgehaven as Buckingham Palace. Now she thought of him and Liz as the King and Queen.

Trip was often away during Diana's first year at Ridgehaven. When he returned, he liked to stand in the front hall, waiting for the sound of Diana's singing. It made coming home much easier. Then he noted that she was singing less frequently. One night he'd worked very late and was finally making his way to his bedroom when he heard the sound of crying. At first he thought it was Decker, but then he realized it was coming from Diana's room. He tapped softly and went in.

She was sitting up in bed, dressed in an old-fashioned flannel nightgown, her hair spilling over her shoulders. Alarmed, she looked up as he came in.

"I heard you crying," he said simply. "What's wrong? Is there anything I can do?"

She shook her head. Large tears were trickling down her cheeks. "I'm sorry I disturbed you. I was trying to cry quietly."

He came over to her and put a comforting arm around her. "Cry as loudly as you like," he said, making her give a weak smile. "Now tell me. What's the problem? It can't be as bad as that."

"I'm just homesick, that's all," she said sadly. "I miss my family. I miss England. I miss going out to buy fish and chips and I miss Marmite sandwiches."

Trip had to smile at her selection. "I can understand that. You've been away quite a while now," he said. "I'll fly you home for a visit if you promise to come back."

"You will?" Her face brightened. "That would be really nice. I'd love to see my mum again, and my little brothers before they're grown up."

"Apart from that, you're happy here, Diana?"

She looked up at him. "Oh, yes, very happy."

"Decker isn't too difficult?"

"She's spirited, and Mrs. Atkins tries to spoil her," she said, "but I manage all right. It's just that she doesn't seem to want to get too close."

"No," he said, realizing the truth of this. Nobody at Ridgehaven liked to get too close.

"And my wife?"

"I don't think she likes me very much," Diana said at last. "I don't know why. I've always tried to be friendly."

"Maybe it's because you're so young and lively and she's not," Trip said.

"I try not to be too lively," Diana said. "At nanny college they were always telling me to act with more dignity, but I can't help it. I'm just naturally that way."

"I wouldn't change it for the world," Trip said. "You've brought a breath of fresh air to this house, Diana. I hope you stay for ever and ever."

"That's very nice of you, sir," she said. "You've always been so kind to me. I'm really grateful . . ."

"Who couldn't be kind to you, Diana?" he asked. "You're so sweet and delightful and . . ." He was suddenly conscious that he was sitting on her bed and that his arm was around her shoulders. "It must be lonely for you here," he said.

She nodded. "Sometimes I'm very lonely. There's no one my age."

"You must go out, go down to the burger place. That's where I believe all the kids hang out. Or go bowling."

"I don't know anything about bowling," she said. "We don't go in for bowling where I come from. I'd look silly."

"You could never look silly."

She turned away from him. "But I'm acting very silly indeed," she said. "A grown girl crying because she misses her mummy and daddy and because it's hard to make friends in another country."

"I understand perfectly," he said.

She was surprised at his tone. "How could you?" she asked, turning her face up to his. "A powerful man like you. You're so strong. I bet you never feel scared or lonely like the rest of us."

He smiled gently. "On the contrary, Diana. I feel lonely most of the time," he said. "There's nobody here I can relate to. At least there wasn't until you came. But I feel . . . close to you, Diana. I feel we're on the same wavelength. Are we?"

She nodded, her eyes shining. Her elfin face was upturned to him, with tears still on her cheeks. Before he could think of what he was doing, he took her chin in his fingers, drew her face toward him and kissed her gently. To his surprise, he felt her respond. He felt desire flame through him as he eased her back onto the pillow, his kiss more demanding now.

"No," Diana said, sitting upright again. She was breathing hard and her face was bright red. "This isn't right," she said firmly. "I must admit that I've always had a crush on you."

"You have?" He was flattered. "I didn't know that."

"Oh, yes. I think you're super—awfully handsome. I even imagined what it would be like . . . you know. But you're Decker's daddy. We were warned at nanny school that there should be no hanky-panky . . ."

He found her confusion delightful. She was so adorable that he hugged her again. "Don't worry," he said as he felt her stiffen in his arms. "This is just a friendly hug. You're absolutely right, Diana. It would not be the wisest thing in the world if we had anything going on between us, however much we're attracted to each other."

"Oh, absolutely," she said. "We must always remember that you're the Mister and I'm the employee."

He got up. "I'd better go before I change my mind," he said, and he tiptoed to the door. "Sleep well," he whispered.

As he closed the door silently, he thought he saw a movement at the end of the hallway, but when he went in that direction, all the doors were closed.

It wasn't long afterward that Liz suggested they try for another child. Trip was more than willing. Decker was already becoming a bossy little madam and he still had dreams of a son. Liz went back to the fertility clinic and her pregnancy was confirmed soon afterward.

Rowan Atkins arrived just after Decker's second birthday, a fine healthy boy with a mop of dark hair, weighing seven and a half pounds. Liz was delighted with him, and so was Trip. His first experiences with

Decker had not been positive ones. When he saw her
she was usually crying and didn't even like to be held.
When Diana passed her across to him, he felt her go
rigid and arch her back, or hold out her arms to get
back to Diana. Rowan was different from the beginning. He looked adorable and smiled a lot. Trip told
himself that he'd spend more time with this child, and
share in his early years, but it just didn't happen. The
trouble was that he had no time. The clinic was almost
too successful. His new tranquilizers and antidepressants were revolutionizing the treatment of depression.
His fertility drug had proved one-hundred-percent
successful in trials. He found himself constantly on
the go between the clinic and Washington, D.C. He
had frequent invitations to address conferences
around the world and was a member of the President's
advisory board on health care. His visits to the nursery
wing at Ridgehaven became fewer and briefer. On the
rare occasions that he did drop in for a visit, Rowan
was scared of the big, blustering stranger and held out
his little arms for Diana or Mommie to take him.

Trip's inability to interact with Rowan annoyed
Trip. He realized that he had little idea of how a father
should behave. His early memories of his own father
were those of a man who swung at him when drunk,
or slept, mouth open, on the sofa. Did they ever play
together, go fishing, or do any of the things fathers
and sons were supposed to do? Trip couldn't remember any such occasion. He remembered his mother
reading to him, but apart from that, his play had been

solitary. He hoped that things would get better as Rowan grew up and that they'd one day be able to share a father-son relationship. He fantasized about taking the boy around the clinic and the factory, showing him what was being done and seeing the boy's bright little face turned up to ask, "What are these machines doing, Daddy?"

"They're making medicines to make people better," Trip would answer.

Rowan would look around, impressed. "Is this all yours, Daddy?"

"Yes," Trip would say proudly, "and one day it will be all yours, Rowan."

His first inkling that Rowan might not be an intellectual giant came on the boy's second birthday. Among the many presents was a pyramid of stacking rings. Rowan sat in the middle of the floor, surrounded by wrapping paper, a pedal fire truck, a tricycle, a little desk and chair, a stuffed panda bigger than he was, and hundreds of smaller, as yet unopened gifts. In one hand he held a yellow stacking ring, in the other the pyramid base on which it was to rest. He tried to make it go all the way to the bottom of the base, but it was the smallest ring and, as such, would fit only at the top of the pyramid.

Trip squatted down beside him, intrigued. The boy made a handsome picture, his little face screwed up in concentration, his dark curls falling forward. "Here, son," Trip said kindly. He held out the biggest ring. "Try this one. The red one goes on first because it's biggest, see?"

Rowan lifted dark eyes to look at him without emotion. "I want dis one," he said firmly, and began trying to cram the smallest ring onto the post again.

"But that one goes on last," Trip snapped, his temper rising. "Can't you see? The biggest one has to go on first and then they get smaller and smaller. Let me show you."

Rowan snatched up the toy and ran to his mother. "No, mine," he said, burying his face in her skirt.

Trip got up, shaking his head in disgust. "You've given birth to a pretty-faced idiot," he said to Liz, and he stalked from the room.

Nothing Rowan did as he grew up made Trip waver from this opinion. People commented on Rowan's beauty, but never on how smart he was. He wouldn't sit still long enough to finish a puzzle or learn his letters. He certainly wasn't stupid, especially if it involved getting his own way. When left unsupervised for a second, he found a way to climb up and get at the cookie jar, and then he carried the cookies all the way back to the nursery closet before eating them. And when he got Diana's makeup off her bathroom shelf and wrote all over the wall with her best lipstick, he blamed it on his baby brother and left the empty lipstick case, as evidence, in his cradle. For Liz had had another baby. The fertility method had worked without a hitch again and she had given birth to Adam, another son.

With Adam Liz finally got the child she dreamed

of. Adam was different from the others from birth. He loved being held. He loved being breast-fed. He would spend hours contentedly lying in his mother's arms, sucking his thumb and gazing at her with dreamy blue eyes. Liz thought he was quite perfect. She left Rowan and Decker entirely to Diana's supervision, although Diana warned that no good could come of making them feel left out and rejected.

"They rejected me," Liz said. "It's not my fault that Adam loves me and they don't."

Diana was shocked. "What a thing to say, Mrs. Atkins," she said. "Of course they love you. It's just that they're very different in personality, that's all."

"Well, Rowan might love me, but not Decker," Liz said. "I believe she was born hating me."

"That's not true," Diana said. "She wants your love more than any of them."

"Then she has a strange way of showing it," Liz replied. "Whenever I'm in the room, she starts acting up. She had a real temper tantrum when I was putting Adam to bed last night."

"Of course she did. She was trying to get you to notice her," Diana explained. "She's just jealous of the time you spend with Adam."

Diana didn't admit that she agreed that Decker was a very difficult child. She wanted all of the attention, all the time. She was jealous of any second that Diana or her parents spent with either Rowan or Adam. On the day Adam was to be baptized, Decker was caught attempting to carry the baby to the window. The fact that the window had bars on it and nothing could have happened didn't alter the fact that Decker had wanted her baby brother out of the way.

Diana kept a very close watch on her after that, which infuriated Decker. What the child really wanted was to be with her father. She had no desire to be close to the other adults in her life. Diana made her do things she didn't want to do. Her mother annoyed her, not just by her silly fussing over the dumb baby, but by the helpless look on her face when Decker had a tantrum. Decker wanted her mother to be strong. When she lay on the floor screaming, she wanted an adult to pick her up and hold her and tell her that she was loved. But her mother always called for Diana.

Her father, on the other hand, had come in once when she was in mid-tantrum. Diana wouldn't let her take her favorite little car to bed with her, so she'd thrown it across the room and was lying on the floor, kicking and screaming, when her father walked in. He went straight over to her, picked her up, gave her a solid whack on her bottom and put her in her bed. "Go to sleep or there will be trouble," he had said. Decker had liked that. Here was an adult who showed he was boss. She wanted her father to be around her more. But the only way she could get him to notice her was by throwing tantrums and Trip, tired and mentally exhausted at the end of a long business day, had no patience to deal with a child he decided was a spoiled brat.

He had little patience with Adam, either. Trip

hadn't found his older children perfect, but he had to admire their spunk. Adam was sensitive by nature, wanting to please and devastated by rejection, and Liz's overprotectiveness had made him hopelessly timid. In the garden he would run back to his mother if a butterfly came near him. He never wanted Liz out of his sight. He'd burst into tears if Rowan or Decker took a toy away from him, but never fight to get it back. He knew that his mommy was right there to scoop him out of trouble, hug him and make everything all right.

Sometimes on Sundays, Trip would attempt an afternoon of family togetherness. Tea would be served out on the lawn and he'd try to play a game with the children. But the afternoons were rarely successful. Trip would try to show Rowan the correct way to catch the ball; Rowan would insist on doing it his way and then drop it. Decker would always get upset if she didn't win and then push over the baby when he held out his hands to catch. It would usually end up with all three of them crying and Trip stalking into the house in disgust.

"Are they always like this?" he'd snap accusingly to Liz. "You're bringing them up to be spoiled brats."

"Maybe if you were a little more patient with them," Liz would snap back. "Rowan's only a baby, you know. You can't expect him to catch like a man."

"He won't learn, that's what I can't stand," Trip said. "And Decker must win at all costs, and Adam sniveled for hours and wouldn't even try again, just because he got a tiny bomp on the nose with a softball."

He always felt guilty afterward. He knew they were his children and he should like them. But he didn't. He hadn't managed to produce the bright, inquisitive, friendly child he had dreamed of and he didn't like to fail. He gave up going to the children's wing altogether.

CHAPTER 29

After that, Trip went on extended business travel to the Orient. There was a new interest in Western medicine in so many countries that Trip found his advice, and his pharmaceutical products, much in demand. After meeting with health leaders in the developing nations, he came home with ideas for cheap contraceptive alternatives for India, China and other countries threatened with terrible overpopulation, and for more broad spectrum antibiotics for attacking the myriad diseases so common in rural Asia.

He came back briefly to the States, stopping over in Lake Success just long enough to meet with key employees and tell them of the latest developments before returning to the Orient. All year he was rarely in Lake Success for more than a few days at a time. When he finally came back to Ridgehaven, it was late summer.

Lake Success was sizzling in the heat. The water was dotted with boats and water skiers. Children ran under lawn sprinklers. Screams and sounds of splashing came from the big public pool. It all seemed very relaxed and carefree after the dreary climate and hurried pace of London, where he'd stayed a week before.

As the car swung through the big gates and headed up the driveway to the house, Trip found that he was almost looking forward to being home. He'd play with his children in the pool and Diana would be there in her tiny bikini, singing and acting like a twelve-year-old. He needed fun and laughter. For the first time, he was feeling distinctly jet-lagged and realized that he was getting older.

He was told by the servants that Liz had been sick again and was resting in her room. He went straight to the children's wing and handed them the presents he'd brought them, though he got the feeling that they were more delighted with the presents than their father's homecoming. Then he handed Diana a package.

"I brought you a little something too."

He noticed that she didn't look as healthy as when he had last seen her. There were dark circles around her eyes, and her cheeks looked hollow.

"I can't accept this, sir," she said in a quiet voice.

"Why on earth not? I've brought presents for everyone else," Trip said. "Go ahead, open it. It's French perfume. All women love French perfume, don't they?"

"Thank you very much, sir," she said without open-

STENN/QUIN-HARKIN

ing it. "When you have a moment, I'd like to speak to you in private."

"Certainly, Diana," he said. "Come to my study right away if you like."

She followed him down the hall. He wondered if Liz had made life uncomfortable for her during his absence. He wondered if she was homesick again. He ushered her into his study and pulled out a chair.

"I'd rather stand, if you don't mind," she said politely. "I can do this better standing."

"What is it, Diana?" he asked gently.

"I want to offer my resignation, as from the end of this month, sir," she stated in a formal voice.

"Your resignation? Diana, aren't you happy here?"

"Oh, yes, sir, very happy."

"But the children love you and everything's running so smoothly. If it's a question of homesickness, I'm sure we could let you have time to fly home . . ."

"No, sir," she said. "It's not a question of homesickness."

"Then what in heaven's name?"

"Please don't ask me, sir. I'd rather not say. I just have to go home at the end of the month."

"My wife!" he exploded. "It's my wife, isn't it?"

"Your wife?"

"Yes. She's always been jealous and suspicious of you. Has she been giving you a hard time?"

"Oh, no, sir. Mrs. Atkins has been in bed most of the past few months. It's . . . a personal problem, sir."

"What sort of personal problem?" Trip insisted.

· 192 ·

"I'm sure there's no personal problem we can't overcome if you'd only tell me about it."

"There's nothing you can do, sir," she said, shaking
her head.

"Rubbish. I'm a powerful man, Diana. Just tell me
who's been upsetting you . . ."

She was biting her lip. "If you really have to know,
sir, I'm pregnant," she said.

"Good God." He had not been prepared for this.
"Who? Why? When . . . I mean, how did it happen,
Diana?"

"How did it happen?"

"I know how it happened!" he stormed. He was
filled with inexplicable rage. He had stayed away
from her, kept his hands off her to preserve her innocence, and then she had done this behind his back!

"I'm sorry sir," she stammered. "I know I was stupid and naive, but it just happened."

"Who's the father? Damned whippersnapper. I'll
make him marry you."

Her gaze was steady now. "I can't tell you that, sir,
and I really don't want to marry him."

"You're not going to tell me?"

"If you'll pardon my impertinence, it's none of
your business, sir," she said, blushing. "I'm very sorry
I let you down after you were so kind to me. And I'll
try to find you a good replacement as soon as I get
home."

"I don't care about the damned replacement,
Diana," he said. He went over and grabbed her shoul-

ders, his fingers digging into her. "I care about you! I don't want this to happen to you…you and some guy …after everything…after I thought…Dammit, Diana, I really cared about you."

"I know," she said. "I've said I was sorry. What else can I say?"

"I own a clinic," Trip said. "You don't have to have this child. If you'd like to go that route—"

"I couldn't, sir," she told him simply. "It wasn't the way I was brought up. I'll just go home to England, and I expect my mother will understand."

"And if she doesn't?"

"Then it's up to me," Diana said. "I made the mistake. It's up to me to handle things."

He looked at her with hurt and longing. "I don't want to let you go, Diana. Would you come back after the baby?"

"I don't see how I can, sir," she replied. "And it wouldn't be wise to come back here."

He stalked over to his desk and opened the center drawer. "If you really insist on this, then here . . ." He scribbled furiously and flung a check across the table at her. Diana picked it up and gasped. "It's for fifty thousand dollars," she said. "I can't take this."

"Take it, damn you!" he shouted. "If you don't take it, I'll ram it down your throat."

"But I can't. I'm the one who let you down. You don't owe me anything."

"I want you to have it," he said, trying to sound calm. He could see her distress. "It would make me feel better if I knew you had enough money to take care of yourself. Please take it."

"If you really insist," she said hesitantly.

"I insist."

She folded the check and put it in her pocket.

Trip intended that the details of that conversation remain a secret between himself and Diana. He announced to the staff that Diana would be leaving at the end of the month because she had personal commitments in England, and that he would be hiring a local replacement.

However, he underestimated the grapevine in the large household. By the end of the day, it was common knowledge that Diana was leaving because she was pregnant, and there was a lot of speculation about the father. None of the other servants knew of any liaisons with town boys. Diana had always kept her activities very much to herself, with no evidence that she had fallen in love. The staff concluded that Trip was the father.

Trip also underestimated Liz. With him she seemed to be in another world most of the time, sleeping or hardly bothering to acknowledge him. During one of her more alert periods, he said that Diana was going home and that he'd find a new nanny for the children. She seemed to accept this, with little more than a nod of the head. But during her lucid periods when the drugs wore off, she began to wonder. She overheard snippets of conversation. She questioned the servants who most liked to gossip, and she came to her own conclusions.

As Trip was escorting Diana down to the car for her journey to the airport, Liz appeared behind them at the top of the stairs.

"So the lovebirds are trying to sneak away!" she cried, making them both spin around.

She looked from one face to the next. "You must think I'm stupid and blind," she said. "You really believed I didn't know what was going on, didn't you?"

"What are you talking about, Elizabeth? Please go back to bed," Trip said evenly.

"Oh, sure. Go back to bed, Liz, so that you can carry on with your young mistress."

"Elizabeth, don't be ridiculous."

Liz gave a snorting laugh. "Oh, don't play innocent with me, Trip. All the staff knows about it. I've heard them talking. You got her pregnant and now you're sending her home in a hurry with a nice fat check in her pocket."

"Liz, that's totally untrue," Trip said.

"Do you deny it, little Miss Innocent?" Liz said, turning her furious gaze on Diana.

Trip put out a restraining hand to Diana. "I'll handle this," he said. "She's all doped up and she doesn't know what she's saying."

"I know very well what I'm saying," Liz said. "I can see now that this is all part of your plan. You've kept me doped so I wouldn't see what was going on. But I've known all along." She pointed an accusing finger at Trip. "I saw you coming out of her bedroom. Don't try and deny it. I saw you and I've been waiting for this moment to get even."

Her voice was rising as she stepped unsteadily toward them, waving her finger threateningly. "I'm going to drag you through the messiest divorce ever printed in the tabloids. I've got the name of every cheap bar floozie you've been to bed with and I'll name them all in court, and then I'll bring little Diana in and tell the judge how you started screwing the teenage baby-sitter while I was in bed, sick in the next room. I don't think you'll get much sympathy, do you? I'll clean you out. I'll take you for every cent you've got, and I'll get the children and the company too. Now you're going to pay for this, Trip Atkins . . . or should I say Woody?"

She looked at his astonished face and started to laugh. "That surprised you, didn't it? But I've known all along who you really are. You've probably always wondered how Alice's parents found out the truth about you. It was me, Trip. I told them. I wanted you for myself, so I told them the truth. And it worked, didn't it? I got you, God help me!"

Her words took time to sink in. All these years of misery, all these years apart from Alice. He gave a cry of rage. "You disgusting, vile . . ." She shrank from him as he stepped forward, his eyes blazing with anger. She lost her balance and teetered backward. For a second she hung, poised, at the edge of the top step. She flailed wildly to regain her balance. Then, with a horrible scream, she fell down the staircase, bouncing over and over like a rag doll until she sprawled, limp, on the floor at the bottom.

Trip and Diana stood rooted in horror at the top of the stairs. A small figure shrank back into the shadows as servants rushed from various parts of the house. Rowan appeared, calling, "Daddy, what was that noise?"

Trip motioned to Diana. "Quick, take him back into his room."

Diana sprang into action as Trip ran down the stairs to join the servants around his fallen wife. "Somebody call an ambulance," he ordered.

William shook his head. "No need, sir. She's already dead."

As he looked at his wife's lifeless body, its limbs twisted in impossible angles, his quick brain was already thinking ahead. He could see the headlines now: DRUG KING PUSHES CRAZY WIFE DOWN-STAIRS TO BE WITH PREGNANT MISTRESS. He knew how newspapers could exploit one single grain of truth.

"Shall I call the police, sir?" William asked finally.

Trip looked from one scared face to the next. "Have all the servants come here," he said. When they were assembled, each taking frightened, sideways glances at the body, he addressed them.

"This could be very unpleasant for all of us if we're

not careful. You and I know that Mrs. Atkins was a very sick woman. It was a terrible accident, but an accident all the same. None of us could have prevented it. But there are bound to be questions asked. I'm reminding you now that you signed an oath of loyalty when you joined me. I expect you to keep that oath. None of you saw anything so none of you has anything to say to the police. Is that clear?"

They nodded with frightened eyes. "Yes, Mr. Atkins."

"Good. I know I can rely on you to make this horrible business go as smoothly as possible. Now please call the police, William."

He had Liz's body covered where it lay, then went upstairs. He found Diana, in the children's bathroom, vomiting and shaking all over. Then he held her in his arms. "Diana, sweetheart, it's okay."

"Is . . . is she dead?"

"Yes. She must have broken her neck in the fall. There was nothing we could do."

She was still shivering violently, but she withdrew from his embrace. "I can't get her face out of my mind, Trip. That look of terror when she knew she was about to fall. I keep thinking that if I'd leaped forward and grabbed her soon enough . . ."

"She might have pulled you down the stairs with her," Trip said quietly, "and then I'd have two corpses on my hands instead of one."

She shuddered. "She was so angry. How terrible to die with so much hate in your heart."

"She was a very sick woman," Trip said. "Pray God she's now at rest."

"Will I still be able to go home?" Diana asked. "They won't keep me here, will they?"

"There's bound to be some sort of inquiry," Trip said. "There always is when rich people are killed. But there were two witnesses. We both saw her fall."

Diana nodded, echoing him. "Yes. We both saw her fall."

Trip put his arm around her shoulder. "I'll try to save you from any unpleasantness."

She pulled away from him. "Maybe it wouldn't be wise to put your arm around me in the near future, not in the circumstances."

"You're right," he said. "I'm afraid people are going to talk, whatever happens. I'll try to get you out of here before there's any publicity."

"You're very good to me, Mr. Atkins, especially since this must be a terrible shock for you."

He looked at her with anguished eyes. "I hate to say this, Diana, but I've waited for this moment. I've wanted it to come for years . . . to free me from this terrible burden. But now that it's happened, I can't feel anything. Not sorrow, not joy. Nothing."

"At least you're free, Mr. Atkins," Diana said. "You can get on with your own life, without worrying about your wife anymore."

Free! The word echoed through his head. Was he really free at last? No more worrying about whether Liz would take too many sleeping pills? No more fake affection around the children, no more nights in her bed with her face turned away and her eyes open? He really was free, and it was just beginning to sink in.

"I think you should go to the children," Diana said softly. "They're really scared. They don't know what's happening. You should tell them yourself."

He shook his head. "I can't," he whispered. "I . . . I don't know how to talk to them. Would you do it for me?"

"If you insist," she said.

Sergeant Bauer of the Lake Success police arrived about fifteen minutes later. He listened to Trip's account of the accident. He examined Liz's body, had pictures taken, and arranged for the coroner's examination. He questioned the staff at length and then thanked Trip for his time. "It must be very distressing for you, sir. I'll let you get some rest and I'll be round again in the morning."

"Is there much more you can do?" Trip demanded sharply. "I should have thought you'd seen all there was to see by now. My wife is often under sedation. She was unsteady and she fell. That's all there was to it. I really don't want my staff subjected to further upsets."

Sergeant Bauer eyed him closely. "It shouldn't take long, sir, if that's all there was to it."

He left then and drove back to the police station to report to Captain Harris. "I don't like it, sir," he said. "It has all the makings of a good juicy murder. The husband and the cute, young baby-sitter just happen to be standing at the top of the stairs when the crazy wife falls down them. And none of the staff heard anything, saw anything, or knew anything. He's bought their silence, you can bet."

Captain Harris got up from his desk and put his hand on the young sergeant's shoulder. "And if there was any question of foul play, how the hell are you going to prove it?" he asked. "And even if you get enough evidence to take him to court, do you really think he'd be found guilty by a jury of twelve of his own employees? The guy owns the town, for Christ's sake, Bauer."

"That doesn't mean he's above the law, sir," Bauer said.

"Of course not. And if I was sure he'd been flaunting the law, I'd try to nail him. But can you really blame the guy? He's stuck with a wife who's nuttier than a fruitcake. Would it really be too terrible if he wanted out?"

"Understandable, sir, but still against the law."

Harris slapped him on the back. "Okay, Bauer. Nose around if you want to. If you can come up with any solid evidence, we'll take it further. If you can't, we'll write 'accident' in the files and close the book on it."

CHAPTER 30

By the end of the week, the Lake Success police department had to admit that they would never find out what really happened at Ridgehaven on the night that Liz Atkins died. None of the staff had heard anything until Liz screamed. She had been confined to her bedroom for long periods and only rarely got up to walk around the house. Most of her meals were taken up to her. The autopsy revealed large quantities of narcotics in her system and her doctor testified that her balance and her spatial perception would have been severely affected. In her condition, she should not have attempted to handle the stairs alone.

"It's all too pat," Sergeant Bauer said, but even he had to agree that they hadn't one shred of evidence to acuse Trip Atkins of pushing her. Reluctantly, they closed the books and gave Diana permission to leave.

* * *

Trip drove her to the airport himself. She looked so young and defenseless sitting beside him, clutching her Elvis collection on her knee—seemingly no older than when she had shown up on his doorstep and thought he was the butler.

Trip swallowed hard. The house would seem so bleak and empty without her, and yet she had refused to stay. He had even considered asking her to marry him and had mentioned this possibility to her. But she had shaken her head firmly. "It's a very kind gesture on your part, sir," she said. "But I don't think it would be wise, considering the circumstances. If you and I were suddenly to marry, the police might well be suspicious. Besides . . ." and she paused to look up at his face with a little smile. "I admire you very much, but I don't love you. When I marry, it's going to be a real love match. And you don't love me either."

He did love her, Trip decided, but more as a daughter. He just didn't want her to go away.

At the airport she took his hand. "Thank you again for everything. I'll never be able to repay you," she said.

"I wish you all the best, Diana," he said gruffly. "I hope you're making the right choice and that everything goes the way you want it to."

"And I wish you all the best too, sir," she said. "You can put all this nasty business behind you and really get on with your life now. You can all make a new beginning at Ridgehaven."

He watched her walk across the tarmac to the waiting plane, pause on the steps once to wave, then go inside. Now he had to make decisions about what to do with the children. Rowan and Decker were almost too old to need a nanny anymore. Should he hire a governess, a tutor? They needed a woman's loving influence, especially after their mother's death had shaken them so profoundly.

Then, like a blinding flash of light, it hit him: he was free! He could go and find Alice and bring her home here as his wife. As far as he knew, she was still married to some West Coast property developer, but she had admitted that she wasn't exactly happy with him. They'd fly to Reno for a quickie divorce and he'd bring her back here. The children would adore her. She'd bring her own light and laughter to the place and he would be happy for the first time in many, many years.

He was like a young boy as he flew out to San Francisco. Should he tell her he was coming? No, he wanted to see her face when he surprised her. He wanted to see the realization and then the glow of happiness. Then he'd take her in his arms and they'd never be apart again! Tears of happiness welled up in his eyes—glad that he was alone, he hastily wiped them away.

The flight to San Francisco seemed to take forever. He arrived in late afternoon and grabbed the first taxi he saw. Her neighborhood was filled with exclusive homes, set back on big, wooded lots with a view over the bay. Her house was almost as grand as Ridgehaven, he noted. She hadn't done badly for herself at all. As he walked up to the front door, he experienced a hundred different emotions, ranging from anticipation to despair. What if she wasn't there? What if she was with her husband in Tokyo and not expected back for months? She had to be there, he told himself. This was finally their moment—she had to be there.

A maid answered the front door and he handed her his card. "Please tell Mrs. Wilson that an old friend wishes to see her."

He waited, holding his breath, surrounded by the scent of jasmine on the front porch, until the woman returned. "Mrs. Wilson will see you out in the sunroom, sir."

He was absurdly disappointed that she hadn't come rushing to the front door to greet him herself. He followed the maid through a lofty entrance hall, an elegant living room, and down some steps to a room that was mainly glass, with white wicker furniture and palms in ceramic pots. The glass ceiling was shaded by a large hibiscus, resplendent with huge yellow flowers. And on the sofa, surrounded by big, flower-print pillows, was Alice.

To Trip, she didn't look a day older. Her hair was still like spun gold, her face devoid of lines. Her smile, when she looked up and saw him, was radiant and made his heart leap like a schoolboy's.

She held out her hand to him. "Why, Trip, what a nice surprise. How kind of you to pay me a visit. Please excuse my not getting up. I'm incapacitated, as you see."

She pointed at the cast on her leg.

"What happened? Nothing serious, I hope?"

"Just my foolishness. Trying to do things that should be left to younger people. We went late-spring skiing and the snow was too slushy and I fell. Simple as that. I'm afraid I find it hard to admit that I'm over the hill."

"You'll never be over the hill," he said. "You're as beautiful as the day I first saw you."

"Thank you," she said. She patted the seat beside her. "I am glad to see you. It's miserable being confined to one spot when I'm so active. Can you stay for dinner? I know that Spencer would love to meet you."

"Spencer?"

"My husband, silly."

"Ah, your husband." Somehow the scene was not adhering to plan. Trip felt a chill of apprehension.

"So what are you in town for this time?" Alice was saying. "Another mega-deal to put a few more millions into the Atkins' pocket?"

He shook his head. "I came to see you, Alice."

"To see me? Why?"

"Lizzy died," he said.

"Oh, Trip, I'm so sorry," she said before he could go on. "What a shock that must have been for you. Or maybe not such a shock, considering her past history. Was it suicide?"

"No, an accident. She fell down the stairs."

"How terrible. Poor Trip. It wasn't the smoothest marriage, was it?"

"It was hell, from start to finish," he said. "I'm only now just beginning to realize that I'm out of it. I can make a new start, Alice. I can begin living my life the way I want it lived."

She was smiling at him. He went on. "That's why I came straight to you. This is our chance, Alice. We can make up for all those missed years. I'm going to take you with me, back to Ridgehaven . . ."

The smile had left her face. "What are you saying, Trip?"

"I'm saying that there's nothing to stop us from being together at last. We can finally be happy, Alice."

"One small point, Trip. I'm already married. Have you forgotten that?"

"Yes, but you admitted you weren't happy with him. Not like you were with me. You actually admitted that."

"That was a long time ago," she said. "And I doubt that a forty-five-year-old woman can ever feel the same rush of ecstasy that an eighteen-year-old feels. I told you I was content with him, and I am. More than content. And he has come to rely on me more and more. We're very compatible and comfortable. Yes, I think that describes it perfectly. Comfortable together. I couldn't leave him, Trip. It would devastate him."

"And what about me?" Trip demanded. "If I can't be with you, it would devastate me."

"You've managed to survive without me all these years," she said, smiling fondly. "We admitted, last time we met, that fate had dealt us some bad cards.

That's what life's like, Trip. You get dealt some bad cards and you make the best of them. My life's really turned out pretty well—too well to consider messing it up. Besides, I have other things to think of . . ."

From outside came a yell, then a scream, then the sound of clattering feet over a patio, before the door burst open.

"Paul's shooting me with the squirt gun again. Make him stop," an annoyed young woman demanded. "He is such a child. Tell him to grow up." She must have been around twelve or thirteen, wearing a print bikini and dripping wet. Trip took in the slender body, the slanted almond eyes and raven-black hair. The boy behind her, around the same age, was a direct contrast to her with his fair hair and blue eyes. He reminded Trip of someone.

"Samantha, you're dripping on the floor," Alice said, "and we have a guest. He'll think I have a couple of spoiled brats for children."

"Sorry." Both young people were instantly aware of him.

"Come and say hello to Mr. Atkins," Alice said. "He's an old friend from my youth. This is Samantha and this is Paul."

Both children mumbled an awkward hello, then excused themselves and ran outside again.

"Your children?" Trip asked.

"Yes." She was not looking at him. "We thought we couldn't have children and we put in to adopt a Korean orphan. We got the notice that we could have

Samantha just about the time I found I was pregnant with Paul. So it all worked out nicely. It was almost like having twins. She's just eight months older than he, and she bosses him mercilessly." She smiled, then looked up at Trip. "Now do you understand why I could never leave? I love my children and they are the apple of their father's eye. He adores them, Trip. I couldn't do anything to disrupt their happiness."

"I understand," he said. "I also have children, but it doesn't seem . . ." He got to his feet.

"Won't you stay for dinner?" she asked. "Spencer is usually home in time to play with them in the pool. They're both terrific swimmers—walls covered with blue ribbons and trophies. Spencer sees them in the Olympics one day." She smiled again.

There was a lump in Trip's throat that wouldn't go away. He felt as if he was talking to a beautiful statue. "I have to catch a plane," he said. "My very best to you, Alice."

"And to you, Trip," she said. "I hope you find what you're looking for from life."

He shook his head. "I found it once and lost it again. Now it's lost forever." He held up his hand. "I can find my own way out."

It was only on the plane home that he realized why the boy had looked familiar. And that Alice had named him Paul: the P in P. Stuart Atkins.

CHAPTER 31

The next year something strange happened in Lake Success: a baby was found abandoned on the steps of the hospital. The event made headlines in the local paper. The police department sprang into action to try to trace the mother, but turned up no clues. Nobody knew of a runaway teen who could have given birth, or of a woman who might have had an unwanted child. In such a family-oriented close-knit community every pregnancy was noticed.

Little Anthony, as the nurses called him, seemed to have been dropped from the sky. And he hadn't come from poverty, either. He was dressed in the best quality baby clothes and wrapped in a Hermes cashmere blanket. Since he was the community's first foundling, it was decided to give him a name starting with A, and the head pediatric nurse was a big fan of Little Anthony and the Imperials. So Little Anthony he became—a sturdy, handsome little boy who was soon put in his first foster home.

A few months later another strange event had Lake Success tongues wagging: Diana reappeared at Ridgehaven. One day, out of the blue, Trip got a letter from her saying that she had changed her mind and wanted to return to work for him. He immediately invited her back as housekeeper and she accepted, looking older, more sophisticated and no longer pregnant. When asked about the baby, she said that she had done what was best for the child and never wanted to discuss it again.

Trip tried to conceal his delight at having her back in the house, but now the children were openly hostile.

"Why are you so mean to Diana?" Adam wanted to know after Decker was so coldly rude that even Diana had blanched.

Decker looked at him scornfully. "Don't you know?" she demanded. "We have to make sure that she's not our new mother. We want to make sure that Dad never marries her. Maybe if we're mean enough, she won't want to stay here and she'll leave."

"Yeah," Rowan agreed. "We don't want her here. We don't need someone bossing us around. We'll be so mean that she'll go home to England."

But Diana didn't leave. She was infuriatingly patient with Decker's tantrums. She hugged Adam when he had nightmares and she sang him back to sleep. Soon he began to soften to her. He needed an affectionate adult, whereas it seemed that Rowan and Decker needed nobody.

But one day Decker came home from school, flung down her bookbag in the front hall and ran up the stairs, passing Diana in the hall.

"Why, Decker, what's wrong?" Diana asked.

"Leave me alone. I hate you!" Decker shouted. "I hate everybody." She ran into her room and slammed the door.

Soon afterward Diana could detect the sound of crying. She waited a while before knocking gently and then entering. As Decker lay across her bed, Diana tiptoed over and put her hand gently on the child's back.

"Decker, what is it? What upset you so much?" she whispered.

"They all hate me," came the muffled response.

"Who do?"

"The girls at school. They've formed a club called the White Unicorns and they won't let me in."

"I wouldn't worry about it," Diana told her soothingly. "Girls of your age are always getting into little cliques. It won't last."

"Yes it will," Decker said hopelessly. "I'll never be one of them, never. They don't like me because I'm rich and I'm different from them and I can't play out in the streets like them."

Diana acknowledged that this was probably true. By other kids' standards Decker wasn't allowed to live a normal life.

"I know it's hard being you," she said, "but you're

going to have to face it. You're always going to be the boss's daughter, the rich kid from the mansion. That doesn't mean that people can't be friends with you, though."

"They don't want to be friends with me," Decker said. "They say I'm spoiled and I boast."

"And do you?"

"I guess," Decker confessed at last. "I have to have something to be good at. I'm not the smartest, I'm not gymnastics champion, but I have more things than they do."

Privately, Diana thought that Decker was probably a real pain at school, but she patted her back as the child sobbed. "I know it's hard, sweetheart," she said, "but one of the most important things to learn as you're growing up is how to get along with other people. It's not easy. It was really hard for me when I came to America and had to leave my country and my family. I was so homesick to start with, but I got over it. You could try being the sort of person the other girls would like as a friend—not by trying to buy them with money, but by listening and caring, the way I'm doing now."

Decker turned a tear-stained face up to her. "Why are you being nice to me, when I'm so mean to you?"

"Because I know it's not really me you're mad at," Diana answered.

"It's not?"

"No. You think you're angry with me, but you're really angry at yourself and your father."

"I am?"

"Yes. You're angry at yourself because you weren't really sorry when your mother died, and you're angry at your father because he doesn't pay enough attention to you."

Decker sniffed hard. "You're right," she said. "He doesn't even notice I'm alive."

"That's because he was never very happy here," Diana said. "Maybe now things will start to get better. Maybe now he'll really be able to start enjoying his family. We'll all have fun here, and turn this place into a happy home, right?"

"Okay," Decker agreed. Cautiously, she sat up and wiped her tears. "I'm glad you're here after all, Diana," she said. "Sometimes I do need somebody." Then unexpectedly she flung her arms around Diana's neck.

CHAPTER 32

LAS VEGAS, 1972.

The floor show at the Desert Inn was nearing its climax. In the middle of the stage, a fountain rose, spouting colored water, while two long lines of leggy showgirls stepped out of a Grecian archway and gracefully descended the sweeping staircase to take up their poses. They were wearing oversized headdresses of colored ostrich plumes, matching G-strings, from which yards of tulle trailed behind them, and little else. Rhinestone collars circled their necks, and their breasts were highlighted with rhinestones glued to the nipples. In their hands they carried ostrich-plume fans, and they spread these across the stairs as the music began to build.

Behind the column of the Grecian arch, Honey Potts waited to make her entrance. Even though she did this same routine night after night, her heart always beat faster as she heard the soaring notes of music rise through the theater. Every few seconds before her cue, she made sure her headdress was in place, then took a deep breath as she stepped out onto the stage. Her costume was essentially the same as the other girls', except that her headdress was even more spectacular, rising like a giant peacock's tail above her head, and ropes of rhinestones criss-crossed around her breasts, accentuating their perfect roundness. Honey had always known that her breasts were one of her best features, along with her wide blue eyes. The blond hair had come later and had definitely completed the package. She had grown used to people telling her she looked like Marilyn Monroe. Personally, she thought she looked better than Marilyn.

Now she stood on the top step, savoring the applause. This was the moment when she told herself that she had finally made it: all her dumb, impractical dreams back in Johnson's Crossing, South Carolina, had finally come true after all. She only wished that Betty Sue Pritchard and the other kids from school would be in the audience one night to see her triumph. They had all laughed when she said she was going to be a star someday. They'd told her she'd marry Ed Hawkins down at the gas station and have a dozen babies by the time she was thirty, just like everyone else, but she had proved them wrong.

From the moment she first bleached her hair at fourteen, everyone had taken her for a typical dumb blond, but she had known from the very beginning where she was going, if not how she was going to get there.

Honey began to walk slowly down the staircase. Fans were whisked away just before she stepped on them. She was extra careful where she put her feet. She intended to keep this job for a long time! One night last fall, one girl hadn't whisked away her fan in time and the star, Charlene du Chame, had toppled down the stairs, breaking her leg. That was when Honey stepped forward and offered her services. She pointed out that she knew all Charlene's routines and could fit into Charlene's costumes. So Honey took over the next performance and hadn't looked back since.

That was her skill, she decided—recognizing opportunities and knowing how to make the most of them. Honey had looked voluptuous and sexy since the age of twelve. The only boy she'd been with had left town as soon as he could. He'd told her he loved her and promised to send for her, but he never did. This made Honey realize that if she wanted anything out of life, she'd have to take it herself. Since then she had never failed to take an opportunity.

There had been a time back on the peanut farm at home—her name had still been Harriet Potts—when things had looked so hopeless that she was really afraid her classmates were right: she'd have to marry Ed Hawkins and be stuck in Johnson's Crossing for the rest of her life. But then Sherman Hayley's car had broken down, right outside her daddy's property. Sherman Hayley was a traveling salesman, middle-aged, saggy-jowled, not much to look at . . . but he was heading for Atlanta. Honey had smiled at him and leaned over to reveal her cleavage while her daddy fixed his car. She had left with Sherman the next morning, hinting at promises of things she never planned to deliver.

She reached the bottom of the staircase and began her walk along the apron of the stage, her arms stretched out wide, her hips swinging seductively. About halfway across, she noticed the man watching her. Of course she was used to most men ogling her, but she could always tell when one was watching her in that special way. Even though she could only make out a light shirt and what looked like blond hair, she could sense his eyes following her every move with appreciation and pleasure. She liked that admiration: it made her feel like a work of art, Venus de Milo or the Mona Lisa. Honey had heard of both, although she decided that if she ever bought a statue, she'd rather have one with arms and legs, and she didn't think Mona Lisa was even pretty.

She glanced down at the guy's table and mouthed him a little kiss. She could see then that there were other men with him. Damn. That usually meant a convention. She hated dealing with men from conventions. They usually wanted to do the strangest things when they were away from their wives, and some of them thought that a couple of drinks, or even dinner at the hotel buffet, would pay for her favors too.

Some of the girls liked the guys attending conventions. They said they were easy to fleece. It was like taking candy from a baby to get them back to a hotel room. Only afterward a girl could mention that the fee was a hundred, or five hundred—whatever she thought the market could bear. If the guy made a fuss about paying up, the girl only had to mention that her boss was with the Mafia and those old suckers couldn't peel off the bills fast enough.

Honey wouldn't do that, even though she knew some of the girls made big bucks at it. She wasn't above giving her body on the right occasion, like to that judge at the Miss Home Appliance contest, which had been her big break, but she had sworn she was never going to do it for money. She was a showgirl, not a tart, and she intended to keep it that way.

If a particular admirer happened to reward her with an expensive gift, that was just fine with Honey. She liked gifts, especially gifts that sparkled, but she'd walked out on several guys who had offered her cold cash. She had her pride, and her dignity too.

At the end of the stage, she swiveled and walked across once more to take up her final pose in front of the fountain.

It was a good audience tonight, cheering and hollering. She wondered what sort of convention was in town: sounded like farmers, but you could never tell. Some of those technical types were wild when they got aroused! Honey gave them all her dazzling smile as the curtain fell. Then she whipped off the headdress. It weighed a ton and gave her a shocking headache if she didn't take it off quickly.

"They were lively out there tonight, weren't they?" she called to Roxanne as they made their way back to the dressing room. Roxanne had started in the show about the same time as Honey, but she was still in the chorus. Honey didn't think Roxanne cared much. She made enough on the side to be able to afford a white Cadillac convertible. There were rumors that she was actually shacking up with Danny de Russo, Mafia kingpin in town, but it didn't do to pry too closely into things like that. Girls who asked too many questions had a tendency to disappear.

"There's two conventions in town, that's why." Roxanne said. "Fertilizers and pharmaceuticals. All those guys and no wives. Should be a busy weekend!" She sat at her stool and started to take off her makeup.

Honey sat beside her. "I hear Frankie's coming into town next week," she said.

"Frankie?"

"Frank Sinatra."

"Since when were you on Frankie terms with him?" Roxanne laughed. "You don't even know the guy."

"I know, but this might be my big chance. I might even get to meet him. I overheard Mr. Davis saying they might use me in one of his numbers. Imagine that, Roxanne. Me and Frankie! And after the show, he might say, 'Hey baby, how about going out for a bite to eat'?"

"Dream on," Roxanne said. "You're too tall, for one thing. Men hate it when the girl is taller. Especially stars. Besides, you wouldn't want to marry him, would you? He changes wives like most guys change library books."

"Who said anything about marriage?" Honey asked. "I'm not intending to marry for years yet. Not until I get too old for this. I'm not giving up stardom to make any guy's scrambled eggs."

Roxanne laughed and unclipped the rhinestones around her neck. Then she tried to remove the two from her nipples. "Ow, that hurts," she complained, "and guys don't like the taste of spirit gum either."

Honey had gotten as far as taking off her own rhinestones when Denise, one of the youngest girls, came up to her. "There's a guy out there wants to see you, Honey."

"What sort of guy?"

"Oldish."

"How old?"

"Over forty maybe."

"Convention?"

"Could be."

"Tell him no thanks. I'm tired tonight. I was planning to get an early night for once. Beauty sleep."

Denise went but soon returned, her face bright red. "He wants you to come tell him yourself. He was real forceful, Honey. He said, 'You get her out here right now, understand? I'm not used to taking no for an answer'."

Honey made a face and reached for her robe. "Probably Mafia then. It doesn't do to turn them down. I'd better go."

She left the dressing room and walked down the hall to the stage door. Several men were standing there, but one caught her eye immediately. It was the guy who had watched her so closely during the show. "Hi," he said. "I knew you couldn't really be giving me the brush-off. I really liked your act. There's something about the way you move. How about coming out for a drink with me?"

She took in what he was wearing. Not flashy enough for Mafia. But no sign of polyester pants either. Probably not convention then. The shirt looked like silk, and there were gold cuff links at his wrists. High class definitely, but then the real high-class guys were not exactly big spenders. The ones who had money didn't like to throw it around. And like Roxanne had said, he wasn't exactly young. Honey sized him up, then she gave him her dazzling smile.

"That's really nice of you, but I'm afraid I've got another engagement tonight."

His eyes looked right through her, as if he knew she was lying.

"Another engagement? I thought you wanted an early night for your beauty sleep."

"Both," she said uneasily. "Another quick engagement and then my beauty sleep."

"I see," he said. "Pity, because I'm not in town often and I hate dining alone."

She could feel herself weakening. Think tough, Honey, she commanded herself. If you start going with every guy who shows up, you won't be any better than the rest of them. He only wants one thing like all the others. It's not your company he's after . . .

"I said I was sorry," she told him. "Some other time maybe."

"I don't expect I'll be in town again for a while."

"You're here on a convention then?"

He smiled. He had a very charming smile. Handsome for an older guy. "Something like that," he said.

At least that settled it. She didn't do conventions!

"Look, I have to go," she said. "Nice meeting you, mister."

He didn't supply his name, and she smiled nervously as she ran back up the hall to her dressing room. There was something about that guy. He wasn't the usual type she saw around here. Maybe it would have been fun to see what he had to offer.

"I think I just might have made a mistake, Roxanne," she said. "I turned him down."

Half an hour later she was about to step into a cab for the ride home when a big black limo pulled up. The back door opened. Honey jumped back nervously. This was how the Mafia did business with you, she'd heard. So when the chauffeur said, "Get in, please," she jumped right in.

She couldn't have been more surprised when she saw that the other occupant of the backseat was the man from the stage door.

"I thought at least I could give you a ride to where you were going," he said.

CHAPTER 33

Trip Atkins didn't like conventions. He saw them as a complete waste of time. Instead of coming to further their knowledge, most delegates came to cram as much fucking and drinking as possible into three days. And they were usually such boring people. As he grew older, Trip had less tolerance for boring people. They hovered around him, flattering him, trying to get him to fund their pet ideas, hire their sons or marry their daughters.

But at this convention too, he was asked to be the keynote speaker—the first time in the history of the convention for a nonmedical man. Too good to turn down, especially with all he wanted to say to the members of his profession. He was becoming more and more concerned about the long-term effects of new drugs. He had been pushing for stricter rules on testing, but shot down by the other drug companies, greedy for profit, and wanting to market new drugs as soon as they proved not to develop cancer in mice.

The thalidomide scandal had really shaken Trip. He'd had a chance to develop a drug similar to thalidomide, but he'd backed off with a gut feeling that he didn't like what he saw. As a result, Decker-Atkins was now one of the few companies with the public's respect and trust.

Trip had flown into Las Vegas earlier that day, met with the convention organizers and settled into a suite at Caesar's Palace. He'd intended to have dinner sent up to his room while he spent the evening perfecting his speech, but the organizers had been insistent about showing him a good time. Trip thought it mildly amusing that they'd want to show off Las Vegas to a man who'd seen everything worth seeing in the world. He doubted that the show would compare to the Folies Bergeres and every other chic nightclub in Europe. But the organizers were so clearly trying to entertain him that he couldn't refuse. Besides, he'd been too much on his own lately.

The show had been pretty much what he expected. A couple of mediocre singers had belted out "Climb Every Mountain" and "My Way," and a lot of dance numbers that relied on costumes and bare breasts for effect.

Then he saw Honey. There had been something about her that had instantly grabbed his attention: a sort of wide-eyed innocence that separated her from the hard faces and supercilious smiles of the other girls. She had moved with a gorgeous, long-legged grace—like a gazelle, Trip thought—and as she walked across the front of the stage, it seemed that she was looking only at him. She even blew him a kiss.

Trip wondered why he was so affected by her. He had no trouble getting any woman he wanted, anywhere in the world. There were always hopeful contenders for the role of Mrs. Atkins as well as those who'd give him a night's pleasure. Failing all else, he had the numbers of the best escort services in every major city.

But to his surprise, this girl had turned him down. Nobody had turned him down in a long while. It was a new sensation; it whetted his appetite and made him hope that perhaps she really was as wide-eyed and clean-cut as she appeared.

He took her rejection as a challenge. In a few minutes he had found out her name, where she lived, her habits, and the fact that she had no steady boyfriend. That was how he came to be waiting outside the right exit at the right time. He beamed with pleasure as he noticed her surprised face. She would soon learn that he wasn't a man to be brushed off lightly!

The car pulled out onto the strip. "Where to, boss?" the driver asked.

Trip looked inquiringly at Honey. "You don't really have another engagement, do you?" he said. "If I'm giving you a ride, the least you can do is come up for a drink."

"Up where?"

"To my hotel room."

"Give me a good reason why I should. You practically kidnapped me."

Trip laughed. "I saw you onstage and I fell in love with you on the spot and I had to meet you. Isn't that a good enough reason?"

"I want you to know right now that I'm not that sort of girl," she said.

"What sort of girl?" His eyes were laughing at her.

She actually blushed. "You know. Sex for money."

"I'm only talking about a drink," he said. "What's the harm in coming up to my room for a drink? There's a lovely view."

The car swung into Caesar's parking lot and drove around to the back of the building. The driver leaped out to open the door for them.

"Who are you, anyway?" she asked.

"Like you said, a guy from a convention," he responded, smiling. "You can call me Trip."

They entered through a rear door and took a back elevator that stopped at an unmarked floor. The door opened directly into a top-floor suite. Honey's blue eyes opened even wider.

"Some convention," she said. "How does a guy from a convention get a suite like this?"

"The company pays for it," Trip said easily. "Good PR for them. Shows they're not about to go broke."

"Oh," she said. "So you must be a top executive type."

"Pretty much."

"I like executives," she said. "It must be fun to make all those decisions."

"Sometimes," he said.

The elevator opened again and a hotel employee appeared with a bottle of champagne on ice, two glasses and a tray of smoked salmon. He opened the champagne, poured it and left without a word.

"I thought you might be hungry," Trip said, handing her the plate of smoked salmon.

"I'm always starving after a performance."

"Then you'll have dinner with me? I haven't eaten yet and I loathe dining alone."

Honey took a sip of her champagne. He had one of those faces that aged well, the lines around his eyes giving him a ruggedly handsome look—like a guy in a cigarette commercial, she thought. He was distinguished-looking too. And he'd had the champagne all ready for her. She liked a guy who knew what he wanted.

"I know a couple of places where they do a good prime rib or T-bone," she said. "It's only ten bucks for the T-bone if both of you order it."

Trip smiled as if she'd said something funny. "I hate eating in restaurants," he said. "Too much noise. And I've already ordered dinner. They'll be sending it up in half an hour."

"You just assumed I'd have dinner with you, without asking?"

Trip nodded.

"Do you always get your own way?"

"Most of the time," Trip said.

He came to sit beside her on the brocade sofa. "So tell me, Honey, why did you turn me down tonight?"

She was flustered, unnerved by his presence. "I didn't exactly—"

"Yes, you did. You turned me down flat. Very bad for a guy's ego, you know."

"It's just that I try to stay away from convention delegates," she said. "I saw a whole bunch of you at the table and I figured that's what you were."

"What's wrong with a good, honest fertilizer sales-man?" he asked.

"They go wild when they get away from their wives, that's what," she said. "They act like animals and want to try all sorts of kinky stuff. Then they think they can buy you with a couple of drinks or ten bucks."

"And how much can they buy you for?"

She turned her wide blue eyes on him. "I don't do it for money," she said.

"What do you do it for?"

The eyes narrowed. "Pleasure," she said.

"Funny, that's what I do it for too," he said. "It might be interesting to see if we both mean the same thing by pleasure." His fingers slid over her hand and began to climb her bare arm. "You don't really need to get home for your beauty sleep, do you?"

She looked through into the bedroom. "You have such a big bed," she said. "Pity not to make the most of it."

LAKE SUCCESS

"And dinner's not being served for half an hour."
His hand had reached the strap of her dress and was
sliding it down over her shoulder. She wasn't wearing
a bra, and her breast was as perfect close up as it had
been on the stage. His hand moved around it as he
pulled her toward him and kissed her. He felt her sigh
as his tongue thrust through her parted lips.

"Who needs a whole half hour?" she whispered as
they broke apart. She took his hand and led him over
to the bed, undressing him skillfully while his eyes
feasted on her body.

"Well, you look like you're ready, willing and
able," she commented with a grin. "I think I underestimated you, Trip."

"You definitely underestimated me," he said. He
took her into his arms, delighting in the feel of the
smooth, naked flesh against him, and fell with her
onto the vast expanse of satin sheets. Their passion
was brief and explosive.

"That was fine for the appetizer," she said as he lay
panting on top of her. "After dinner I'll do it to you
and we'll take our time."

They had slipped into robes when the waiter
arrived to serve dinner, and Trip delighted in the
glimpses of her naked breasts each time she bent forward to take a bite of food.

"You weren't kidding, you really were starving,"
he commented as she worked her way steadily through
each course.

"I've always been known for my healthy appetite,"

she said. "The steak's pretty good, but that stuff on top makes it taste funny."

Trip laughed. "That stuff on top is truffles, my dear. They are a special mushroom from France that can be found only by trained dogs under oak trees."

"Geez," she said. "Are you a professor or something? You sure know a lot."

"I've traveled a bit in my life."

"I'd love to travel," she said dreamily. "I've seen all the Cinerama movies. I love the bit where they're flying over the Swiss Alps. And going under the Bridge of Sighs in Venice. I'd love to see Venice. It must be so romantic."

"Have you ever traveled, Honey?"

"Atlanta, Dallas, Las Vegas," she said. "Those've been the high points of my travels so far."

"I'd hate to ask what the low points are," he said, laughing.

"I can tell you the low point. Johnson's Crossing, South Carolina. You can't get much lower than that," she said. "We had a dirt floor in our house, we were so poor. There were five of us kids and we all had to share a room. We used to steal corncobs from the neighbor's farm. Many's the time I've been to bed hungry . . ." She broke off. "I don't suppose you can understand what it's like to be really poor. You probably think that poor is only able to afford a Buick instead of a Cadillac."

He looked at her steadily. "I know what it's like to be poor," he said. "I once had to grovel down a drain to get a quarter a rich kid had thrown to me. Oh yes, I can remember what it's like."

"You were poor once? Tell me about it."

He found himself describing that tenement where they had lived and the patches on his clothes and his drunken father. He hadn't mentioned any of these to anyone else in thirty years, and yet here he was telling them to a showgirl who could have made a nice amount of money by giving the scoop to the National Enquirer. But that never entered his head. He saw that she was really interested. She wanted to know and share his story. Her eyes were full of tears. "Trip— you and me should both be proud of ourselves," she said. "We both were dealt bad cards and we made it to the top anyway."

Trip was amused. "You feel you've made it to the top?"

"Oh, yes. Lead showgirl at twenty-four? It doesn't get much better than that. Of course I'd have liked to star in one of those movies, like they made in the thirties, you know, with the revolving stages and lines of chorus girls. But then, I can't dance like Ginger Rogers and I can't swim like Esther Williams, so maybe I'm better off where I am."

"And what about marriage?" he asked. "What if a rich guy were to come here and sweep you off your feet?"

"I'm not interested in marriage," she said. "No thank you. No siree! That's not in my plan, not for a long while yet. I want to enjoy my success, not have to wait on some spoiled mama's boy, however rich he is. Besides, sex gets boring if you have to do it with the same guy."

Trip laughed. "Honey, you are the most interesting person I've met in years," he said. "Does it get boring if you do it with the same guy more than once?"

"I'll let you know when I get bored," she said, "but I don't think it will be for a while yet." She stood up and let the robe slip from her shoulders. Then she walked back to the bed. "Lie down," she said. "This time is my treat."

Afterward they lay side by side, their legs touching as if they didn't want to break the contact.

"I bet your wife would be surprised if she could have seen you," Honey said. "I bet you don't do it like this at home."

"No," he said regretfully. "I've never done it like this at home. This has been one of the most pleasurable nights of my life, Honey. Thank you." He leaned over and gave her a delicate kiss on her forehead. Honey felt tears coming into her eyes. It was the nicest thing that anyone had done for her.

In the morning he was still asleep when she woke at seven. She dressed and took the elevator down without waking him. Then she took a cab home. She didn't want to spoil his fantasy by making him face her in the daylight.

CHAPTER 34

After she had showered and washed her hair, Honey took a cab back to the Desert Inn for morning rehearsals. They didn't tolerate lateness. As she walked through the lobby, she glanced at the posters advertising today's events, and a picture caught her eye. "National Pharmaceutical Convention. Today: Grand Ballroom. Keynote Speech by P. Stuart Atkins III, founder, chairman and CEO of Decker-Atkins." Underneath was Trip's photo.

Honey ran all the way to the dressing room. "Holy cow, Roxanne, I've just found out that I spent all last night fucking a billionaire!" she exclaimed.

"Who?" Roxanne yelled.

"P. Stuart Atkins, that's who. And I didn't know."

"Jeez, Honey, how could you be so dumb? If I'd spent the night with P. Stuart Atkins, I wouldn't have left this morning until I'd gotten a wedding ring on my finger."

"He's not married?"

"What were you—born yesterday?" Roxanne demanded.

"I could kick myself," Honey said, sinking into a chair. "What a dummy I was. You know, I thought he looked familiar. And now I've totally blown it. I told him that I wasn't interested in doing it with the same guy more than once and that I had no interest in getting married. And I left without saying good-bye. God, Roxanne, I'm such a fool."

"Did he give you anything?" Roxanne asked.

"No, he said he didn't want to insult me by giving me money."

"Then the guy's a tightwad," Roxanne concluded. "Lots of millionaires are. They hang on to all that lovely money once they get it."

"He bought me dinner and champagne."

"Big deal," Roxanne said. "Oh well, at least you can always boast now that you did it with a billionaire. I bet that's something not many girls can claim. What was it like?"

"Fantastic, Roxanne. I tell you, I thought from his age and everything that he'd be one of these boring, inhibited suburban types, but he was pretty good. And considerate, too. I mean, he waited for me to get something out of it, which is unusual for the guys we meet, isn't it?"

"No kidding," Roxanne said. "Talk about wham, bam, thank you ma'am."

"He was special, Roxie."

"No kidding. A couple of billion always makes a guy special."

"No, I mean really special," Honey said. "I mean, he treated me with respect. Like a person who mattered."

"Well, I wouldn't go all dewy-eyed over him, Honey," Roxanne advised. "He'll fly out after his speech today and you'll never see him again, so forget it. Concentrate into getting into your leotards and getting your little tush out there on that practice floor or you'll be unemployed as well as heartbroken."

Honey was halfway into her leotards when a messenger boy came into the dressing room, blushing as he made his way past the half-naked bodies. "Miss Honey Potts?" he called. "Flowers for you."

He handed her five dozen long-stemmed roses and a small box of chocolates in a gold foil box.

Honey's face flushed with excitement. "Did the gentleman deliver them in person?"

"No, miss. They came from the florist's."

"Oh." Honey's face fell. A thank-you gift then. Thoughtful, she supposed. There was a card attached and she opened it.

"Thank you. That was the best night in many years," was written in small, neat letters. Then, underneath, "On second thought, maybe tonight will be even better. P.S. Having seen you eat last night, I know you're not on a diet, otherwise I wouldn't have risked this."

"What does he mean by that, do you think?" Honey asked.

"He wouldn't have sent you the candies, I suppose," Roxanne said.

The other girls had clustered around.

"Well, I don't usually eat candies," Honey said.

"It's not even a very big box," Roxanne commented. "See, I told you—cheapskate."

"But there's a whole lot of roses here. They must have cost a bundle."

"If you don't really like candies, can I have one?" another of the girls asked. "I didn't get breakfast and I'm dying."

Honey opened the box and there was a collective gasp as they saw that the center chocolate had been replaced by a heart-shaped velvet box.

"Ohmigod," Honey said.

"Go on, open it!" Roxanne commanded.

Honey's fingers were trembling as she pushed it open. Inside was a very large diamond. A small slip of paper was folded beside it. It read: "Sorry. Best I could do at nine in the morning."

"Do you think it's real?" one of the girls asked.

Roxanne picked it up and examined it. "You bet your boots it's real. Honey, I think you hit pay dirt last night!"

"I did, didn't I?" Honey exclaimed, her face flushed with excitement. She took the diamond and slipped it onto her finger. If this was a dream, then she never wanted to wake up.

* * *

She was in the middle of rehearsal when a messenger called her over. "There's a man on the phone, Honey. He said he has to speak to you. It's a matter of life and death."

Honey ran down the hall to the phone.

"Good morning," Trip's voice came down the line. "You left without saying good-bye."

"I'm sorry. I didn't want to wake you."

"Very considerate. How are you?"

"Just fine. No, that's not true. I can't get over what you sent me...I mean, I never dreamed...in my whole life...I really shouldn't accept. It's too good for me. I don't know how to thank you."

"You can thank me by having lunch with me. My car will pick you up in half an hour."

"But I've got rehearsal."

"Damn rehearsal. Cut it."

"I might be fired."

"So be fired. See you in half an hour."

Her cheeks still flaming, she ran up to the rehearsal director. "I have to go. It's an emergency," she said and fled before he could say anything.

The other girls looked at each other and grinned. They could guess what the emergency was. They wished that kind of emergency would come up someday for them.

Honey changed out of her practice clothes. She wished she had time to go home and put on something more elegant than her usual denim shorts and halter top. What if he wanted to take her to a fancy place for lunch?

The black limo was waiting and the door opened for her as she came out into the dazzling heat of mid-day. Trip was sitting in the backseat and his face lit up as she slid in beside him.

"Hi," he said. "You look even more beautiful than I remembered."

"Don't say that. I look a mess," she said, putting her hand up to her hair. "I was in rehearsal."

"I decided I couldn't wait until tonight to see you again," he said. "Let's go back to my place for lunch."

Honey glanced at her watch. "Okay, but it has to be a quick lunch. Wednesday is always full-day rehearsal. Run-through starts at one-thirty."

"I don't think we'll take too long," Trip said, his eyes full of meaning.

The elevator doors had scarcely closed when he took her into his arms, his lips crushing down on hers.

"You're a very impatient man, Mr. Atkins," Honey panted.

He raised an eyebrow. "So you found out who I was."

"It wasn't hard to do. Your picture is all over the hotel."

"Of course. So does that change anything between us?"

Honey wrapped her arms around his neck. "You're still a man and I'm still a woman," she said. "That's all that really matters, isn't it?"

This time they couldn't wait to undress. Clothes flew in all directions before they fell onto the bed together, making love with urgency, as if they had been parted for years.

"This is crazy, Honey," Trip said afterward. "I feel like I'm eighteen again."

"You act like you're eighteen again," Honey said. "I've got bruises all over from last night."

"I'm sorry."

"Don't be. I enjoyed it as much as you," she said, laughing.

"You really are quite a girl," Trip said, shaking his head in wonder. "I suppose now you're starving for lunch."

Honey glanced at the bedside clock. "It better be something quick. I haven't got long. I can't be late for rehearsal."

"Sure you can."

"They'll fire me."

"Not for being late once."

"And what about you? I saw you had to make a speech at two."

"So I'll be late too. Let 'em wait," Trip said. "Let them all wait, Honey. What the hell do rehearsals and conventions matter anyway?"

"I have to pay the rent next month," Honey said, "and I've worked awful hard to be lead showgirl."

"Is that really what you want for the rest of your life?" Trip asked. "Is lead showgirl enough to make you happy?"

"It's pretty good for someone like me, isn't it?" she asked.

"Yes, it's very good. But won't you get lonely someday? Will different men every night make you happy?"

She looked at him earnestly. "I don't know that any man will make me truly happy. Not now, after this."

"Flatterer," he said, laughing.

"I mean it, Trip," she said. "You and I—we have something special, don't we? I mean, it probably doesn't feel special to you. You can have your pick of women…"

"It does feel special, Honey. Very special indeed. I've done nothing but think about you all morning. Usually I can shut out everything when I've got business to attend to. But I daydreamed all the way through a meeting, like a lovesick kid." He took her hand. "Do you think it's really possible that we're in love, Honey? It seems absurd, doesn't it, but I think it has to be true."

"Just like in the movies," Honey said.

He grabbed her hands. "I know. Let's fan the convention and the rehearsal. My private jet is waiting at the airport. Let's fly out of here and let me show you Venice and Paris and anywhere else you want to go!"

Honey giggled unsteadily. "This is crazy," she said. "I can't just give up my career, just like that. You're a very powerful man. It's okay for you if you skip one convention. But they'll fire me, and then I'll never get to be lead showgirl again. I'll be finished."

He took her face in his hands. "Honey, it doesn't matter if you never get to be lead showgirl again, does it? You've got me now. You'll never need to worry about money again."

Honey lowered her eyes. "But you might get tired of me. I might just be the flavor of the month for someone like you. How do I know? I'm just a simple girl from Johnson's Crossing."

"I suppose the question is, Honey," Trip said slowly, "would you rather be a lead showgirl at the Desert Inn, or be with me?"

She looked up at him again with big, clear-blue eyes. "If I could be sure that I wouldn't find myself dumped in the middle of nowhere when you got tired of me—"

"I'm not going to get tired of you, Honey."

"You say that now…" She rested her hand lightly on his arm. "Trip, I really want to be with you. You're the most fantastic thing that's ever happened to me. It's just that I can't help being scared. I never want to go back to being dirt poor again."

"You won't, Honey. I promise you that. If it makes you feel better, we'll get married."

"Married?"

"Yes, let's do it, Honey. This is Las Vegas, isn't it? We can get married right away. I'll call and have a judge sent over to the room." He jumped up, snatched his bathrobe and put it on, pacing up and down. "I wonder how soon he can get here. You're not married, are you?"

"Of course not."

"That's okay then. No cause or just impediment. Terrific. We'll get married and then we'll fly out right away. Where do you want to go? We only have to tell my pilot and he can file the flight plan. New York first and then Europe, or Hawaii first and then Asia or Australia?"

Honey put her hands to her face. "Don't, Trip," she said. "It's too much. A girl can't take all this at once. I just can't believe it's true."

He went over and knelt beside her. "It's true, Honey," he said. "I love you and I want to spend the rest of my life with you. Now, there's the matter of the ring—"

"You already gave me one ring today," Honey said, laughing through her tears.

"That was a friendship ring. Now we need a wedding band," Trip said. "I'll have the jeweler come around with the judge. Now, anything else we need to think of? Oh, yes." He went over to the phone. "Miss Johnson, please pass a message to the Desert Inn. Please tell them that Miss Honey Potts will not be returning for rehearsal today, or ever again."

He hung up the phone with satisfaction.

CHAPTER 35

It was three weeks later that the new Mrs. Atkins first saw her new home.

"Holy cow, Trip," she exclaimed. "It's like one of those European castles, only bigger!"

"Not exactly," he said, smiling at her amazement. Everything she did gave him such pleasure. In a world full of rich, bored people, it was a delight to watch her eyes open wide at things like a ride up the Eiffel Tower or a plate of fresh strawberries out of season—things he had taken for granted ever since he married Liz. He hoped she would be like a breath of fresh air blowing through Ridgehaven, taking away all his sadness and coldness.

He led Honey into the entrance hall. "How do you like it?" he asked as she gazed around her.

"It's like a frigging museum, Trip," she said. "I mean, don't get me wrong. I'm not criticizing, but jeez, Trip, there's no friendly touches, are there? I mean, can anyone actually feel at home with a suit of armor?"

Trip laughed. "It's your home now. Go ahead and decorate as you like."

"No kidding? Really?"

He took her up the stairs and opened the door onto the bedroom that used to belong to Liz. "This will be your bedroom," he said. "Mine is through this adjoining door."

"I bet you won't be in yours much," Honey said with a sly wink. "But I can tell you something else. This is the room I'm going to start redecorating first. Talk about gloomy and boring. Gives me the creeps. You wait until I tell you what I'm going to do to it."

Trip smiled indulgently. "Later, okay?" he told her. "Now I'd like you to meet the staff and the children."

Diana was waiting for them in the hall outside. "Welcome home, sir, madam," she said in her most impeccable English accent. Honey's jaw dropped.

"This is Diana Westley," Trip said. "She keeps the place running smoothly."

"How do you do, Mrs. Atkins. Welcome to Ridgehaven," Diana replied with frosty politeness.

Honey managed a smile, but as soon as Diana had left to summon the staff, Honey grabbed Trip's arm. "Who's that—the frigging Queen of England?"

"She's the housekeeper, Honey," Trip answered, smiling at her horrified face.

"We don't need a housekeeper anymore now that

I'm here, do we? I can run this place for you now."

"Not need Diana? Of course we need Diana," Trip said.

"But she gives me the willies," Honey protested. "That superior way she looks at me and talks all superior."

"She's just English, Honey. That's how she talks. She's a very kind, warm person. I know she'll be a big help to you in understanding how this place is run."

"So I can't fire her if I want to?"

"No," Trip said. "Under no circumstances will Diana be fired. I suggest you get along with her, Honey."

Honey sulked as they walked along the hallways to the children's wing. It was the first time that Trip hadn't given in to her. She was sure that Diana Westley didn't like her and would make things difficult. Honey was sure that she'd be shown up as common and uneducated every time she opened her mouth around Diana. But it looked like she was stuck with her, at least for the time being. Maybe one day, when she had settled in and learned to manipulate her new husband, she'd find a way to get rid of Diana.

"Don't worry if the children aren't too friendly to start with," Trip said. "It's bound to be hard for them to have to get used to a new mother."

"I'm sure they'll love me," Honey said. "Kids always do. I was real good with my own brothers and sisters."

He opened the door and ushered her into their play-room. Adam jumped up. "Daddy!" he cried, his eyes shining. "Daddy's back," he called. The two older ones appeared.

"Hi, kids," Trip said.

"Hi," Decker and Rowan replied in unison.

"Did you bring us anything?" Decker asked.

"You bet I did," Trip said. "Something more special than you can imagine. I brought you a new mother. Children, I want you to say hello to Honey."

Three pairs of eyes looked at her with suspicion. She was different from any woman they had seen: her platinum-blond hair was teased into a mountain of curls, she wore long, fake eyelashes, long, red finger-nails, and her skirt was halfway up her thigh. She looked at the children and opened her arms dramati-cally. "Come and give your new mommy a big hug," she said.

Nobody moved.

"Go ahead, children. Give Honey a hug," Trip instructed. Adam went over to her. Rowan followed. Decker hung back. Honey hugged the two boys. "Well, aren't you the little man," she said, eyeing Rowan with appreciation. "Look at those muscles. I bet you work out, right?"

"A little," Rowan said.

"I've got muscles too," Adam bragged, displaying his biceps.

Rowan laughed. "Those aren't muscles, they're peas!"

Honey turned to Decker. "Don't you want to come say hi, sweetie pie?" she asked. "You and I are going to be big buddies. We can have girl talks together and I can fix your hair real pretty and show you how to paint your fingernails. I can tell you haven't had a mommy's care for a while. Those shorts don't make you look at all feminine, but tell you what—we'll go out shopping and we'll get you some real pretty dresses, and stuff for your hair...what do you say?"

Decker's eyes were cold. "We don't want a new mother, and I wouldn't wear anything you bought me if it was the last piece of clothing on earth," she said.

"Decker!" Trip snapped. "Apologize at once."

"I don't see why," Decker said. "We don't want her here, and there's no way she can ever be our mother, and there's no way I'd ever want to look like she does."

"Go to your room!" Trip yelled.

"Gladly!" Decker shot him a look of pure venom. "And I'll stay there until she's out of the house!"

She ran out, slamming the door behind her. Trip looked at Honey and tried to give her an encouraging smile. "I think you've got your hands full," he said.

"Don't worry, I'll soon win her around," Honey said.

CHAPTER 36

For a month, Honey genuinely tried to win over the children. Adam responded almost immediately. He loved to curl up on the smooth satin quilt of her new bed while she told him stories about her life in South Carolina and Las Vegas. The other two called him traitor and wouldn't speak to him. There was no way they were going to make Honey feel at home.

After a month of impasse, Honey went into Trip's study one evening. "I've been thinking," she said. "Those kids have been allowed to run wild too long."

"I wouldn't say they've run wild," Trip said quickly. "Diana is quite strict with them."

"But they're not as social as they should be," Honey argued. "This place isn't right for them—not considering what they're going to grow up to be."

"What are you saying, Honey?" Trip asked.

"I'm saying that it's an unnatural life, shut away

from the world up here in this museum. And when they do get out and mix, it's with the wrong people, Trip. Oh, don't get me wrong. I'm sure your employees are a nice enough bunch, but they're not the level of people I'd want for my kids if I was a millionaire. I mean, shucks, Decker could grow up to marry a Kennedy someday. Your boys could go into politics. This small-town atmosphere ain't right for them, Trip. They're teenagers now. You wouldn't want to find that Decker is dating the guy from the gas station or that Rowan has his eye on the little piece at Burgerhaven."

"So what do you think we should do?" Trip asked.

"I think we should give them the advantages we never had, that's what. I think we should send them to the best schools money can buy, so that they're mixing with the top-notch cream of society."

Trip looked up, interested. "Maybe you're right, Honey. I've always kept them at home because Liz wanted them close to her, and then Diana was a comfort to them after their mother's death. But perhaps they do need to spread their wings now. I'll get Diana to look into schools, shall I?"

"Don't let her handle it," Honey said. "What the hell does she know about American schools? And I'm not having them sent over to England and come back speaking like pansies. I may not have been to the best schools, but I've read enough in the society pages. I know where the best people send their sons and daughters."

"And where's that?"

"There's a military academy in Virginia that's about as snobby as you can get," Honey said. "They wear the cutest gray uniforms. I bet Rowan would look swell with all that braid."

"And the discipline couldn't hurt him either," Trip agreed. "He's a lazy so-and-so."

"And Adam could go along with him to keep him company."

"Good idea," Trip said. "That child is too sensitive for a boy. Maybe military school will toughen him up."

"And for Decker there's only one place," Honey announced. "A finishing school in Switzerland. That's where all the European royalty send their daughters. We might even get her married to a prince and she can have one of those fairy-tale weddings."

"I can't see any prince in his right mind wanting to take on Decker," Trip said, laughing, "but it might be good for her. It will teach her manners and grace, both of which she sadly lacks at the moment." He went over to Honey and kissed her lightly on the forehead. "I'm glad we had this little talk. Everything you said makes a lot of sense to me. I'll get my secretary to find me the addresses and I'll call the schools in the morning."

"And in the meantime," Honey cooed, "come and see how my bedroom is coming along."

She took his hand and led him down the hall. Replacing the antique rosewood bed was now a giant circular one, draped in white satin. A canopy of white satin, tied at the sides with big bows, hung from a crown on the ceiling above it. Across the room a white, lace-draped vanity was topped by three big mirrors. There was another gilt-framed mirror on the wall and yet a third on the ceiling. On a pedestal in the corner was a huge display of gold- and silver-sprayed artificial flowers.

"So how do you like it?" she asked Trip.

"When did all this get here?"

"I ordered it, from a catalogue," Honey said triumphantly. "It cost a whole bunch of money. I hope you don't mind."

"Not if you're happy," Trip said. "Spend what you like."

Downstairs, Diana walked into the kitchen to catch the staff whispering. They broke off when they saw her.

"What is it?" she asked.

"We were just talking about the new bedroom," Consuela said. "I got a glimpse of it today and I've never seen anything like it outside of the movies."

"It's not up to us to comment on how Mrs. Atkins decorates her private room," Diana said primly.

"Yes, but what if she starts on the rest of the house?" Martha demanded. "Is Mr. Atkins going to let her put plastic flamingos on the lawns and cherubs that pee colored water in the drawing room?"

The other staff members giggled. Diana frowned.

"That's enough, Martha. As I said, it's not up to us to comment."

But she made sure she intercepted Trip as he came home that night. "Excuse me, sir, but I foresee a problem developing," she said.

"Oh, yes, Diana? What is it?"

"Your wife's taste in furnishings," she said. "The staff is afraid that the boudoir look will spread to the rest of the house. They see the artworks replaced with illuminated plastic Venus de Milos."

Trip grinned. "The bedroom is a bit much, isn't it?" he said. "But it's made her happy. Between us, Diana," and he drew her closer, "I'm hoping that you'll be able to educate my wife in the art of gracious living."

"I hardly think so, sir, since she clearly loathes me," Diana said.

"She's just scared of you, Diana."

"Scared of me? What for?"

"She's overawed by your accent and your upper-crust manners. If you can just let her know that there's a friendly person underneath that frosty exterior . . . I know, why don't you take her shopping in New York or London? That would give you two girls a good chance to get to know each other."

Diana couldn't hide the wince. "Is that part of the job description, sir?" she asked.

"What's wrong with it?"

"I hardly think that Mrs. Atkins and I would want to visit the same shops," Diana said. "Maybe Frederick's of Hollywood would be more to the point."

"Good idea," Trip said, grinning at her discomfort. "Maybe Honey can get you to try one of those negligee sets to replace that flannel monstrosity."

"Huh!" Diana said, and not finding an answer, walked away.

It was Diana who broke the news to the children that they were to go to boarding school. Privately, she thought it was a good idea. They had grown up too sheltered, convinced that the universe revolved around them. Learning to get along with other children would be good for all three of them. But the children looked at her in horror.

"I knew I hated her," Decker exploded. "But I thought you were on my side, Diana."

"I am, Decker."

"No, you're not. You've let her trick Daddy into sending us away. She's been all sweet and nice, and at the same time, scheming to get us out of here."

"I only agreed because it's in your best interests, sweetheart," Diana said. But Decker turned away. "You're a traitor too. There's nobody we can trust around here."

She ran to tell her father what she thought of him, but he couldn't see why she wasn't excited about the thought of school in Switzerland.

"You love her better than us," Decker said, determined not to cry in front of him. "You never loved our mother and you've never loved us."

"Decker, that's not true," Trip called, but she had already run from the room.

It was true, he thought. He did love Honey. He would have done anything to make her happy. Since she had arrived at Ridgehaven, his life had been new and different and exciting. For the first time ever, he hadn't shown up at the office at eight-thirty every morning, ready to get down to work. Work didn't seem quite so important when Honey's naked body lay beside him, ready to be aroused at any given moment. She had only to stretch out her hand to him and murmur, "Do you really have to go so soon, sugar?" and Trip would decide that he didn't. He hadn't been away on a business trip since she arrived.

"Are you happy here, Honey?" he asked her as they lay in bed sipping coffee one morning.

"Are you kidding? If I'd pinched myself every time I thought this couldn't be true, I'd be black and blue by now," she said. "I still can't get over it, Trip. I mean, to have a private plane waiting for me. To be able to go to the best department stores in New York and point to a mink coat and say, 'Charge it to my account'. Shoot, Trip, I can still remember when I couldn't go to a dance because I didn't have a pair of shoes."

"And I couldn't go because I couldn't afford to rent a tux," Trip said. "We really are two of a kind, Honey."

Honey put down her coffee cup. "And I'd say we go together real well in other ways too," she whispered.

"Careful," he laughed. "You're making me spill my coffee."

"Then put down your damned cup," she said, laughing too as she began to climb onto him.

At the military school in Virginia, Rowan stood before the mirror, studying himself in the ridiculous uniform. He looked like an extra from a Civil War movie, he decided. This whole thing was a farce. He had determined to be so bad that he'd be expelled within a week and could go home. Of course that would leave Adam there alone, but he didn't care. Adam needed shaping up anyway. He was a little whiner. When orders were given, Rowan quietly ignored them and did his own thing.

"Yo, Atkins, didn't you hear that bugle?" his dorm corporal demanded.

"I'm not a dog. I don't come to whistles," Rowan said, and started to walk away.

"You obey all orders, like everyone else," the corporal yelled.

Rowan looked at him scornfully. "My father pays big bucks for me to be here. I know he wouldn't want me to do stuff I didn't want to do."

When the corporal reported this to the headmaster, the staff was given a directive. "I want you to break those Atkins boys within a week. We're not going to put up with any of their insubordinate crap here at Greenbriar. Do what you like, but break them."

At the end of the first week Rowan and Adam were

kidnapped from their dorms at night. "New-kid initiation ritual," they were told. "Every new boy has to go through it."

They were led across the compound to the old laundry. "You have to crawl from one side of the building to the other through that crawl space underneath the floorboards," they were directed. "Watch out for snakes and spiders. They breed under there like crazy. They like the damp from the washing machines."

Rowan drew two of the oldest boys aside. "Look," he said, "I get a very generous allowance from my father. How much would it take to get out of this crawling nonsense?"

The boys eyed each other speculatively. "What sort of allowance, Atkins?"

"I'm sure we can agree to terms," Rowan said. "Money's really no object."

The older boys returned to the others. "Atkins major is going to do it another night," one of them said. "Atkins minor can do it now."

Adam shot Rowan a terrified look. Rowan just smiled. Later they had to forcibly drag Adam out of the last few feet of the crawl space, screaming and sobbing. They carried him back to his bed, where he lay curled in a tight little ball, his thumb in his mouth.

In Switzerland, Decker was determined to hate everything about Mont Clair Academy. She complained that there wasn't a TV in her room and the mattress was lumpy. The other girls seemed very immature and stupid. Her roommate, Sabrina, a gorgeous Italian countess, was horrified by her outspokenness and constant criticism.

"You just insulted Princess Sophia of Belgium," she whispered in a horrified voice.

Decker looked amused. "My father has enough money to buy Belgium," she said.

Sabrina gasped. "Look, Decker," she said. "It really might be a good idea to get along with other girls here. Otherwise, you will not have an agreeable time."

"I don't intend to have an agreeable time," Decker said. "I intend to hate every minute here."

Back at Ridgehaven, Honey had announced to a surprised and delighted Trip that she was pregnant. Every time he looked at her swelling body, he felt absurdly young and potent. For the first time, he was present at the delivery, and he held the squalling, red-faced Suzanne Atkins tentatively in his arms. Honey lay back white-faced on the delivery table.

"Shoot, Trip," she said in a weak voice, "I don't think this motherhood crap is all it's cracked up to be!"

CHAPTER 37

After Suzy was born, Honey began to appreciate having Diana around. She was proud of herself for producing a pretty baby daughter and she enjoyed watching Trip's delight in the child, but her first assessment had been correct. Motherhood was not something that came naturally to her. She had little patience and she hated getting messy. She soon weaned Suzy to the bottle because breast-feeding was making her breasts sag. She hated changing dirty diapers, and she didn't like being awakened at two in the morning. Diana was only too glad to move back to the children's wing and take full responsibility for little Suzy. Honey loved dressing up her daughter in frilly dresses, putting a bow in her hair and playing with her, but she always handed her back to Diana when she cried or spat up.

A year later, Honey found herself pregnant again.

"This breedin' nonsense has got to stop," she said to Trip. "It's not as if I'm a prize sow or something. After this, I get my tubes tied. You're too darned virile for your own good—you should know better, a guy of your age."

Trip just smiled to himself. He was enjoying this second go-round of fatherhood, experiencing all the facets he had missed with Liz. He was filled with awe when he put his face to Honey's belly and felt the fluttering kick against his cheek. He was filled with the same awe when Suzy grasped his finger in her tiny hand, looked up at him and smiled. He was over the moon the first time she said "da-da".

"She doesn't know what she's saying. All kids make noises like that," Honey said, annoyed that her first word hadn't been "ma-ma." When the fine, dark-haired boy was born, looking remarkably like his Irish grandfather, Trip called him P. Stuart Atkins, IV, an act that annoyed Rowan intensely. He was the oldest son. He should have inherited the title. He complained bitterly over the phone, not listening to Trip's explanation that Rowan had been Liz's choice of name and it had been impossible to stop Liz from getting her way.

Little Stew was handed over to Diana as soon as Honey came home from the hospital. The two children settled into a serene, ordered life in the nursery, visited occasionally by their mother and father, but most of the time held and rocked by Diana. They were both handsome and sweet-natured and became the darlings of the entire staff.

Motherhood safely behind her, Honey now went back to her first love, shopping. Now secure in her status as adored wife and mother, she was no longer hesitant about using the private jet to go to New York or Los Angeles whenever the mood took her.

That mood took her more and more frequently. As the children grew up, secure in Diana's care, Trip threw himself with renewed enthusiasm into his business, and Honey herself tired of trying to turn Ridgehaven into a Walt Disney version of Windsor Castle. Trip was glad to see that she had gained confidence and taste from her travels. He sensed no danger when Honey kissed him good-bye and said she was going to New York to take in a Broadway musical and do a little Christmas shopping.

In Switzerland, Decker was reading the overseas edition of *The New York Times* when she let out a great yell of glee.

"What is it?" the other girls in the common room asked. Decker had jumped up and was waving the paper excitedly. "There is justice in the world after all!" she screamed. "My wicked stepmother has been kidnapped!"

The girls crowded around to read the paper. It was only a small item at the bottom of a column, but it stated that Mrs. Honey Atkins, wife of the pharmaceutical giant P. Stuart Atkins, had disappeared during a flight home to Lake Success from New York.

"How could I have been so dumb?" Decker yelled. "I should have thought of it and arranged it myself years ago!"

* * *

Ridgehaven was in turmoil. Policemen were swarming all over the house and grounds. The staff was questioned, and questioned again. Every inch of the airport was searched for clues, but there was no shred of evidence.

"It doesn't make sense, sir," Captain Bauer said to Trip. He had been promoted after the retirement of Captain Harris. "She was the only passenger on a private plane. The plane landed safely at the airport and the pilot swears that he saw Mrs. Atkins disembark, but the chauffeur swears that he never saw her come out of the terminal to the car. It's not like it's Kennedy or O'Hare, Mr. Atkins. You just can't get lost in the Lake Success terminal."

"My wife did," Trip said. "Somehow, someone managed to kidnap her between the entrance and the exit. Whoever it was must have been very smart and knew her movements exactly. It must have been someone close to us. Honey made a spur-of-the-moment decision to go to New York. It wasn't planned in advance. No one outside the house knew she had gone, so how the hell did anyone know when she was returning?"

"We've double-checked all the employees who would have access to knowledge about Mrs. Atkins' visit to New York," Captain Bauer said, shaking his head. "They've all been with you for years, sir. We can't come up with anybody with motive or opportunity or criminal connections."

"And nobody around town saw anything? It was late afternoon, for Christ's sake," Trip said angrily. "Somebody must have seen something. If she was kidnapped in the terminal, she must have been brought out and driven somewhere. Somebody must have seen her."

"I bet that Tony Parrish kid knows something," Captain Bauer said. "They say he cuts classes to watch the planes at the airport."

"Tony Parrish?"

"You remember—Little Anthony. The kid found on the hospital steps. Spent his first years in a succession of foster homes. Never stayed long because he was a little firecracker—too much for most folks to handle. Anyway, now he's been adopted by the Parrishes. Nice couple, but the kid's still wild. Had a few run-ins with the police."

"Let me see him," Trip said. "Maybe he'll talk to me."

Tony Parrish, his eleven-year-old face defiant, was brought to Trip. "I didn't do anything," he said.

"Nobody says you did, Tony," Trip said. "All I want is your help. My wife has disappeared, and Captain Bauer says you were out at the airport on Tuesday afternoon when it must have happened. Maybe you saw something that can help us?"

The child looked away. "I wasn't anywhere near the airport," he said. "I was in school."

Nothing Trip said could make Tony change his story. Trip fought to keep his temper, although his nerves were stretched to the breaking point. He hadn't slept a wink for two nights now. It was all he could do to stop himself from wringing Tony Parrish's neck and making him talk.

"He's played truant once too often," Bauer said after he was ushered out, still defiant. "He's scared that his new family will be mad at him. They're very hot about schooling and not cutting class. But he let slip to a friend that he saw a big black car out at the back of the airport and he thought Mrs. Atkins was in it." Bauer shrugged. "He might just have been shooting his mouth off to impress his friends. He's that kind of kid. But even if he saw something, I doubt he'll tell us any more."

After Tony had been shown out, Trip sank his head onto his desk with a sigh. "What do we do next, Bauer?"

"If it is a kidnapping, we wait for a ransom note. One should show up pretty soon."

"If? If?" Trip demanded. "What could it be but a kidnapping? My wife has disappeared without a trace, Bauer." He got up and began pacing. "I feel so damn powerless," he said. "And I tell you something else. If a ransom note appears, you're staying out of it. I'm paying whatever it takes to get her back."

"Unfortunately, paying ransom isn't always a guarantee of safety," Bauer said cautiously.

"Surely even the most underhanded criminal wouldn't take the money and then kill Honey?" Trip, for all his sophistication, was incredulous.

"If she had seen his face, or if he'd given too much away," Bauer said. "Why don't you give us a couple more days at least, sir? We need to search for tire tracks in the hills, check all the gas stations and motels on routes out of town, check the flights out of Denver and Salt Lake City. It's not like a big city—she can't just have gone underground. We can almost guarantee that she's not still in town, in which case, there are only a limited number of ways out. If she really was in a big black car, someone must have noticed her."

"Then why hasn't anyone come forward?" Trip asked. "God knows, the TV stations have given us enough publicity. It's in every newspaper. My wife is a very striking-looking woman. Someone must have seen her!"

But the days went by and no news came in. No ransom note appeared.

"What do we do now?" Trip demanded. "If they've taken her, why the hell haven't they sent me a demand for money?"

He noted Bauer's face. "You don't think she was kidnapped for money, do you?"

"It's five days now, Mr. Atkins. If a note hasn't appeared, I don't think it's going to. I don't want to be pessimistic, but I'd say her chances are slim."

"Oh, God," Trip groaned, hiding his face in his hands.

CHAPTER 38

Trip sank further and further into depression. He hired his own detectives to cover both the States and Europe. He found it hard to sleep or eat or concentrate. He stopped going into the office, instead waiting at home by the phone for news. Diana watched him patiently, until one day she sat on the bed beside him.

"Come on, sir. This isn't like you," she said. "You have to buck up and get on with your life."

"How can I, when all the time I'm imagining my poor wife buried alive, or locked in a cellar, or worse than that. Do you really think she could still be alive, Diana? Really in your heart of hearts?"

Diana looked away. "Did it ever occur to you, sir," she said hesitantly, "that she might have staged this whole thing herself?"

"Staged it herself? What are you talking about?"

"I was just suggesting a possibility."

"Of course it's not a possibility," he roared. "What a heartless thing to say. She adored me. Why would she want to get away?"

"Because she was bored? Because she didn't like being tied down by responsibility? Because she was a fish out of water in this sort of life?"

"What a stupid, hurtful thing to say," he yelled. "She loved it here. She loved me! I thought you were my most loyal employee."

"I am, sir."

"Making damned spiteful suggestions about my wife is not what I call loyal. I always knew you resented her from the moment I brought her here. You never could look past her exterior to her sweet, gentle nature, could you? She might have been rough around the edges, but she was a warm, loving, simple woman who adored me."

"Maybe I could see more clearly than you, sir," she said. "Maybe I could see who she really was when you were blinded by that helpless look and those great legs."

"I run a billion-dollar business. I'm not fooled by anybody!" He was yelling again.

"Not until now!" Diana found herself yelling back. "Everybody else could see through her when she played sweet and helpless. She wasn't exactly giving an Oscar-winning performance."

"Get out of here right now. You're fired. Go home to England and take your goddamned suspicious mind with you," he shouted.

"Very good, sir, if that's what you want," Diana said.

She walked to the door, her lips pressed together, her head held high, and went to her room to pack.

Late that night there was a tap on her door. She opened it to find Trip standing there.

"May I come in?" he asked.

"It's your house," she said frostily, holding open the door for him.

"I'm sorry," he said. "Please don't go. You're all I've got now."

"I'm sorry too," Diana said. "I had no right to say what I did. And it was very silly of me to upset you further. I'm probably completely wrong, as you say. So don't give up hope. She may still be found."

He shook his head. "I have a premonition I'll never see her again." He walked over to the window and pulled back the drapes. "The worst thing is that a nagging little voice in my head says you may be right—and I can't bear to think of it. I think that knowing she was dead would be easier to bear than knowing she deliberately tried to escape."

He turned to look at her helplessly.

"God, Diana, I'd have given her her freedom if she'd asked for it. If that's what she wanted to make her happy. I'd have given her the world. Oh, God, Diana. I really loved that woman. How can she do this to me?" He buried his face in the drapes.

Diana went over and put an arm around him. He

turned to her and crushed her in a fierce, desperate embrace. He buried his face in her shoulder.

"Please don't leave me," he whispered.

"I'll stay as long as you want me to," she said, "and I'll pray every night that they find her."

CHAPTER 39

B
ut Honey was not found and certain facts that supported Diana's theory came to light: a block of Decker-Atkins stock in Honey's name was sold. She had taken all her valuable jewelry out of the safe. Trip tried to deaden the pain by throwing himself feverishly into his work, obsessed with finding cures within his lifetime for every incurable disease. He followed up leads on plants in the Amazon and on herbal medicines in China, flitting from one continent to the next with no rest. His face began to look old and haggard.

One day he called Diana into his study.

"I have to start facing facts and get on with my life," he said. "I'm never going to see her again, am I?"

"I really don't think so, sir," Diana said. "I can't help feeling that if there had been a body, it would have been found by now. They usually are, you know."

"Which means she's alive, living a new identity somewhere."

"It's possible."

"I still don't understand how she could do it, how I could have been so easily taken in by her."

"She was very beautiful, sir. And she did have that helpless look."

"I suppose I'm an old fool." He looked at her with a pained smile.

"You're neither old nor a fool, Mr. Atkins," Diana said. "You just need to put this episode behind you. You still have so much to give the world."

"You're right, Diana," he said. "I've come through a lot in my life and nothing made me crack before. I'm ashamed that I finally went to pieces over a woman— over that woman—when I kept going after..." He shook his head. "Never mind," he said. "I want you to do something for me."

"Yes?"

"I want those children out of here."

"Which children?"

"Her children. Suzy and Stew."

Diana looked horrified. "But they're your children too."

"And they remind me of her every day. They torment me, Diana. I love them, but I can't stand to look at them. I want them to have a chance to lead normal lives. Find them good schools to go to, will you? Not ridiculous establishments like Honey chose for the older kids. I don't care two hoots about braided uniforms. I want them to get the best education in warm, caring surroundings—far from here."

Diana got to her feet. "Maybe it would be for the best," she said. "This house has never had the right sort of atmosphere for children to flourish in. I'm very fond of Suzy and Stew. Very fond indeed, but I want the best for them. I'm willing to send them away if that can give them a chance at normal lives."

As a result, Suzy and Stew were sent to the same boarding school on the East Coast. Diana flew there with them herself, trying not to show her own hurt at leaving them so far away. "You'll love Southampton," she said in her bright English voice. "There are ponies to ride and a great art department, and they take you on outings to museums and theaters . . ."

They didn't complain and rebel as Decker and Rowan had. They sat there side by side on the plane, staring straight ahead of them. Diana felt her heart would break.

"And you'll be home for holidays," she said. "It won't be long until Thanksgiving—"

"Father doesn't want us home, does he?" Suzy asked in a small voice. "He doesn't like us."

"He loves you very much, Suzy," Diana said. "It's just that . . . he's still very upset. He loved your mother and he still misses her. He knows he can't be a good father to you right now, so he wants you to be somewhere where you're happier. And I'm sure you will be happier at Southampton. It seems like a nice, friendly place . . . but if you're not happy, you write and tell me. I'm not leaving you anywhere that you're not happy. Understand that."

"Thank you, Diana," Suzy said politely. "I'm sure we'll be just fine, won't we, Stew?"

Stew nodded.

That was the last time in many years that the children returned to the house. Trip arranged for them to go straight to summer camps from school and didn't see them growing from shy, scared children to confident, bright young people, relying on each other because they had nobody else.

CHAPTER 40

In 1981, seven years after her disappearance, Honey was declared legally dead. When the court date was announced, Trip had been secretly hoping that she would choose the occasion to make a dramatic reappearance, if she was still alive. But when he heard the judge announce Honey's status Trip felt a physical pain around his heart. He had to get out of that courtroom and fast. It felt as if the walls were closing in on him and he couldn't breathe. He got to his feet, the words still singing in his head. The singing grew and grew. Spots of light were dancing in front of his eyes. He loosened his necktie but he still couldn't breathe. He clutched at his throat and fell to the floor.

When he awoke, he was lying in the intensive care unit of his own medical center.

"Well, this is novel," he joked to Dr. Amsden, the

head physician. "Patient instead of administrator. Now you see to what lengths I go to achieve quality-control and check things out for myself."

Dr. Amsden didn't smile. "You gave us a pretty big scare, Mr. Atkins," he said. "It wasn't huge as heart attacks go, but big enough to give you a warning to start taking care of yourself."

"I take care of myself."

"When did you last have a full physical? Not on my records. You're no longer a young man. You can't keep up this punishing schedule. The next heart attack may kill you."

"But my company is all I have to live for," Trip said. "My work is even more important to me now that..." His voice trailed off. He couldn't even speak her name.

"I understand that your oldest children are out of school now. Bring them home, have a family around you again, get interested in their futures. You need family and stability right now."

"Family and stability," Trip said with a sigh. "What I've always wanted. It just never seemed to be there. But maybe you're right. Maybe I will give it another try. Rowan's busy racing yachts on the East Coast. Maybe I should try to teach him the business. And Decker's been in Switzerland long enough. I'll get Diana to write to them."

Dr. Amsden forbade Trip from going back to work for at least a month. Trip hated this enforced idleness.

He had never learned to enjoy doing nothing. He sat up in bed, looking out over the lawns of Ridgehaven, surrounded by piles of medical journals. At least he was going to keep his brain in top gear.

The heart attack had been a terrible shock to him; until then, he had believed that he would go on forever. He'd never felt old. Apart from a twinge of arthritis after a long tennis game, he still thought of himself as a young man. But now he had only to look in the mirror to see that he was old. His face was lined, from the frown lines on his forehead to the deeply etched grooves running down from his mouth. An old man's face. What's more, the face of a man with nothing left to live for.

"I can't die without making my contribution," he told himself. He had always dreamed of coming up with the drug, the one simple ingredient that would change the course of humanity. He wanted future generations to read in the history books, "Before Trip Atkins discovered the miracle drug, there was no cure for cancer or degenerative diseases, or even for dementia."

It should be possible, surely. He had continued to assemble the best brains money could buy. He had provided them with the best facilities and equipment. But all the recent products of Decker-Atkins had been very routine. They made money, but they hadn't changed the world.

While browsing through the medical journals Trip first came upon the article on Dr. Martin Goldman. It seemed that the young research associate had been conducting revolutionary experiments at a small private university and producing preliminary results that had shocked the medical establishment. He was working on synthesizing a human growth hormone; if the concept actually worked, human cells could be continually renewed.

Trip became increasingly excited as the possibilities became clear to him: brain cells that kept the thought processes of an eighty-year-old as keen as those of a twenty-year-old, but coupled them with the wisdom of age; athletes who had muscles that never faded, allowing them to break records into their fifties and sixties. Just how long could the growth hormone go on prolonging life? For twenty years? A hundred? Forever?

He knew right then that he had to have this Martin Goldman working for him. Trip would certainly go down in the history books if he created eternal life!

Dr. Goldman was a pleasant, unassuming young man in his early thirties. He sat before Trip in his white lab coat, from which a conservatively striped tie peeped, and stared earnestly from behind dark-rimmed glasses while Trip explained what he had in mind. At the end, Dr. Goldman said, "Thank you. I'm flattered, but I'm very happy here."

Trip looked around at the antiquated lab. "How could you be happy here?" he asked. "Look at your equipment—held together with string!"

"Not quite as bad as that," Martin Goldman said with a smile. "We manage."

"So you're telling me that the research wouldn't go ahead any faster if you had the best equipment money could buy at your disposal."

"Undoubtedly it could," Martin said.

"Then why in heaven's name don't you want to come to Lake Success? Is there a love interest on the East Coast that's keeping you? Fear of being too far from civilization?"

"Nothing like that," Dr. Goldman replied. "When I'm working, I think of nothing outside my work. I'm afraid I don't have time for women or Broadway in my life."

"Then what, for God's sake?"

Martin turned serious eyes on him. "You must forgive me if I'm being rude," he said, "but I seriously believe that I have a duty to humanity. I've been given a good brain for a purpose—to make life better for future generations. I don't want what I'm doing cheapened and commercialized, as it certainly would be if it was sponsored by one of the big drug companies like Decker-Atkins. You'd use it as the biggest PR scoop of the century if I perfected Vital-A."

"Vital-A?"

"That's the code name I've given my experiments," he said. "Look, Mr. Atkins, I know how drug companies work. You produce something that nobody else has got and your first thought is the enormous profits because you've cornered the market. If I finally create

Vital-A, I want every patient who is dying from Lou Gehrig's disease to be able to afford it, every Alzheimer's sufferer, every young person with MS. I'm afraid I'm not for sale, Mr. Atkins."

"I don't think you understand, Doctor Goldman," Trip said. "I'm not interested in the commercial aspects of Vital-A either. I've just had a heart attack. My doctors have told me to take it easy, or else. I'd never thought about dying before and quite frankly, it scares me."

"So it's self-preservation you're interested in?" Dr. Goldman asked.

"Not for me personally," Trip said. "But I don't want to die without having made my mark. I want to have helped create something really worthwhile—oh, I know I've done a bit for the treatment of mental health. I've improved tranquilizers and antidepressants. But nothing that will make Decker-Atkins go down in the history books. I'd like to do that, Doctor Goldman. And I expect you'd like a Nobel prize. Come to me and you'll get it, while you're still young enough to enjoy it!"

Dr. Goldman took off his spectacles and polished them on his lab coat. "And if I came to you, what would you offer me that I'm not getting here?"

"Your own lab, designed to your own specifications," Trip said. "Unlimited budget for staff and equipment, the best team of world brains money can buy, and a salary of, shall we say, a million?"

"The salary's not important to me," Martin said,

"but I have to admit that the other aspects do tempt me."

Trip slapped him on the back. "Then fly back with me today and take a look at the place. My private jet is outside. You can be back here by this evening if you don't like what you see."

Dr. Goldman spread his hands. "How can I refuse?" he asked.

CHAPTER 41

A month later Dr. Goldman packed up his facility on the East Coast and went to work for Trip. Sometimes his conscience murmured that he had given in to big business and the lure of money, thus betraying the cause of pure science, but he had only to look around at his new lab to realize that he could accomplish here in months what would have previously taken him years.

He felt excited and hopeful as he started his job at Decker-Atkins. If Trip Atkins' name went down in the history books, so too would his! He could almost smell that Nobel prize. He threw himself with enthusiasm into his work, glad that the tiresome details of day-to-day living, like looking for a house and unpacking his things, could be put off for a while. For Trip had generously suggested that he live up at Ridgehaven until he found a house he liked.

"The place is empty, apart from myself and the

housekeeper," Trip said. "We rattle around like ghosts in all those rooms. Frankly, I'd enjoy the company, and I keep a good wine cellar."

Martin liked Ridgehaven. He liked the quiet tranquillity and old-fashioned elegance of the place. Every trace of Honey's extravagance and lack of taste had been removed by Diana, except for her bedroom. Trip had had it locked up, just the way it was. He couldn't bring himself to touch it or to throw anything away. It remained, a shrine to tackiness, amid the tasteful artwork and subdued elegance of the central wing.

Decker looked out of the plane window as it approached the runway. There was her town, nestled among its hills, its Lake Success glistening, in the sunshine. Her first thought was, how small it is. She was now so used to Europe, where one town or village was never more than a stone's throw from the next, that the vast, open spaces around Lake Success reminded her that it was completely cut off from the real world. She noted the newness, too. She had grown used to houses that had stood for hundreds of years, so long that they seemed to be part of the landscape. The houses in Lake Success sat on the hillsides like children's building blocks, bright and tasteless after the somber European stone.

All the same, she was glad to be back. It would be good to be in a place where she didn't feel like an outsider, at a disadvantage. The girls at Mont Clair

Academy had grown up with such a vast knowledge of European culture and history that Decker had felt like the Ugly American every time she opened her mouth. How was she to know that Celts lived in Switzerland as well as Ireland, that the Holy Roman Emperor didn't live in Rome, that all those countries that called themselves republics were still full of nobles, who expected to be treated like nobles? She hated the looks the girls gave her—that clearly said, "She's American. She can't be expected to understand."

What's more, they were not impressed by her money. Money didn't matter to the girls she mixed with. They had grown up in families who had been rich for generations. Money had always been there—it just wasn't something that one talked about.

Over the years, Decker had gradually acquired European elegance and turned into a beautiful young woman. She spoke excellent French and German, and passable Italian. She knew how to move with grace, how to create the perfect dinner party and how to discuss art. She also learned how to attract men. Since leaving school, she had partied on the Riviera with the liveliest young jet-setters. She was used to being the center of attention among the young men. She was blasé about being proposed to.

She smiled to herself as she sat on the plane. What would her father say if he knew that she had been toying with proposals from a second cousin of the Windsors, the son of an Argentine cattle baron, and the heir to an oil fortune? Not that she had seriously considered marrying any of them. The Windsor was boring, the Argentinian was arrogant, and the oil heir was a real mama's boy. When she married, it would be to a man she could respect without being dominated and whom she could love as much as he loved her.

The plane made its landing and Decker strode through the terminal and out to the waiting car. She was absurdly disappointed to find that her father hadn't come to meet her.

"I'm afraid your father has been very busy lately, Miss Decker," the chauffeur told her. "He's up to his eyes in some new hush-hush project."

"Which he cares about more than his daughter," Decker said coldly. "At least Diana might have come to the airport."

"She was making sure everything was just so at the house," the chauffeur responded. "She's looking forward to having you home again."

The electronic security gates opened silently and the car swung up the driveway. Ridgehaven stood before her, as imposing as the châteaus she had grown used to. She got out of the car and went up the steps. The front door opened and she stepped inside, savoring the unique smell of home—the smell of polish and old wood, the mustiness of the ancient tapestries. She was about to call for Diana when a young man appeared, crossing the hall with a newspaper in his hands.

"Oh, good," Decker said. "I was just about to call for someone. You must be new. I'm Decker Atkins. Would you bring my bags up to my room? I'm going to find Diana."

She started up the stairs. The young man watched her with amusement, then put down the newspaper and went to get her bags.

Decker found Diana plumping the pillows in her room. Diana looked up with surprise and delight. "Decker. I didn't expect you so soon. How lovely you look. Come and give me a hug."

"Hello, Diana," Decker said, walking toward her outstretched arms. "You don't look a day older."

"Nice of you to say so. I don't actually feel a day older. It's something about this climate."

Decker walked over to the window and looked out. "Nothing seems to have changed," she said. "Except that I hope you've thrown out those ridiculous frilly dresses Honey bought for me."

"I've thrown out everything Honey bought," Diana said. "The house is back to normal." The two women exchanged grins.

"So how was Switzerland? Are you glad to be out of school?"

"I couldn't wait another second," Decker said. "But guess what, Diana. I got proposed to by Viscount Albury."

"Good heavens, did you accept?"

"No way." Decker made a face. "He was chinless and he had a silly laugh. I also had two other proposals, but I'm turning both of them down."

"Quite right," Diana said. "You're too young to marry."

"Not if I found the right man, which I haven't," Decker said. "How's Father?"

"Better now. He gave us a scare with that heart attack. But he's still not right. The doctor wants him to go in for further tests. He gets tired so quickly."

"He always did do too much."

"Yes, he still drives himself hard," Diana said. "I don't think he'll be able to make it for dinner tonight. He has people flying in for a meeting. But that's good. It will give you time to rest. There will be only the three of us."

"Three?"

"Yes, you, me and Doctor Goldman."

"Doctor who?"

"I told you about him in my letter. He's the brilliant young man your father has lured from the East Coast. He's staying at Ridgehaven until he finds a place of his own."

Decker had gone very pink. "Why, Decker, what's the matter?" Diana asked.

"I think I just put my foot in it," Decker said. "I thought he was a new household employee. I told him to bring up my bags. I'd better stop him…" She ran out. The young man had just come up the stairs with a large suitcase in each hand. He was panting under the strain.

"I'm so sorry," Decker said, scarlet with embarrassment. "You're Doctor Goldman. I didn't realize. I thought you were a new valet or something."

He smiled, which transformed his serious face. "No problem," he said. "Delighted to be able to be of help. I needed the exercise."

"I hear you've just arrived here," Decker said. "I'd be happy to show you around after dinner. The nightspots weren't anything to shout about before I left, but we could go check them out."

"Thanks all the same," Dr. Goldman said, "but I have some reading I should catch up on. And you probably need an early night after all that traveling. I'll see you at dinner, then."

He gave her a polite nod and walked away. Decker stood there watching him go. It took her a few seconds to realize he had turned her down. It was a novel sensation for her, and made Dr. Goldman all the more intriguing.

CHAPTER 42

Over the next few days, Martin Goldman was pleasant to Decker but refused to be bowled over by her charm. Decker, who could have had her pick of nobles and tycoons, now saw it as a personal insult that he wasn't instantly attracted to her. But at the same time, she found herself admiring him. It was rather tiresome being constantly hovered over by empty-headed young men and spoken to by brainy men as if she were an airhead. At least Dr. Goldman seemed to consider her a human being. He knew a lot about Europe. He liked art, and discussed it with Decker. He even liked the Impressionists, Decker's favorites.

On Sunday she suggested that they go out riding in the hills together.

"I'm sorry," Martin Goldman said, "but I don't ride."

"I could teach you."

"I think it's a little late to learn. Besides, I've never had any great love for horses since one bit me when I was a little kid." He grinned. Decker thought he had a very appealing smile.

"So come sailing with me instead. It's a beautiful day and you only have to sit there, if you don't know how to sail."

"Actually, I do know how to sail," Martin said. "All right, you've talked me into it."

Decker bounded upstairs to change and felt triumphant all the way down to the dock. It was a perfect day. Just a slight breeze ruffled the waters, and the lake was dotted with various pleasure boats.

"I must say, this is very nice," Martin said as the boat slipped away from the dock. "It's been a long time since I've taken any form of recreation."

"My whole life seems to be nothing else," Decker said.

"Don't you find that boring?"

"Very, but I haven't yet decided what to do with myself. I presume we'll be called upon to take over the business someday."

"How would you feel about that?"

"I wouldn't mind the business side," Decker responded. "But I find the science bit totally boring... Whoops, sorry, I shouldn't have said that to you."

"It's all right. It would be a very dull world if we all liked the same things." He sat up suddenly. "Hey, watch out for that rock."

Decker swung the tiller. "Where did that come

from? It was never there before," she said.

"I gather the water level is particularly low this year. We've had a drought," Martin said.

"I'd better pay attention then," Decker said. "I didn't expect I'd have to be on the lookout for rocks—"

"And powerboats," Martin said as one whizzed past them. "That guy's going awfully fast on such a small lake."

"Lunatic," Decker muttered.

"He's coming back in our direction," Martin warned.

"He'd better remember that sail takes precedence over power," Decker said, continuing her course.

"It doesn't look as if he knows that," Martin told her nervously.

"Then he'll have to learn, won't he?" Decker said smoothly, her hand on the tiller and keeping her tack.

The powerboat appeared to realize at the last moment that she wasn't about to change course. It swerved to the right and struck the rock Decker had just missed. There was a splintering crash, followed by the boom of an explosion. A ball of fire shot up, black smoke billowed. Bodies seemed to fly out and land in the water.

"Oh, my God!" Decker screamed. She swung the tiller around to go back to the burning craft. "That poor person's going to get burned!" The fire was already spreading across the oil-slicked water. "What are we going to do?"

Without warning, Martin dove over the side and

started swimming powerfully toward the floating body.

"Martin, no, come back, you'll get burned too!" she screamed. Then, as he ignored her, she flung out the anchor and dove in after him. He had reached the first victim, an older woman, and had maneuvered her into shallower water. "She's still alive," he said, "but badly burned. We have to get her to the hospital." He turned to Decker. "Can you hold her head above water? Here, like this, under her neck. Try not to move her too much."

"Okay." Decker could feel herself trembling but she did as he said. Her heart was pounding so loudly that she was sure it must be echoing out all over the lake. She tried not to look at the blackened, bleeding person who lay moaning in her arms. "It's all right," she tried to say soothingly. "You're going to be all right."

Martin plunged into the flames, pulled another person free, towed him to shore and started immediate CPR. Decker stood, waist-deep, keeping the woman afloat.

When she had met Martin the night before, he had seemed to be one of the ordinary, harmless, inoffensive scientists who worked at Decker-Atkins. Now she was impressed by his power and determination. Other people arrived. When paramedics came, Martin Goldman directed them calmly, as if this was just another Sunday at the lake and he hadn't almost been burned to death. Technicians took over the body on the shore and Martin waded out to Decker.

"Quickly, Martin. We must do something for her right away. She looks terrible," Decker said. "Can you do CPR or something? God, I feel so stupid. I don't know what to do."

Martin looked down. "I'm afraid there's not too much hope," he said. "She's been badly burned, but I'm sure they'll do what they can."

Paramedics slipped a backboard under the woman and towed her in to shore. Filled with compassion, Martin didn't tell Decker that the woman was already dead.

"Those poor people." Decker was crying. "You were wonderful, Martin."

"You were pretty good yourself," Martin comforted her. "You didn't panic. Lots of girls your age would have." He took her elbow, steadying her as she came from the water. "Are you okay?"

"Yes, I'm fine," she stammered. "It's just that I've never seen . . . never had to . . ." She started shaking again. "Martin, hold me," she whispered.

His arms went around her. "It's all right, Decker. I'm here," he whispered.

She could feel his arms warm against her cold body—strong, safe arms that she never wanted to leave again. At that moment she knew that she wanted Martin Goldman. What was more, she was going to get him. She nestled her head against his shoulder. "Don't let go of me, Martin," she murmured.

"I won't," he said. He couldn't believe that he was holding this adorable, beautiful creature in his arms. It was the sort of fantasy that didn't often enter Martin Goldman's head.

The boating accident made headlines in all the Lake Success media. It was the first fatal accident on the lake and was particularly sad because the victims were the Parrishes—a well-liked, middle-aged couple who had just bought their first boat. They were still inexperienced sailors, and it appeared that their throttle had jammed open.

"Parrish?" Trip asked his secretary. "Wasn't that the name of the couple who adopted that kid?"

"Little Anthony? Yes, that's right."

"How did he make out? He was a little scamp, I seem to remember. Always playing truant and in trouble."

"Turned out just fine, so I hear," the secretary said. "The Parrishes did a wonderful job with him. He's just graduated from high school and he's heading to Dartmouth on a scholarship."

"Send him to see me," Trip said. "I'd like to know if there's anything I can do."

The tall, dark-haired young man in the leather jacket was very different from the former scruffy youngster with the darting eyes. He shook Trip's hand firmly.

"I'm very sorry about your parents, Tony," Trip said. "I'm banning all powerboats from the lake. I don't want anything like this to happen again."

"It was a freak accident," he said. "But it happened to the only two people I had in the world."

"You were heading off to college. How will you manage?"

"I'll manage," Tony said. "I'm determined to make something of myself, Mr. Atkins. I want to make them proud of me. It's even more important now they're gone."

"I'd like to help, Tony," Trip said. "I'd like to cover anything that the scholarship doesn't."

"That's very generous of you, sir," Tony said, "but I'm sure I can handle it. I intend to work during the vacations."

"Let me do this, Tony," Trip insisted. "I can afford it and it would make me feel better. I can't help feeling partially responsible for the accident. I knew that the lake level was low. I should have thought—"

"Of course you weren't responsible, Mr. Atkins." Tony finally yielded. "But I will accept some financial help, if it makes you happy."

"Good boy," Trip said. "You've done your adopted family proud, I hear."

"Yes, sir. They believed in me," Tony said. "That was all I needed."

He headed for the door, then he looked back. "By the way," he told Trip tentatively, "I'm pretty sure it was Mrs. Atkins that day at the airport. She was driving herself away."

Then he hurried from the room.

CHAPTER 43

A week later Trip stormed out of his study and called to Diana down the hall, "Where's Doctor Goldman? They say he's not in his lab. He's not here, is he?"

"No. His room's empty," Diana said. "He wasn't here for breakfast." A strange look came over her face. "Funny—Decker wasn't here either. Maybe they went out for a walk together—"

"Decker and Martin Goldman. Surely not. What could those two possibly have in common?"

"He's a man and she's a woman," Diana suggested.

"If she's going to try to distract him from his work," Trip snapped, "I should never have brought her home."

"He is an attractive, single man," Diana pointed out. "He does have a private life."

"Not when he works for me," Trip retorted.

"You're unusually grouchy today, sir," Diana

observed. "Is something wrong?"

"The doctor wants me to go for more of those damned tests," Trip said. "Why can't the fools find out what's wrong with me? I don't like not feeling one-hundred-percent. It slows down my work if I keep getting tired like this."

"You are at an age when many people have retired, sir," Diana reminded him.

"Baloney. I've still got so much to do. Where's that damned Goldman?"

A maid came out of Decker's room. "There's a note for you, Miss Westley," she said. "It was on Miss Decker's bed."

Diana opened the note. Then she looked up incredulously at Trip. "They've run away to Reno to get married!" she exclaimed.

"Decker and Martin?" Trip was astounded. "She must be joking. He's the last sort of person I'd expect her to marry, and she's certainly the last person he'd want as a wife."

But they weren't joking. That night Ridgehaven got a call from Decker, who was now Mrs. Martin Goldman. The newlyweds arrived back three days later, Decker glowing with triumph and Martin still looking slightly bemused by the whole thing, as if he couldn't believe what had happened to him.

In Palm Beach, Florida, Rowan read the news of Decker's marriage. "Marrying a doctor who works for my father—she must be out of her mind," he reflected.

"That doesn't sound like Decker's style at all. Maybe she's pregnant." He didn't give the matter anymore thought until much later. Then one day, waking up with a particularly bad hangover, he began to wonder about his life and where it was going. Since leaving school, his life had consisted entirely of racing yachts and parties, up and down the East Coast. It had been fun, but it was beginning to bore him. He thought of Decker and the young doctor, Trip's own choice, both of them at home, being groomed to take over from an ailing old man. Suddenly Rowan realized that he'd been away from home too long. If he wasn't careful, he'd find himself squeezed out of the future of Decker-Atkins.

He looked down from his balcony at the girls lying in the shade by the pool. He had to plan wisely. He wanted to make sure that he was financially independent of his father. If Father really did hand over the business to Decker and Martin, Rowan was pretty sure that Decker would shut him out. One of the guys cannonballed from the diving board, sending a shower of spray over the girls by the pool. They jumped up, screaming. Not Denise, Rowan thought. Not Sarah or Jamie. They were all too flighty and they liked spending money too much. He'd never know whose bed they were jumping into behind his back.

But Corinne . . . his gaze lingered on Corinne Hayes. She wasn't exactly the life of the party. She was pretty naive compared to the other girls, but she was reputed to be stinking rich. As the only daughter of a Midwestern shopping-mall magnate, Corinne was probably worth as much as Decker-Atkins. And she had a big crush on him, too. In fact it shouldn't be at all hard. Rowan combed his hair and wrapped a towel around his waist before he went down to her.

Three months later, in the fall of 1983, Rowan and Corinne arrived in Lake Success, married.

"Isn't this nice?" Diana said, welcoming the new bride into the entrance hall. "The gathering of the clans. Pretty soon this gloomy old place will be echoing to the patter of tiny feet."

Corinne gazed up at Rowan adoringly. "Oh, I do hope so," she said.

Rowan swallowed nervously. He was already getting bored with Corinne. It had only just struck him that he'd now be expected to spend the rest of his life with her. He was angry too; she had waited until after the wedding before letting on that she couldn't touch her fortune until she turned forty. Twenty years with a girl who giggled and chattered meaninglessly—would he be able to hang on that long, he wondered.

The two young couples set up their own apartments in different wings of the house while they looked for sites for their own houses. Diana hoped this would take a long time. She liked the house full of people again. She hoped that one day the Mister would want Suzy and Stew back home, and Adam too. She worried about Adam. He had been such a warm, sensitive little boy, but he had stopped writing home almost as soon as he had gone to boarding school. Each time she had seen him after that, he seemed to have withdrawn deeper into himself.

Diana sat down and wrote him a cheerful letter, describing the arrival of the newlyweds and suggesting that he might like to be among his family again. She got no reply but one day, a month later, she came out of an upstairs room to see a figure standing in the shadows. He had a hollow, haunted look and for a second Diana's heart lurched, as if she were seeing a ghost.

"What do you want? Who are you?" she demanded.

"Diana—it's Adam," he said.

"Adam, my dear boy, welcome home!" she said. "The others will be so delighted—"

He grabbed her arm and drew her aside. "I don't want the others to know I'm here yet," he confided. "Especially not Father."

"Why not? Is something wrong?"

He looked at her with tortured eyes. This was Diana, the one stable person in a miserable, lonely life. All the way home he had made up his mind to tell her the truth, the awful truth that had been tormenting him since that day years ago. He knew he was too young to remember what happened, but he did remember, and it still haunted his dreams. Somehow, some time he had to be free of it, and Diana had been there. Diana could tell him what really happened. But when he came to say it, out loud, he clammed up again, not able to voice his worst fears.

"Me. I'm wrong," he said. "I've been getting these nightmares. I can't sleep, Diana, and then I take things to make me sleep. God, Diana, I'm a mess. I'm scared I'm turning into my mother." He looked at her with imploring eyes. "I don't want to go crazy, Diana. I need help. Help me."

Diana put her arms around him awkwardly. With her British reserve, hugging didn't come naturally, but she could tell that what Adam needed right now was to be held. "Of course we'll help you, Adam. Your father has the best rehab clinic in the world here. I'll talk to him—"

"No, I don't want him told until I've licked this," he said. "I know he never did think much of me. I was always too weak, too soft, for him. That's why he sent me to that military school, wasn't it? He wanted to make a man of me. Well, I guess I'm a man now, but not his sort of man. I don't want him to know I'm here until I can face him. I hoped you could get me into the clinic under a false name."

"I'll do what I can, Adam," Diana told him gently, "but I think you're wrong about your father. Deep down I'm sure he loves you."

"If only I could believe that," he said. "I've grown up believing that nobody cared a damn whether I was alive or dead."

"That's all behind you now," Diana reassured him warmly. "This is a new beginning for all of us. We're going to make Ridgehaven into a happy place."

"A place full of Atkinses happy?" Adam laughed

cynically. "You should know us better by now. We feed off each other, like sharks—only I'm the family guppy. They all feed off me. I really don't think anything will change just because Decker and Rowan are married and Father's getting older. This never was a happy house. I don't think it ever will be."

CHAPTER 44

Old Man Atkins—that's what they called him now. Not to his face, of course, but he'd heard it enough behind his back.

"I *am* old," Trip thought, alone in his study. Old and worn out and dying. In the twelve years since his heart attack, his health had steadily deteriorated. Nothing more to give after all. No page in the history books, no happy ending. He stared out of the window at windsurfers racing across the lake. How easy it looked, skimming over the glassy surface with no apparent effort. He wished he'd tried that, one of many things that had come too late in his life. He wished he'd learned more about computers, but they'd arrived too late, as well; he could never feel comfortable with them. And, if the tests proved successful, his new life-prolonging drug, Vital-A, would come too late as well.

He glanced down at the will he had just begun and

sighed. He didn't know what he wanted. A light tap on his door made him start. Without waiting for a word from him, the door opened and Diana came in. "I made you a cup of tea, sir," she said. "That's what my mother always did back home when she wanted to cheer somebody up. It didn't matter what was wrong—death in the family, war, fire, invasion of mice—tea would put it right."

Trip smiled. "It must be powerful stuff. Maybe I've been marketing the wrong things all these years."

She put the tea down in front of him. "You've produced a lot of good things over the years," she said. "A lot of people are alive and healthy today, thanks to you."

"Yes, but I wanted so much more, Diana," he said. "I had such great dreams, and now . . ." He held out the piece of paper to her. "You know about this?"

"I heard," she said. "Martin told me. Not very encouraging news, I gather."

"I'm dying, Diana. That's what it amounts to." He looked up at her hopelessly. "I hadn't realized until now what a mess I'd made of my life."

"A billion dollars, one of the premier medical facilities in the world, and Lake Success—you call that failure?"

He managed a smile. "Oh, I've done better than I thought I would when I set out from home all those years ago. I've done better than most people, but at what price, Diana? My personal life is a complete failure, I've a power-mad daughter, a lazy, devious son, a junkie son, and two kids who are probably as crooked as their two-bit mother."

"That's not true, Mister Atkins," Diana defended her charges. "Suzy and Stew are delightful young people. They're done very well in school, too. It's time you got to know them again. You think you're dying, then send for them. Get to know your children before you make any decisions."

"You're bossier than you were when you first arrived here," he recalled, "clutching your Elvis records and thinking I was the butler."

Diana smiled at the memory. "I've grown so fond of you all. You are my family. That's why I hate to see you like this. You've given up, haven't you? You get one piece of paper and you give up. Well, that's not the Mister I know. The Mister who opened that door twenty-five years ago would have looked upon this as a challenge. You used to love a challenge—the more impossible it looked, the more you loved it."

He gave a tired smile. "You're right, Diana. I hated anything to get the better of me. I had to fight to get Lake Success built, but I did it, didn't I?"

"Then fight now," Diana said. "Those medical men aren't always right. Get those tests on your secret life-drug speeded up." She saw his surprised face. "Ah, you didn't think I knew about that, did you? There's not much gets past me in Lake Success." She nodded knowingly. "Who knows, maybe the breakthrough will come in time for you. You can be the first proof that the drug works and you'll live to a hundred."

"I wish I could believe that, Diana," he said. "There are a lot of things I want to make right. I don't like the way Rowan has turned out, or Decker, or Adam, for that matter. Do you think Suzy and Stew have a chance of turning out any better? Are they better off in their own environment or should I have them brought home again?"

"At least you should make contact with them," Diana told him firmly. "You are their father, the only parent they have. They think you've completely rejected them and they can't understand why."

"I was selfish," Trip said in a low voice. "Their mother hurt me so badly that I couldn't stand to be reminded of her. That was small of me. I was wrong." He stared past Diana, out of the window again. A jet was landing at Lake Success airport. "Do you think she's still alive, Diana?" he asked softly. "The worst part is not knowing."

"I don't think we'll ever find out now, sir," Diana said.

"I was a fool, wasn't I? To fall so heavily for a woman like that."

"She was very beautiful, sir. More men than you have been dazzled by a pretty face and a great body."

"She made me feel like a king," he admitted. "In bed she made me feel like the best lover in the universe. It sounds foolish now, but I still miss her."

"Of course you do," Diana said. "We never get over the great loves of our life."

"Did you ever have a great love in your life, Diana?"

"Ah, that would be telling, sir," Diana teased him.

"I did," he said, "and her name wasn't Honey." Diana looked at him, surprised. "I've never told anyone here about her," he confided. "I shut her from my mind long ago and I haven't thought of her in years. But now I realize that compared to her, Honey was like polyester compared to pure silk."

"Did this all happen long ago, sir?" Diana asked.

He looked at her with a wicked smile. "I'll tell you all about mine if you tell me about yours," he invited.

"I think we'll keep them secrets for now," Diana said. "If you're still alive in five years, we'll sit down for another cup of tea and we'll tell each other all the details. Until then, they'll just remain two more secrets of Lake Success." She raised her teacup to him across the table.

"The secrets of Lake Success," Trip said, laughing. He picked up his own teacup. "I'll drink to that."

What had really happened to Honey? Who was the father of Diana's baby and what was the true identity of the foundling Tony Parrish? There are still many secrets of Lake Success waiting to be answered in the upcoming TV drama on NBC this fall.